"I didn't expect to see you... so soon."

"Oh. Does that mean you were thinking of looking me up?"

Maggie heard her own scorn and was surprised by the fresh anger bubbling to the surface even after all this time.

"No." Tanner was definite. "But I knew we'd run into each other eventually. I understand my daughter went to see you today."

"She told you?"

"You're surprised?"

"A little."

It was scary how the years seemed to have fallen away. She could be seventeen again, meeting him in front of his house.

"Do you mind helping her?"

"Of course not. But she obviously resents my help."

"She doesn't know about you and me."

Maggie's head whipped around. "I never thought she did. There's nothing to know anyway. The past is long over."

Dear Reader,

Spellbinders! That's what we're striving for. The editors at Silhouette are determined to capture your imagination and win your heart with every single book we publish. Each month, six Special Editions are chosen with *you* in mind.

Our authors are our inspiration. Writers such as Nora Roberts, Tracy Sinclair, Kathleen Eagle, Carole Halston and Linda Howard—to name but a few—are masters at creating endearing characters and heartrending love stories. Their characters are everyday people—just like you and me—whose lives have been touched by love, whose dreams and desires suddenly come true!

So find a cozy, quiet place to read, and create your own special moment with a Silhouette Special Edition.

Sincerely,

The Editors
SILHOUETTE BOOKS

NATALIE BISHOP
Summertime Blues

Silhouette Special Edition

Published by Silhouette Books New York

America's Publisher of Contemporary Romance

SILHOUETTE BOOKS
300 East 42nd St., New York, N.Y. 10017

ISBN: 0-373-09401-9

First Silhouette Books printing August 1987

America's Publisher of Contemporary Romance

Printed in the U.S.A.

Books by Natalie Bishop

Silhouette Special Edition

NATALIE BISHOP

lives within a stone's throw of her sister, Lisa Jackson, who is also a Silhouette author. Natalie and Lisa spend many afternoons together developing new plots and reading their best lines to each other.

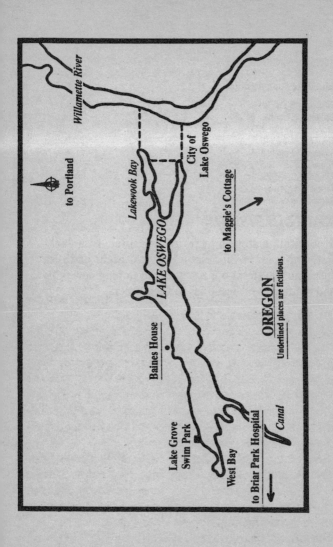

Willamette River

to Portland

Lakewook Bay

City of
Lake Oswego

to Maggie's Cottage

LAKE OSWEGO

Baines House

Lake Grove
Swim Park

West Bay

Canal

to Briar Park Hospital

OREGON
Underlined places are fictitious.

Chapter One

The first time Maggie Holt met Tanner Baines was in his bedroom—when she was fifteen years old.

If she let herself, she could still feel the scrape of bark from the gnarled oak beneath Tanner's window as she shimmied up the tree; the thrill of danger as she hung from the upper limb, her toe searching for the windowsill; the shock of sliding inside to find that Tanner was silently waiting for her. She remembered his surprise at her sudden entrance and could still hear him asking in his drawling way, "And who the hell are you?"

He'd been naked to the waist, clad only in a pair of disreputable jeans, and it had been some time before Maggie could explain why she'd come. Even then he'd regarded her with narrow-eyed suspicion, certain she'd had some ulterior motive beyond the one she'd stated.

But after fourteen years it was Tanner's face that was still the easiest to recall: high cheekbones defined against a lean, determined jaw; skin the color of teak; hair a straight, sun-streaked blond; tawny eyes shadowed by thick gold-tipped lashes; a mouth that was a slash of purpose. Maggie had been stunned by their first meeting, and she'd reacted like the tongue-tied child she'd been. But time, in its inevitable way, had altered her feelings, and she'd learned to appreciate and admire him, and by the time she was seventeen she'd fallen head over heels in love.

Now, staring into the eyes of his adolescent daughter, she searched for some resemblance between Shelley Baines and her father. But there was little to distinguish her as Tanner's child. The pale, somewhat sullen girl casting her resentful glances from behind a curtain of long brown hair was nothing like Maggie's memory of Tanner. Shelley's resemblance to her mother, Tricia Wellesley Baines, was far more apparent.

And it made Maggie uncomfortable.

Clearing her throat, she flipped through the papers in Shelley's file. "Dr. Kempwood sent you straight over from the hospital to see me. She notes here that you were diagnosed as diabetic several years ago but have just recently been having trouble with dizziness. She wants me to check your diet."

Shelley regarded Maggie with bored eyes and said nothing.

"You've just moved here, I understand. Do you feel the change has interrupted your usual habits, both with meals and your insulin intake?"

"I told the doctor everything already."

Maggie managed a smile. "Maybe you could help me out with the same information. Your file's still incomplete."

The girl's eyes dropped to the pin on Maggie's lab coat. It read MAGGIE HOLT, R.D., and though Maggie was certain she must already know what it stood for, she said, "I'm a registered dietitian and I'm Briar Park Medical Center's nutrition consultant."

"Well, I don't need help."

Shelley's rebellion was more in her tone than her words. Her teeth were set, her young body was stiff with affront and she looked anywhere but directly at Maggie.

Sighing inwardly, Maggie asked quietly, "Are you here by yourself, or is your mother... or father... with you?"

"My mother's dead."

Shocked, Maggie couldn't prevent her stare of disbelief. Tricia dead? How? Why? *From last fall's car accident?*

The news swept over her like a wave, the same wave of unreality that had nearly drowned her when she'd found out that Tanner was back in Portland. She'd heard tales about the accident, of course, but after the first buzz of gossip had died down she'd been left with the impression that Tricia Baines had been unscathed—while Tanner, one of Boston's most noted surgeons, had lost the use of his right hand... and therefore his career.

Silence lengthened in the room. While Maggie tried to pull her thoughts in order, she saw the gleam of triumph in Shelley's eyes. If it hadn't been for the fear lurking there, too, she might have felt little sympathy for the girl. As it was, her sorrow was immense and she had to swallow before saying. "I'm sorry. I didn't know. Is your father here, then?"

"No. I came with Mrs. Greer, our housekeeper. Dad is—my father doesn't go out much."

It was another piece of information Maggie didn't want to hear. The hairs on the back of her neck rose. *Doesn't go out much.* The sound of that made her uneasy.

What was happening to Tanner?

Drifting memories passed over her, snatches of conversation she'd heard, malicious bits of gossip that had nevertheless been burned into Maggie's brain.

"The bones of his hand were crushed to dust..."

"His surgical career is over, completely over..."

"Looks like Lake Oswego's shining star finally got what he deserved..."

She looked down at the open file again. Shelley's home was typed in as Boston and no Oregon address was listed. Yet Dr. Kempwood wouldn't have bothered sending her to Maggie if Tanner wasn't planning on staying.

With slightly unsteady hands Maggie closed the manila folder. "Well, then, maybe I can set the appointments up with you. I'll give you these sheets and I want you to write down everything you eat for the next few days. Try to watch the carbohydrates—especially sugar. We want to find out exactly what your stability level is. Don't be foolish, Shelley," she added, seeing how hard the girl was trying to close her out. "I'm sure you know the dos and don'ts already. I'll go over your history with Dr. Kempwood, and then could you and I meet again on Thursday, say around two o'clock?"

Shelley shrugged and rose from her chair, grudgingly reaching for the information held out to her. Without a goodbye she passed through the outer office, and Mrs. Greer, the housekeeper Maggie had once known as intimately as Shelley did now, put down her magazine and followed the dark-haired girl out into the warm June sunshine.

The smells of summer flowed through the open window of Maggie's car—dust, dry grass and the occasional sweet scent from the heavy-headed roses. It was the kind of day that tugged at her memories; the kind of day she dreaded.

She breathed deeply and her mind swirled with images from her youth, as if the very act of inhaling brought the past touchably close.

She wished Tanner had stayed in Boston where he belonged.

Unscrewing the sunroof of her Volkswagen, she kept just ahead of the speed limit around Lake Oswego, the cool air fanning her hot cheeks, her mind clearing a bit with each passing mile. But driven by some unhealthy interest she took a side route, winding up the back hills that looked over the lake, turning down the street where Tanner's home had once been.

It had been years since she'd really allowed herself to feel these emotions. Her romance with Tanner was long over and she'd built a satisfying life for herself since their brief, disastrous affair. She seldom brooded about "what could have been." The past was the past. Yet she couldn't forget it completely.

She parked across the street from the white colonial house and leaned her arms on the steering wheel. Heat settled inside and she felt her hair stick to the back of her neck. Who lived here now? she wondered idly. Tanner's father had left town not long after his son's marriage to Tricia Wellesley.

Tricia Wellesley. *My God, was she really dead?* It seemed impossible to believe that the young woman Maggie had wasted such bitter tears over, had hated with all the intensity of her adolescent heart, could be gone. Regret slid over her, deep and profound. Tricia had only loved the same man she had; it was hardly a crime.

Sighing, Maggie let her eyes travel over the familiar three-story structure. It had been a cabin once, like so many other homes around the lake, but Tanner's father, Dr. Gerrard Baines, had renovated it into its current, imposing condition. It was undoubtedly worth a small fortune now.

The gnarled oak tree still reached around the corner and up the side of the house and over the roof. How old was it? she wondered. A hundred years? Two hundred? Someone had once told her an oak tree lives six hundred years: two hundred to grow, two hundred to live, two hundred to die. It would probably be there long after her life was over, and it humbled her to think how futile and unimportant her own existence was.

Shifting gears, Maggie was on the road again, driving blindly down the switchback lanes. To the right and far below, a scintillating blur of green and blue flashed between the droopy-limbed firs. Lake Oswego, the man-made lake that had given the surrounding town its name, ran beside Maggie's car like a mocking shadow.

A dry ache filled her, the kind of ache that never seemed to go away. It surprised her because she hadn't even known it existed until now. She tried not to dwell too closely on the origins of her pain and concentrated instead on making the correct turns to her own home. Fifteen minutes later she was pulling into the drive of her cottage on the outskirts of the city.

She snatched the note taped onto her front door and frowned as she turned the lock. It was typical of Chad and she read his nearly illegible scrawl with a feeling of frustration:

Am going to be late. Can you meet me at Maxwell's? I'll be there around six-thirty. I love you, Chad.

The note was already crumpled in her palm before Maggie realized what she'd done. In astonishment, she smoothed it out and laid it on her kitchen counter.

I love you.

It seemed like a terrible travesty to read those three careless little words. Dr. Chad Collins offered them so easily and with no compunction. It was as simple for him as breathing, and he had yet to notice that Maggie had difficulty saying them back. They stuck in her throat, and only Chad's lack of perception saved her from having to explain why she had such a phobia about repeating them to him.

With a realization she'd tried to ignore for weeks she knew she was going to have to stop seeing Chad. Their relationship was at a stalemate; it had been for months. She'd hoped time would alter her feelings, but now she knew it wasn't going to happen. Maybe tonight would be a good time to face the truth with him.

She glanced at the clock. Five-thirty. She had just enough time to shower and change to meet Chad by six-thirty. With a grimace meant for life in general, she prepared herself for the task she dreaded, knowing Chad wouldn't want to hear that his "almost" fiancée wasn't in love with him.

"If everything goes well the community will raise the money for the new obstetric wing by the end of the year," Chad said to the group at the table. "That'll bring a lot of money into the hospital. They'll have to add more staff, too."

Sandy Francis, a surgical resident at Briar Park Hospital, looked pensive. "What if we don't get the money?"

"We will. Have some confidence." Chad's smile was wide. "And then who knows," he murmured, slipping an arm over Maggie's shoulders. "The sky's the limit."

Maggie managed a smile, but her thoughts were elsewhere. As soon as she'd realized she and Chad weren't going to have some time alone she'd had to change her plans. Now was not the time and place to end their relationship.

The table was comfortably crowded, with several of Briar Park's bright young doctors discussing the upcoming expansion with an eagerness born of selfishness. More facilities meant more prestige—and a way to speed up the long trek to the top. And Chad was more than ready to assume additional responsibility and acquire some name recognition along the way.

Maggie didn't have any feelings about the expansion one way or another. She was happy with her small offices, glad that the doctors understood her expertise and treated her with respect and interest. To her, the political movements within the hospital made little difference, and her only concern was whether the new addition would improve patient care.

"I heard there'll be some new administrative positions open," Sandy said reflectively. "Maybe they'll shift some of the department heads around."

"Sandy's hoping Samuelson will be moved out of surgery, giving her a chance to shine," Dr. Jeff Hall, Briar Park's junior pathologist, said with a smirk that earned him a glare from Sandy.

"I don't blame her," Chad said. "We'd all like Samuelson out of the way. He's holding back the whole department with his outdated ideas."

"And who would you like to be the next head of the department?" Jeff asked innocently. "As if we all didn't know, Dr. Collins!"

Chad shrugged. "I've made no bones about what I want."

"You'd be good," Sandy told him. "Wouldn't he?"

She looked around the table, her sharp eyes asking for support. Maggie smiled in agreement, but she wondered if it was really true. Chad's lack of depth was one of the reasons their relationship had failed. Wouldn't that same flaw affect his performance as head of a whole department?

The discussion continued, but Maggie's attention drifted. For some reason her thoughts centered on Shelley Baines, Tanner's daughter. Now there was a problem worth solving. How difficult would it be to help her? she wondered, especially since Shelley's problem seemed as much one of attitude as anything else. And then there was Tanner himself. Maggie was fully aware that she would have to deal with him at some point in the future.

"There may be a hitch to your plan," Jeff said with the air of someone imparting important news. "What about our illustrious Dr. Baines? I hear he's just moved back to the area."

Maggie shot a startled glance toward Jeff. She was surprised his thoughts were also on the Baines family.

"What about him?" Chad asked, unimpressed. "His hand's ruined. He's not going to be performing surgery again, as I hear it."

"No, but he could still be department head."

"Not in any functioning capacity," Chad insisted. "Tanner Baines is finished as a surgeon. It's too damn bad, really. He was one of the best. But he's no threat to anyone's career at Briar Park."

Tanner Baines is finished . . .

"Excuse me," Maggie said, scraping back her chair. Chad's words had depressed her and she itched to be away. She headed in the direction of the women's room, barely noticing the trays of Maxwell's famous triple-layered desserts beneath the glass counter near the entryway. Her mind was filled with confusing thoughts.

Staring at her reflection in the bathroom mirror, Maggie wondered, *What's wrong with me?* She hadn't thought of Tanner in years. At least not *that* way. But seeing his daughter on a warm June day and then listening to his name dropped in the middle of the avid discussion at Maxwell's had brought back a spate of unwelcome memories.

A part of her had never gotten over Tanner. There was a corner of her heart that still responded whenever she heard his name. For a thirty-one-year-old woman, it was difficult to admit she still suffered the pangs of an adolescent romance, but there was no denying how she felt. Her relationships with men since had never had that same breath-catching intensity, and she knew part of her problem with Chad was she expected to be swept off her feet again.

Maggie pulled out her brush and ran it through her hair until the long reddish brown strands crackled with static electricity. But after replacing it in her purse, she continued to stand in front of the mirror, seeing not her own solemn green eyes, but a past she had buried since the summer before her eighteenth birthday.

"I'm marrying Tricia Wellesley," Tanner had told her the morning after she'd lain with him under the sweeping arms of a majestic fir, learning the pleasures of loving and being in love.

They were on his back deck, Tanner leaning against the white wooden rails, Maggie behind him, her arms around his waist. She'd been too insanely happy to notice his distance that morning. When she'd left him the night before the future had been as open and untouched as a windswept beach.

"Very funny," she answered, smiling, stuffing her face into the back of his neck.

She felt his shaky intake of breath, the pause that painfully followed. And then she knew he was in deadly earnest. Her arms fell to her sides in disbelief.

Tanner half turned, his face gaunt and older than she had ever seen it. "Tricia and I are getting married," he said again, as if he, too, were having trouble believing it.

"You can't." Maggie's voice was a whisper. "It's impossible."

He didn't answer. He just looked past the firs that thrust arrogantly through the cedar planks of his back deck and focused on the lake far below. Maggie numbly followed his gaze, seeing sunlight dance on the water, smelling the verdant scent of fir and pine, feeling her crown heat under the early morning sunshine while her insides shivered with cold.

"I'm sorry about us, Maggie," he said in a strained voice. "Things went too far last night. It's my fault. For that I'll always be sorry."

Her shock disappeared under an avalanche of anger and pain. "Sorry. *Sorry?*" She grabbed his arm and shook it hard, glad to see him flinch at her sarcasm. "Well, I won't be. I'll never be!"

Emotion flashed across his face and she dimly realized there was something he hadn't told her. "It's because of your father, isn't it?" she accused, guessing. "*Isn't it?* I'm not good enough. The Holts aren't good enough!"

"No."

"That's why you're marrying Tricia Wellesley. I was just available, gullible—" she lowered her voice but it throbbed with intensity "—*easy.*"

"*No!*"

"Then what?" Tears stood in her eyes. "Tanner, I love you. You know I do. And you said you loved me, too."

She had expected some kind of response, hoped he would tell her the same. But he didn't answer, and apart from a tensing of his jaw, he didn't even move. Maggie wanted to kill him, to beat her fists against his chest and demand that he take everything back. But all she did was cry—huge, silent tears that ran down her cheeks and dropped unheeded to the white-painted decking.

When he finally turned to look at her, his lips slackened in regret. He reached for her, but she swiftly backed away.

"Don't try to make me understand," she said unevenly. "I can't. How *could* you wait until now to tell me?"

"Oh, Maggie..."

Tanner looked terrible, wrung out, as if wracked by some inner torment, but Maggie was too wounded to care. She sensed him working himself up to tell her more, but she couldn't stand to hear it. With a choked cry she turned on her heel and left him, walking stiffly through his home, glad Tanner's father wasn't there to witness her devastation. Blinded by tears, she drove wildly to her own home on the outskirts of the city, the poorest section surrounding Lake Oswego.

For a time, a part of her had believed he would phone and tell her it was all a terrible mistake. She'd half expected he would call her up and beg her to come back. To ease her pain she'd looked forward to that moment of power, that moment when she would make him suffer just as she'd suffered, only to throw herself back into his arms, enjoying the forgiveness that much more.

But that moment had never come. A month after Tanner had told Maggie he was going to marry Tricia Wellesley, he did, and shortly after that he'd left for medical school in Boston. He'd never come back to Oregon as far as she knew. And she'd never understood what had gone wrong between them.

She supposed she never would.

With a last sigh for her misspent youth, Maggie wove her way back to the table where Chad and his associates still waited. She apologized for her long absence, pleading a headache, and was glad when shortly afterward Chad walked her to her car, holding open the door as she slid inside.

"You sure you're okay?" he inquired solicitously. "You look kind of pale."

"Do I? It's been a long day."

"I want to talk a little longer to Sandy and Jeff. How about if I stop by your office tomorrow?"

"Fine." Chad closed the door and Maggie rolled down the window, cowardly relieved that she wouldn't have to tell him their relationship was over just yet. There was always tomorrow, after all, and she didn't want to think about Chad tonight.

He kissed her on the cheek and Maggie eased out of the parking lot, waving a goodbye. In her rearview mirror she saw him head back toward Maxwell's neon-trimmed door.

Restlessness overcame her as soon as she reached Oswego's city limits. She drove by the familiar storefronts, glimpsing the lake between the buildings where the railroad tracks cut through the center street and wound along the edge of the lake. Lake Oswego, an oasis of affluence, snobbery and beauty, just south of Portland, had changed very little since Maggie's childhood. The only difference was then she'd been a poor outsider looking in, now she could afford the area, but for reasons rooted in Tanner's rejection, she felt she could never quite fit in.

It was a trick of fate, she decided later, that made her drive past her turnoff, choosing instead the meandering roads that threaded through the hills around the lake. There was no rhyme or reason to the roads; they'd been put down by necessity and, to the first-time traveler, were a confusing web with no particular direction. The problem was the lake itself. You had to drive all the way around it to get from Point A to Point B, and the narrow lanes around its banks twisted in and out, like some master plan of braiding gone awry.

Maggie knew Lake Oswego well. She circled around North Shore, crossed a low-walled bridge that provided a barrier from the main lake's slapping waves, saw the flickering reflection of the houseboat lights shimmering in the dark waters, drove over the railroad tracks again and wound her way higher until once again she was on the skyline road to Tanner's old house.

A rueful smile crossed her face, acknowledgment of her own weakness. What was this crazy urge to relive old memories? She'd gotten over her love for Tanner years ago, yet now she seemed obsessed with dragging it all up again.

The car glided to a stop, and with a sigh Maggie leaned her elbow against the window's warm metal frame. Sweet, sultry scents rode on a soft breeze, filling her head, reminding her of another time. Summer and Tanner Baines. For three summers she'd lived with him in her every thought, and the seasons in between hadn't been able to erase those summer memories. She'd savored each incident with him through autumn, winter and spring, and looked forward to June, when Tanner's next college vacation would begin, waiting expectantly for that first sighting, first call.

Maggie lay her head against the cushions of the seat and listened to the cricket's song. Since her expedition up the oak tree—her first real meeting with Tanner—she'd been smitten. Cupid had done his job well, she mused wryly. At least on her part. Tanner's feelings had always been more difficult to place.

It still hurt a little to think back, and Maggie, never one to dwell too long on the irretrievable, reached for the ignition. Someone else lived here now. She could practically feel the hominess as another lamp in the house was switched on, a rectangle of golden light spilling through the window into the soft night. So much for memories, she thought. But as the engine caught she saw the porch light come on and the front door open.

She was in the act of putting the car in gear, when she recognized the man on the porch. *Tanner.* Stunned, Maggie froze, her fingers still on the keys. Her memory was too sharp, she realized, for even through the darkness she knew him. She saw his easy grace, the way he moved, the turn of his head under the yellow porch light. Her heart pounded wildly.

The little Volkswagen revved in the summer stillness and Maggie drew a breath, shaking off the past. For reasons unknown even to herself she cut the engine, pocketed the keys and stepped out into the deepening shadows.

Time ran backward. In breathless expectancy she waited by the side of her car, feeling years slide away as Tanner looked up, saw her and began moving toward her with familiar, assured strides, the early moonlight flickering silver through his blond hair.

She didn't know what to expect. She just stood in frozen silence as he crossed the narrow street and stopped a few feet in front of her.

She heard his swift intake of air. "Maggie?" he asked disbelievingly.

"Hello, Tanner." She was surprised at how controlled her voice was.

"What are you doing here?"

He sounded dazed, and she felt much the same way. "I, uh, didn't know you lived here."

It was hardly a worthy answer, but Tanner didn't seem to notice. His eyes were searching her face in a way that stripped her to the bone.

He shifted his weight. "I didn't expect to see you—so soon."

"Oh. Does that mean you were thinking of looking me up?" She heard her scorn and was surprised by the fresh anger bubbling to the surface even after all this time. What was wrong with her?

"No." Tanner was definite. "But I knew we'd run into each other eventually."

"Well, thanks for telling me. I wouldn't want to make another mistake."

"Maggie..." He sighed.

"I can't believe I'm standing here having this conversation. I must be out of my mind." She made a move toward the car, but Tanner stepped in front of her. She saw then that one hand, his right hand, was tucked deeply into his pocket. She couldn't remember if he'd come out of the house that way, or if he'd hidden the evidence of his accident because of her.

Her anger melted into regret. A part of her longed to help so badly she could already taste the bitter flavor of defeat.

"There's no getting around having to face each other," he said. "I understand my daughter went to see you today."

"She told you?"

"You're surprised?"

"A little."

It was scary how the years seemed to have fallen away. She could be seventeen again, meeting him in front of his house. Maggie glanced away, trying to gain some perspective, and found her eyes drawn to his shadow, falling across the hood of her car.

The shadow moved. "Do you mind helping her?"

"Of course not. But she obviously resents me helping her."

"She doesn't know about you and me."

Maggie's head whipped around. "I never thought she did. There's nothing to know anyway. The past is long over."

Tanner nodded grimly.

That part of her that still cherished her youth finally withered and died, turning to dust like the wildflowers she'd pressed between the pages of a book of love poems so long ago. She hadn't realized how much she'd still cared until this moment.

"Goodbye, Tanner," she said.

"Maggie..." His good hand snaked out and grasped her wrist. She felt him searching for words and she gently, but firmly pulled her hand from his. "Why did you come here?" he asked.

"Nostalgia." She tried not to think about his other hand, about the end to his career. She tried not to care too much about what would happen to him now. "I really didn't think you lived here."

"My father never sold the place. He gave it to me when he moved to the East Coast, and I never got around to giving it up."

Maggie opened the car door. "I'm sorry about Tricia," she said unevenly. "I didn't realize she hadn't recovered until Shelley told me. I'd heard—she was getting better— after the accident..."

"She was. Her injuries were mainly superficial." Tanner's voice was terse. "She had a cerebral hemorrhage months later and no one knows for certain if it was caused by the accident or something else. It happened fast."

There was a dreamlike quality to their conversation. Maggie felt as if they were covering old ground, not speaking for the first time in fourteen years.

"You never married," he said, and it was these final words that gave Maggie the strength to leave.

"I'm engaged, Tanner," she said as she slipped inside the driver's seat. It wasn't exactly true, but she needed to say it. Pride at its worst, she decided, but didn't care.

He rested one hand on the hood of her car. "I'm glad. I hope you're happy."

Happy? She didn't think she could really ascribe that word to how she felt. "Goodbye," she said, and put the car in gear before the conversation slipped into one of those dangerous areas she sensed hovering just outside their words.

"Goodbye, Maggie...." she heard through her open window as she drove down the curving road, cresting the hill that dropped steeply toward the moon-washed shores of Lake Oswego.

Chapter Two

Thursday morning Maggie's nose was deep inside a file when she heard a familiar voice from the other room.

"If you scowl like that much longer you're going to permanently crease your forehead."

She looked up, self-consciously clearing her brow as Chad, who'd ducked his head inside her door, now came inside, dropping indolently into one of the two chairs grouped on the opposite side of her desk.

"But it's okay, you're still beautiful to me," he added with a grin.

Maggie closed Shelley Baines's file. She felt uncomfortable, as if she were deliberately leading Chad on, yet now was not the right time to end their relationship, either. Shelley was due to arrive in fifteen minutes. "How was your morning?" she asked, instead, thinking hard.

"Tiring, but terrific." Chad folded his hands behind his head. "Two surgeries back to back, but no complications. Have you heard the news yet? Samuelson's stepping down as administrative head of surgery.''

"No kidding?"

"No kidding," Chad said with pleasure.

She couldn't share his enthusiasm. Unlike Chad, she regretted seeing the end of an era, and Dr. Edmund Samuelson represented a time when the patient always came first. He'd been an excellent surgeon and an even better administrator, and she'd always felt the tireless old curmudgeon would be around for many years to come.

"With the expansion pending, he didn't want to be in charge anymore. Too much work. The chief of staff's going to appoint someone else."

"You?"

Chad gave her a gratified glance. "If only," he said on a sigh. "I'm certainly going to give it my best shot." Looking toward the doorway, he said, "Tonight Jeff and Sandy and I are going to celebrate Samuelson's retirement. Want to come? I told them you'd be there."

"I can't, Chad. Not tonight."

Maggie's answer had been instinctive, and Chad was surprised at how adamant she sounded.

"What? Too much work?" he asked, glancing at the closed file beneath Maggie's hands.

"Something like that."

"Problems?" he asked, inclining his head toward the file. "That the one you were scowling over?"

"Yes." She felt reluctant about discussing Shelley's case with Chad—some misguided loyalty to the past, she supposed. Yet she honestly needed a sounding board and Chad was an excellent candidate. Plunging in, Maggie said, "This girl's a diabetic and she's suddenly having strong reactions—dizziness, faintness, etcetera. Dr. Kempwood feels it's diet related and doesn't want to change her insulin intake. I agree. But I don't know...it's more than that, too." With a hollow laugh she added, "Woman's intuition, right?"

"Maybe. What's wrong?"

Maggie sighed. "I don't know. It's Shelley's attitude. I've only met her once, but I get this feeling she's deliberately thwarting medical advice. She barely listens. She just—tolerates."

"Well, you can only do what you can do, Maggie. The rest is up to her." Chad rose from his chair. "Want some advice from a friend? Don't let your overactive emotions get you involved with this girl. It's not your job, and besides, you haven't got the time." He leaned over to give her a kiss. "Save those feelings for me, okay?"

Maggie smiled, but the corners of her mouth tightened. He didn't realize how he'd unwittingly underscored all that was basically wrong between them.

"Look, I've got to get back. You sure you can't make it tonight?"

"I'm sure."

"You're not mad, are you?"

"No." It was true. As quickly as her resentment had sprung up it was gone. Chad's advice had been well meant, whether she believed in it or not.

"There isn't something you're not telling me, is there? Something I've done?"

"No."

"Okay. Then I guess I'll see you tomorrow."

"Chad...?"

"Hmm?"

"Could we get together tomorrow...alone?"

His drifting attention came back to her with a bang. "There is something wrong, isn't there? You've been awfully distant lately."

Maggie didn't answer. She knew he was right.

"Well, okay. I'll come over to your house after work tomorrow. We'll get it all sorted out then."

If only she could be so blithely sure the future would resolve itself, she thought after he'd gone. It would certainly make life easier. She fervently hoped Chad would understand her decision.

Stretching, Maggie walked to the window, looking across the parkway that separated her offices from Briar Park Hospital next door. Flowering cherry trees, their spring blossoms exchanged for summer leaves, their trunks surrounded by circular wooden benches, were spaced along the brick walkway. It was a common practice for staff members to brown-bag it in the summertime and several people were sitting on the benches, dawdling over their lunches, feeding crumbs to the robins and sparrows and raucous jays.

An old familiar longing rose inside Maggie. A longing for something she couldn't quite name. It was a feeling that waxed and waned, that had returned this summer with a vengeance that could have only one source: Tanner. It was silly, she knew, but her nameless craving seemed tantalizingly within reach, like a word that hovered on the tip of her tongue. She felt that if she just tried a little harder she could have what she most desperately wanted.

If only she knew what that was.

A soft rap beside her open doorway caught her attention.

"Shelley Baines is here," Karen, Maggie's receptionist, announced. "Oh, and your brother called."

Connor. Maggie felt a flush of pleasure. He'd been the father she'd never really had, and since her mother's death he was her only remaining family. Though he lived in Los

Angeles, she still kept in constant contact with him, and it was always good to hear from him. "What did he say?"

"That he'd call you tonight."

"Great."

Maggie was still smiling when Shelley appeared a few moments later. But her smile fell as she saw the girl's wary glance skate over the appointments of her office—just as it had on their first meeting. No progress there.

"Have a chair," Maggie invited, and Shelley perched on the edge of the blue cushion. "Did your father come with you?" she asked carefully, "or your housekeeper?"

"Mrs. Greer dropped me off. She'll be back."

Maggie nodded, unable to get her mind off Tanner. Why wouldn't he come with Shelley? She knew better than anyone how caring and loving Tanner could be, and she didn't believe he would abandon his daughter when she needed him most. The girl's mother had died scant months before and she was now having trouble with her diabetes. Surely Tanner could understand her needs as a man and a father. And he was a doctor, for God's sake! Where was he?

"Did you bring the food sheets with you?" Maggie asked encouragingly.

A look crossed Shelley's face for just a moment, a look Maggie couldn't quite interpret. Then she pulled a folded piece of paper from her pocket and handed it over.

"How have you been feeling?" Maggie unfolded the paper.

"Okay."

"No more dizziness?"

"Some."

"You're seeing Dr. Kempwood again tomorrow, right?"

"Uh-huh."

Glancing at the paper, Maggie felt her heart stop for an instant, then anger slowly heated her blood. She was beginning to understand Shelley better than she'd expected to. "This is what you've eaten the past three days?" she questioned, regarding her steadily.

Shelley nodded, waiting.

Without a word Maggie pulled out a white folder, the nutritional guide used by Briar Park Hospital and especially by Dr. Kempwood. She turned to the page that listed a possible diet plan and pushed it in front of Shelley's nose. "I think you copied this diet plan word for word, Shelley Baines," Maggie said. "I don't think you ate any of these foods."

"I did eat them."

"Every last item on this menu?" Maggie stabbed a finger at Plan A.

"Every one."

"Nothing else? Just what's on this plan?"

"Nothing else."

It was a stalemate. Short of calling the girl a liar or waiting for Mrs. Greer to appear and offer testimony, there was nothing she could do but accept Shelley's story. But instinct and the look of smugness around Shelley's mouth told a different tale.

"I'm not going to waste your time and mine by arguing with you. If you followed this menu and are still experiencing dizzy spells then your problems probably won't be solved by diet alone. I think I should say as much to your father."

"He won't come here."

Maggie had been reaching for the phone, but the girl was so positive she hesitated over the receiver. Shelley's gaze was bland, but Maggie instinctively felt the challenge underneath. Deciding that if this was going to be a battle of wills she wasn't going to give up yet, Maggie glanced at Shelley's home number in the file, quickly stabbing out the buttons. She mentally braced herself for Tanner to answer.

"Hello?"

The cadence of his voice was enough to make her break into a nervous sweat. Digging into her reserves of poise, she said, "Dr. Baines? This is Maggie Holt, nutritionist for Briar Park Hospital. Your daughter's here visiting me today, but I would like to see you, too."

A long pause ensued while Maggie's heart beat double-time. Shelley leaned forward on her chair, all ears. Dimly Maggie realized this was the showdown the girl had wanted.

"What's wrong?" Tanner asked.

"Nothing that I can find. That's what I want to talk to you about. Preferably in person."

She heard him inhale between his teeth. "If there's nothing wrong, why do I need to see you?"

Maggie could scarcely believe her ears. If Shelley had been her own daughter she'd be moving heaven and earth to find out how to help her. What was wrong with him?

"I'd like to talk over her diabetes."

His indecision could be felt. Even so, when he finally answered it was still a surprise. "No, Maggie. I can't see you. If dealing with Shelley is too difficult, just tell me and I'll move her somewhere else."

She blinked in disbelief. If it hadn't been for his daughter's avid interest she would have blasted Tanner right then and there for his insensitivity to her problems.

"I'll think about it," she said crisply. "Goodbye."

"What did he say?"

There was the tiniest flicker of hope in the depths of Shelley's eyes, almost a desperate expectancy. Gently Maggie said, "He can't come to my office right now."

The hope died. Shelley turned her face to the wall and sullenly said, "See?"

Damn you, Tanner, Maggie thought violently. How could he do this? How could he not see Shelley was crying for attention?

"Shelley," Maggie offered awkwardly, "be careful about what you eat. You're only hurting yourself in the long run."

"It's *your* diet!" Shelley picked up the pamphlet and sailed it across to Maggie. The pages fluttered wildly as she attempted to grab it before it hit the floor. "If it's no good, it's your fault. Your fault!"

Before Maggie could react Shelley twisted out of the chair and ran from the office. Maggie followed in time to see her yank open the reception room door and run blindly across the lawn, reaching the first bench just as Mrs. Greer approached the front step. With a wordless glance at Maggie that could have meant anything, the housekeeper walked slowly toward her young charge, putting an arm over Shelley's tense shoulders and urging her back toward the car.

It was difficult for Maggie to face the rest of her day after the emotional scene with Shelley, but she had two more appointments before she could leave. With a groan she read the names from her scheduling list: Mrs. Tindale and Mr. Rookheiser. Mrs. Tindale was a wonderfully fun woman who was trying to lose weight before surgery, but Mr. Rookheiser was a royal pain in the neck. He was a nutritionist's nightmare, a faddist who believed that megadoses of vitamins and minerals cured everything from baldness to cancer. Why he insisted on seeing Maggie when she refuted all his claims was a mystery, but he kept right on coming. No amount of discouragement could keep him from consulting her, and after a time Maggie had quit trying. Secretly she felt the older man had few friends and simply enjoyed the company. Now, as she smiled a greeting to Mrs. Tindale, she mentally braced herself for the interview that would follow.

"I don't feel I'm making much progress," Alice Tindale said on a sigh, slipping off her shoes in front of the scale. "And I haven't cheated once this month."

"You've lost forty pounds already. That's progress," Maggie assured her.

"But it takes forever."

Maggie nodded and said ruefully, "Yes, it does."

The heavier woman gave her a look. "Have you ever tried to lose weight?"

"A few pounds here and there, and even that was hard."

"I'm going to lose it all, you know," she said with a return of spirit.

"Absolutely. I have complete faith in you."

Mrs. Tindale watched the electronic numbers on the scale, her face registering her anxiety. But when the numbers stopped she was pleased by the result. "Well, what do you know."

"It's coming off." Maggie, too, was happy at her progress. "It's just at a slower rate than it was at first."

"After surgery I'm not putting it back on. I'm gonna keep it off."

"Good for you," Maggie said, and meant it.

Mr. Rookheiser was impatiently shifting from one foot to the other as Mrs. Tindale left the reception area. He was sniffing the air, as if he suspected someone had disregarded the No Smoking sign, and he gave Karen, the receptionist, a suspicious look as he strutted into Maggie's office. He was fit and lean for his seventy plus years, and he pinned Maggie with bright blue eyes, his bushy brows drawn into a line of displeasure. "Can't people read?" he demanded. "No Smoking means no smoking."

"I don't think anyone's been smoking."

"Well, I have a sensitive nose. I can tell." He glared once more in Karen's direction and Maggie had to hide a smile.

"How are you doing?" she asked him.

"That's what I came to talk to you about. I'm doing terrible. Sulfides in everything. I can't eat." He carefully brushed off the seat cushion before he sat down.

"But we determined you're not sulfide sensitive."

"Girl, I know what I am. And I can't stick to your diet plan," he complained. "Red meat clogs the arteries. Eggs are loaded with cholesterol. I'd swear you're trying to kill me."

Maggie was divided, as ever, between exasperation and amusement. "As I recall, red meat isn't on your diet. Protein is, and you can substitute, chicken, fish, beans—"

"You know what your problem is? You can't admit when you're wrong. Why don't you recommend vitamin E? I've seen what it can do. A man I know grew his hair back, and it had been gone for fifteen years!"

"Vitamin E is being researched all the time, Mr. Rookheiser, just as all vitamins and minerals are, but there's no evidence that—"

"What kind of evidence do you need, girl? A man grows his hair back! That's evidence enough for me."

Maggie stared into her patient's bulldog face and counted to ten. "Maybe you could bring your friend in so I could meet him. Then I could see the results, too."

"Oh, no." He wagged a finger in front of her nose. "You'll find some way to discredit him. You're too cautious, that's what you are."

She knew the procedure well enough to realize the battle was over—at least for today. When it came to specifics, Mr. Rookheiser couldn't produce, but he enjoyed the debate all the same. It was the argument itself that stimulated him, she'd determined, and any time he could mix up a conversation he was happy. A wealthy man, he had little to occupy his time, and he spent most of it arguing the pros and cons of his health.

But this day, after relating his various reactions to certain foods, he had something else to fret over. "New people moved in down the street from me, and they've got teenagers. Music all night long and cars roaring up and down the street. No supervision anywhere. And the man calls himself a doctor." He sniffed.

"The man?" Maggie glanced at the clock. It was almost five o'clock and she was anxious to leave.

"Baines. Dr. Baines. The one from Boston who crippled his hand. You know who I mean. He was a hooligan as a kid and he's no better now. I remember when he and his friends would roar up and down the street, and it hasn't changed a bit since..."

His voice droned on about Tanner's wild youth and about the state of the country's children in general, but Maggie's brain ceased functioning. Was there no getting away from Tanner?

She waited for an opening and then interjected, "You live near Dr. Baines?"

"Sure. Don't you know it? He lives on Skyridge. I'm on the side street. Better location on the lake," he added with another sniff.

She'd known Mr. Rookheiser lived on the lake, but she hadn't thought about how close he was to Tanner. Why should she? Tanner hadn't occupied the house for years. She'd assumed it was owned by someone else.

"And that daughter of his. I've seen her with boys twice her age until all hours of the night. I'd bet her dad isn't even home. If she were my daughter I'd teach her a thing or two, I'll tell ya."

Though Maggie knew how he exaggerated, she couldn't help feeling a fresh wave of worry and regret. What was going on with Tanner? What was happening with Shelley?

She suddenly wanted to see Tanner again, to assure herself that all was well and that her nebulous fears were just a hangover from when she'd loved him. She didn't understand his refusal to see her any more now than she had fourteen years before, but she was bound and determined to find out.

"Thanks for coming in," she said distractedly to a surprised Mr. Rookheiser after his session was over. "I'll see you next week."

Chad had warned her not to get involved with patients, but Maggie found it nearly impossible to be so detached. She enjoyed working with them, reveling in their triumphs and sharing their failures and disappointments. Shelley Baines's case would have normally interested her anyway; the fact that she was Tanner's daughter only piqued Maggie's interest all the more.

She glanced at her watch and made a rueful face at her reflection in the windshield as she eased her car to a stop across the road from Tanner's house. She was crazy to be here, but damn it all, Shelley deserved better than Tanner was giving her. And besides, Maggie could admit, she had a few things to straighten out with him herself.

She slammed the door shut and walked down the flagstone path to the front porch. Weeds had multiplied between the stones, and the grass around the path looked dry and crackly. How long had it been since someone had cared for the place? Since Tanner's father, Dr. Gerrard Baines, had moved out?

Her palms were moist and it took several moments before she could find the courage to ring the bell. Fourteen years earlier she'd fled this house in misery; she wondered how she would feel reentering it now.

Shelley herself opened the door, eyes widening at the sight of Maggie.

"Hello," Maggie said. "Is your father home?"

"Er, yes . . . in the study."

"Could you tell him I'm here?"

She was left in the elegant foyer—only now it wasn't quite so elegant. The white balustrade that curved to the upper hallway had yellowed with neglect and the carpet runner over the oak stairs had faded. But the furniture and walls looked clean and polished, and with Mrs. Greer on duty, Maggie wouldn't have expected less. Still, the house had been empty for many years, and it showed in the dingy wallpaper and corroded brass around the base of the crystal chandelier. Only the wood floor gleamed with care, new cream-and-pink Oriental rugs covering its bare length.

She heard Tanner's footsteps creak on the planks before he came into view. Throat dry, Maggie watched him walk into the room and stop dead near the spiraled end of the banister.

He didn't say anything.

"If the mountain won't come to Muhammad . . ." Maggie said with a slight shrug.

"You're here because of Shelley."

Though it wasn't a question, Maggie knew there was a seed of doubt underneath. She understood. "Yes."

Tanner inhaled a long, silent breath and turned his head, frowning as he looked toward the empty living room. It was all Maggie could do to drop her eyes from his profile. That indefinable, mesmerizing quality he'd had when he was young was still there. He'd always had it; it was part of his makeup—unconscious and unwanted. It had trapped Maggie's heart and Tricia Wellesley's, too, and it still had the power to draw her just as irresistibly now.

His face was lean, hollowed out and more mature, but his hair was still the sun-streaked gold she remembered, his skin still seemingly too dark for that pale mane. He wore a lightweight summer jacket over a T-shirt and jeans, his hands thrust deeply in the pockets. He could have been twenty-two again except for the lines of disenchantment around his mouth and the faint webbing of crow's feet radiating from his eyes. What he didn't appear like was the respected surgeon he was—or had been—and Maggie tried to think of him in those terms, and failed.

"Maybe you'd better tell me what's on your mind," he said, sounding grim, and after a pause he headed toward the living room, waiting while Maggie passed through the archway ahead of him.

Given the floor, she hardly knew how to start. She stood helplessly in the center of the room, watching as Tanner, after turning on a corner lamp, leaned against the wall, his arms behind him, his ankles crossed.

"I haven't really talked to you much about Shelley's diabetes," she said awkwardly. "I'd—like to know your own feelings about it."

"Tricia and I learned about it a few years ago, just when Shelley was entering junior high. We were worried, naturally." He moved his jaw. "But Shelley seemed to take it in stride, and it hasn't been a problem to her."

"You mean it wasn't a problem until you moved here."

"Is it a problem now?"

"Well, yes . . ." Didn't he know? "That's why she came to me, isn't it?"

Tanner made an exasperated sound. "She didn't consult me about you—just went ahead and made the appointment. She's very independent. Had I known she was going to . . ."

His voice trailed off, but Maggie, her sixth sense still very strong where he was concerned, picked up the thread instantly and finished, "You never would have let her come see Maggie Holt."

When he didn't answer she felt those embers of anger that had never quite died grow hot again. "Someday maybe you'll tell me just what I did to make you hate me so much," she said tautly. "But right now I don't have time to figure it out. All I want to do is help your daughter. Something you don't seem to care to do."

"I love my daughter, Maggie," he said. "And I don't hate you."

In the lamplight she could see how tense he was, but she didn't care about his demons. "Do you want to hear about Shelley, or not?"

He waved a hand in surrender, then ran it across his forehead, a surprisingly vulnerable gesture.

"I don't know her very well yet," Maggie said, "but she's crying out for attention. She wanted you to come to my office—I could see that. But you wouldn't, and by her reaction, I'd say it's not the first time you've let her down." Maggie took a deep breath and plunged on recklessly. "I don't know what's going on between the two of you, but I've got a pretty good idea Shelley's recent problems with her diabetes are a result of it. She doesn't need me—she needs a psychologist. I'm no expert, but I think she's purposely not eating right."

"That's ridiculous!" Tanner looked stunned.

"You think so?" Maggie was glad to get some kind of reaction from him. Searching through her purse, she said, "I asked her to give me a list of foods she'd eaten the past few days and she gave me this." Crossing the room, she held out the folded paper to him. Tanner gave her a sweeping glance from his tawny eyes before accepting it. "Is that what she's had to eat?" Maggie asked. "If so, it's Plan A, food for food, the menu in my nutrition pamphlet."

"She lied to you." He didn't seem particularly surprised.

"And why would she do that, since you yourself said *she* made the appointment to come see me?"

Tanner's lips tightened, but he said nothing.

Pressing her advantage, Maggie implored, "What's going on? She's playing with fire—her own health, for God's sake!"

"I'll talk to her."

I'll talk to her. How could he be so blind? To Maggie, who'd only seen Shelley a few times, the problem was glaringly clear, and one that wouldn't be resolved with a good old heart-to-heart.

She stared at him in total bewilderment. "I don't—think—it's that simple," she said haltingly. "Tanner..."

His name was a soft sigh on her lips, and surprisingly, it got the greatest reaction out of him. "Go away, Maggie," he muttered tersely. "Thanks for telling me about Shelley, but just—go away."

"I don't understand."

"I don't want you here," he said flatly. "Is that clear enough? Although I appreciate what you've done for Shelley, I don't want to see you again."

Tears filled her eyes. It was amazing, but he still had the power to hurt her with a few cutting words. Turning toward the door, she felt his hand close over her arm. She stiffened. In a voice rough with unshed tears she said, "Let go of me. If you want me to leave, let go of me!"

"Damn it all," he muttered.

"I don't understand you! And I don't think I like you very much."

She would have jerked away, but his other hand came out to grab her, and when she still tried to twist from his grasp he turned her around, forcing her to meet his tortured gaze. "I'd hoped things would be different by now. But they're not!"

"For you, maybe." Maggie was adamant. "My life's totally different than it was."

"That's not what I mean."

"I don't care what you mean."

Her bravado was the result of fourteen years of hurt. She hadn't known she'd hurt so much, and for so long, but she had. He'd wounded her when she was so young and impressionable that the memory refused to fade.

His own anger seemed to melt in the face of such stern opposition. "God, Maggie," he said tiredly. "What are we doing?"

"We're making the past more important than it was," she said bitterly, looking away from the familiar planes of his face. He still affected her. Too much for her own good.

Her eyes drifted downward and in the dim light she saw his hand on her bare arm. His right hand. Only it was a mass of scars and puckered flesh, the skin still red from surgery only a few months before. Shocked, her eyes flew to his, and mistakenly he read pity in her gaze.

He let go of her so fast she stood blinking and dazed, swaying on her feet. "Tanner," she whispered, shattered.

"Didn't you know?" His tone was scathing.

"Well, yes, but..."

"Look, Maggie, I came back to Oregon to put my career behind me. It's over, just like a lot of things. No, don't say anything," he enunciated clearly. "Okay? Nothing."

"Tanner—"

"Just go away. I'll take care of Shelley. She won't be seeing you again."

"You're so damn good at pushing me away!" she cried.

"Not good enough," he retorted grimly, and walked brusquely toward the front door. Maggie had no recourse but to follow, her own steps slow and disjointed. In the foyer, the chandelier gently tinkling above her head, she turned to him, meeting his gaze in wordless regret.

There was nothing more to say. Maggie could read that in Tanner's face. With a feeling the past would never set her free, she left, walking down the pathway toward her car, unable to prevent looking back to the gnarled oak that had been her indoctrination into Tanner's life. Because she couldn't help herself, she thought back to those long-ago days, remembering the first time she'd met him, the first time they'd kissed, the first and only time they'd made love.

As she drove home her mind was filled with memories, and for the first time in a long time she let herself recall every detail....

Chapter Three

At fifteen Maggie Holt was more interested in finding a part-time summer job to help pay for college than in thinking about boys. Her divorced mother, who worked long hours in the local grocery store, was able to take care of Maggie and her brother, Connor, but there was no extra money to be had. So when Con suggested a way she might be able to get on at the cannery with him, she jumped at the chance.

There was just one little catch.

"I want you to do something for me," he said, rubbing the still tender ankle he'd injured that spring. "I'm—in a little trouble and I need your help."

"What kind of trouble?"

"Nothing major," he assured her. "Just listen. I need to get a message to one of my friends. I want you to take it to him."

Her curiosity piqued, Maggie asked, "Which friend?"

"His name's Tanner. You don't know him. He lives on the lake."

"Forget it." Maggie instantly lost interest. Connor was always seeking acceptance with the elite Lake Oswego crowd, and to her it was like selling out. His injured ankle was even testimony to his social climbing; he'd broken it on a skiing trip with some of his new, so-called friends.

"Would you just listen?" he demanded insistently. "I've got to talk to Tanner *tonight*. It's important, okay? His old man's got it in for me and won't let me see him."

"Why?"

Connor's look was straight. "Because I'm not good enough."

Not good enough. Anger burned in Maggie's chest. She could put down Connor all she liked, but no one, especially lake people, treated her brother that way. She began to listen with more interest.

"Dr. Baines is a royal pain in the ass," Connor said feelingly. "He's got a choke hold on Tanner. He's so afraid of losing face in the community that when Tanner's home from college he practically chains him to his room. I swear he listens in on his phone calls, too."

"Why does this Tanner put up with it?"

"He doesn't." A smile curved the corners of Connor's mouth. "He's been doing what he likes on the sly. It's been great." He made a face. "But last night we got caught and boy, it's a mess...."

While Maggie wondered what kind of trouble she might be letting herself into, Con laid out his plans. "There's an oak tree on the side of the house. It goes up to the second floor and it's right outside Tanner's bedroom window. We've talked about using it before but haven't had the chance."

"No way. I'm not crazy."

"All you have to do is climb up and drop this message in his room. Simple." He pulled a sealed envelope from his pocket.

"Climb the tree yourself."

"Very funny," he said, and as if thinking she required more proof of his injury, he took off his shoe and sock and unwrapped the bandage, showing her irrefutably that the puffiness around his foot was no joke.

"Call him, then. Maybe he'll answer the phone."

Connor made a deprecatory sound. "Not a chance. After last night he'll be lucky to be alive. His dad'll pick up the phone for sure. This note is a plan to get him out of the house. Come on, Maggie. Help me and I'll help you."

Later she couldn't remember actually agreeing to help him, but before she knew it she and Con were in his pickup and he was pulling up near the Baines house on Skyridge Drive. With an air of stealth he let himself out into the sultry night, and when Maggie, riddled by second thoughts, didn't move, he impatiently motioned her to follow suit.

"Come on," he urged when they were walking through the tall grass at the side of the road. "It'll be a cinch. Just climb up the tree, deliver the note and climb back down. I'll do the rest."

"The rest?"

"Getting Tanner out of the house. Don't worry. I'll take you home first."

"I don't know why I'm doing this," Maggie muttered, and stopped dead at the edge of the Baineses' manicured lawn.

"The whole thing's so damned ridiculous," Con said in an angry undertone. "He's almost twenty. Okay, Maggie. See that window, the one on the second floor? That's his."

Maggie's eye followed her brother's pointing finger. She saw the lichened oak, its branches reaching toward the house like welcoming arms. The upstairs window was dark except for a faint illumination that meant, Connor explained, the bedroom door was open to the hall.

"This is crazy," Maggie muttered. "You're crazy."

"Here." Connor stuffed the envelope in her hand and Maggie slid it into the pocket of her jeans. "Come on."

He took off in a gimping run, head and shoulders bent against possible detection. Maggie, too afraid to be left alone, hurried after him, heart pounding madly.

The trunk was high and Connor positioned his back against it, linking his palms together for a leg up. Maggie took several deep breaths and put her tennis-shoed foot in his hands.

"Step on my shoulders," he whispered tautly as he strained to hold her weight.

Fingers grappling for a hold on the rough bark, Maggie teetered, and she heard Connor groan as he had to shift his weight to his weak ankle. Anxious for him as well as herself, she got her arms around the first branch and gently swung from his grasp, her fingers digging into the bark.

It was at that moment the porch light came on.

Connor backed around the trunk, into the shadows, but Maggie hung, legs down, from a branch bathed in unforgiving light.

She was afraid to move, pinned by her own fear.

Tanner's father, Dr. Gerrard Baines, came into Maggie's view. His back was toward her and he was smoking a cigarette, staring across the road to the low-slung car parked there. He stopped halfway across the yard.

Perspiration broke out on Maggie's forehead. Her fingers slipped. Knowing she was going to fall, she closed her eyes and held on by sheer willpower, freezing her muscles.

Then abruptly Gerrard Baines turned back toward the house. She heard his footsteps and risked opening one eye in time to see him furiously grind out his cigarette as he headed back inside, never once looking in Maggie's direction.

As soon as he was out of sight she hiked up her arms and swung her legs to the branch, giving her aching muscles a moment to recover.

"I'm not doing this," she hissed down at Con.

He was laughing shakily. "Jeez, that man is tough. I think he hates Tanner. Did you see the way he looked at his car? God."

"Did you hear me? I'm not doing this!"

"Come on, Maggie. Buck up. I've almost talked the cannery into letting you help out a little. Jay's for it."

She hauled herself upright on the branch. A job. A real job. It was tough to find anyone who would hire a fifteen-year-old. "You mean it?" she demanded suspiciously.

"Cross my heart and hope to die."

"At this rate you will before the end of the summer," she muttered, and she glanced down while she climbed higher to see her brother's rakish grin.

With determination Maggie eyed the distance to Tanner's bedroom window and scrambled up one more branch. Waiting several moments, gathering strength and courage, she crawled toward the end of the branch until it began to dip, then she swung downward, scooting her hands farther along until the branch was near breaking, and she reached with her toe for the sill.

"Hallelujah." Con's soft voice filtered upward as Maggie, with a teenager's blind belief in her own infallibility, dropped inside Tanner's room.

Dusting off her hands, she hurriedly reached inside her pocket, her heart pumping double-time. All she wanted to do was get back on the ground safe and sound.

"And who the hell are you?"

The voice froze Maggie where she stood. She'd thought she was alone. Her head whipped up instinctively, eyes scared, and in the dim light she saw him, leaning against the panels of the open door, his chest bare, his arms folded in judgment. Tanner Baines.

Relief flooded through her. Thank God it wasn't his father!

His brows were lifted in surprise and his eyes studied her carefully, finding, Maggie was sure, something lacking in the gangly girl in bark-strewn T-shirt and jeans.

"I'm Maggie Holt," she whispered quickly, distractedly brushing off her clothes. "Connor's sister."

"Really."

"Look, I don't want to be here, either. I was supposed to give you this." She walked softly across the room, throwing a glance toward the open doorway before stepping across that path of illumination.

Tanner took the envelope but didn't open it. He seemed unsure how to deal with her. "I didn't know Con had a sister."

"Well, he does."

"I see."

His skin looked dark, but his hair was pale, a sun-streaked tangle that touched something inside her she'd never felt before. He moved and she saw muscles glide beneath his skin, and as she watched him slowly shut the door, her eyes were mesmerized by the play of light on the supple strength of his back and shoulders.

The door clicked shut and it was dark, and Maggie's pulse began pounding again. She was crazy to be here.

Crazy! Instinctively she sidled toward the window, at the same time sensing, rather than seeing, Tanner move to the other side of the room.

He switched on a bedside lamp and Maggie blinked. "What's Con doing?" he asked.

"I don't know. Read the note." She glanced out the window and saw Con's shadowy figure outside. "He said something about wanting you to come out tonight. He said you'd gotten into some kind of trouble last night and I— well, I don't know...it's in the note."

With a narrow-eyed look that said judgment would be reserved where she was concerned, he ripped open the envelope. As he read, a small smile touched the corners of his mouth.

"Tanner!" Dr. Baines's voice rang through the lower hallway and Maggie nearly jumped from her skin.

She was already scrambling out the window when she felt his hands circle her waist, dragging her back in. "Shh," he hissed in her ear and, still holding her captive, yelled back, "What?" in a distinctly resentful tone.

"Come on down here. *Now.*"

She felt the rage of emotion that went through him, and for some strange reason her heart went out to him. Dr. Baines, apparently, was an autocratic parent who refused to treat his son with adult respect.

"In a minute," Tanner yelled.

"Now!"

"You'd better go," he said, his hands pushing her with controlled urgency. "I'll wait until you're safe on the ground."

She felt his touch against her bare skin as her shirt separated from her jeans. It was warm and hard and did things to her nerve endings that baffled her. "Tanner...?" Maggie twisted around.

"Yeah?" He was distracted, his gaze locked on his bedroom door.

Maggie didn't know what she wanted to say. Something. Something important. She was close enough to see the strange shade of gold his eyes were, the tawny lashes surrounding them, the dark texture of his skin and the evening stubble on his jaw. Inside herself she felt a change, a recognition, and for the first time in her life she couldn't express exactly what she felt.

Her silence brought his head around, prompting a likewise inspection from him. She was embarrassed when his gaze slid over her face: her serious eyes, her cheekbones, the parted curves of her mouth. What did he see? A tomboy whose only remarkable feature was rich auburn, tousled shoulder-length hair?

"How old are you?" he asked.

She wanted to lie but knew Connor would tell him the truth anyway. "Fifteen."

"Good God! Get out of here before you get us both in trouble."

He practically pushed her out the window in his haste, but one arm held onto her until she'd gotten a strong hold on the branch. It was a guiding hand, one meant to make certain she wouldn't fall, but its imprint was felt long after Maggie slid down the tree trunk.

Connor waved to Tanner and he signaled back, ducking his golden head back inside as her brother's strong fingers urged her across the sweeping Baines lawn. Maggie went willingly, but she couldn't resist several backward glances.

At the car Connor asked, "Did you give him the note? What did he say?"

"He just—smiled."

"Good. Good." His head bobbed up and down, then suddenly noticing Maggie's distraction, he peered at her closely and asked, "You okay?"

"Sure. Why wouldn't I be?"

He spread his hands. "Beats me."

They made it the rest of the way home without mishap, and Connor, true to his word, got her a "helping-out" job at the cannery. She worked hard, saving every penny for the college fund she knew she would have to create herself. But meeting Tanner Baines gave her a new and disturbing perspective on her future, and almost against her will she found herself seeking her brother's company whenever she could, casually inserting questions about what he was doing and whom he was doing it with, hoping to hear news of Tanner.

But summer ended and the seasons changed. It wasn't until the next summer, Maggie's sixteenth, that she got to see him again.

She and Con were both working at the cannery and didn't have much of a social life, but one morning, as he and Maggie were walking to the truck, Connor let it out that he was going waterskiing with Tanner Baines after after work.

It was the opportunity she'd been looking for. All day she made plans, and when Con drove her home she begged him to take her to the swim park and drop her off. Grudgingly he acquiesced.

At the swim park Maggie walked to the outermost section of the floating wooden dock, took off her cover-up, and dangled her feet in the water, waiting for Tanner's boat to go by. It bothered her a little, the lengths she would go to just for a glimpse of the man she'd met so briefly, but her feelings were too strong for her to dwell on them long.

She'd been there about an hour, when a white boat with a slashing red stripe zipped by, pulling a skier. She saw the foaming wake and the sheet of water fan out beneath the fiberglass ski, recognized the dark hair of her brother, and swung her gaze to the driver. Tanner was at the wheel, watching the water, the muscles of his bare back working with the effort of keeping the boat on course, his eyes glancing back occasionally to see that Connor was still upright.

It took a moment or two for her to realize they weren't alone. A girl with lustrous black hair sat on one of the red cushions, her arms thrown out over the boat's gunwale, her face turned to the sky.

Maggie stared at her in bewilderment, followed by rising self-anger as she realized how utterly insane she'd been. Of course he had a girlfriend. He was a man, while she was still a girl. What had she expected?

Then Tanner's blond head turned and his gaze swept over her. Maggie cringed inside, sure she was as transparent as her childish feelings. He looked away, then back again quickly. The boat swung in a slow, wide arc and Maggie realized he was coming in to dock. Scrambling to her feet, she suddenly wished there were somewhere to hide, but there was nothing she could do. As the boat drew near she saw the curves and rounded softness of the other girl and silently added the resentment of her own firm, tall build to her already deep misery.

"Maggie, isn't it?" Tanner said over the engine's throbbing idle, his eyes filled with lazy amusement.

She could have died. He wasn't making fun of her—not really—but she could have died all the same. Connor, who'd sunk in the water at the sudden stop, yelled at Tanner and swam to the dock, glaring at Maggie as he shook water from his black hair.

"What the hell are you doing?" he demanded of her.

"Swimming." She squinted against the light, refusing to buckle under to the insecurities clamoring inside her. "I see you got out of the house," she said to Tanner.

"Even my father can't keep me locked up for a year," was the sardonic reply.

Before she could say anything more, Connor tossed the skis into the back of the boat and agilely jumped in beside the black-haired girl. He threw his cold, wet arms around her and she shrieked and leaped from the cushion, glaring at him.

"Damn you, Connor!" She sidled next to Tanner and said acidly, "He's such a barbarian."

Tanner laughed. "And you love it." Cocking his head toward Maggie, he asked, "Want to come along?"

It was exactly what she wanted, but Connor's look of incredulity, as if Tanner had suddenly lost his mind, and the other girl's lack of enthusiasm, made her feel like an unwanted intruder. "I . . . don't know. I can't ski."

"I'll teach you how." He held out a hand to help her aboard and Maggie tentatively took it. For just an instant his eyes met hers and she saw genuine liking in their clear amber depths. With a return of spirit she hopped into the boat.

"This is Tricia Wellesley. Tricia, Maggie Holt, Connor's little sister."

Tricia examined her critically but without apparent malice. "I didn't know Con had a sister."

"I'm a well-kept secret, obviously."

Connor said pointedly, "Who should be kept a secret."

"Oh, I don't know," Tanner drawled, then added, "There's an extra seat over here, Maggie."

She accepted the chair, conscious of how close Tanner's long legs were to her own. He was standing at the wheel, and as he pushed the throttle forward he shifted position and his calves brushed her shins. The boat pulled slowly away from the dock, but when they were outside the safety speed zone he thrust the throttle full ahead. The boat rose out of the water with an angry growl and skimmed across the lake's shining green surface.

"We'll start you in the water," he hollered over the noise. "I'll get in with you and make sure you're positioned right."

"But I don't know how," Maggie screamed back, trying to hold on to her wildly whipping hair.

He looked back with a grin. "Don't worry. I'll take care of that. Connor can drive the boat and I'll personally make sure you get up on skis today."

Maggie's inherent athletic ability and Tanner's expert instruction ensured that she learned to water-ski almost instantly. Con, after his initial disgust at having to drag along his little sister, even treated her with grudging respect. Only Tricia's feelings about her had been hard to decipher. But she didn't worry about the other girl unduly. To Maggie, the day had been a sheer delight, and she'd reveled in the feel of Tanner's hands on her as he'd showed her how to water-ski.

Long after the lesson was over she thought back to the way he touched her to get her to bend her knees just right, the way he held his arms around hers to explain the tension needed to keep upright, the way his laughter rumbled from his chest, low and thrillingly masculine.

She was determined to see him again.

Later that summer they had one day alone waterskiing together—a time out of time when everything fell into place. A time when, to Maggie's secret pleasure, Tanner invited them all skiing but neither Tricia nor Con could join them.

She had him all to herself.

Maggie sat in the front swivel chair next to Tanner in his boat, her eyes on the sun-sparkled water. It seemed like no one was about; she could have been alone in the world with Tanner Baines.

While Tanner drove the boat over the water, a thousand questions buzzed through her mind. What was his relationship with Tricia? Did he really want to become a doctor? Why didn't he and his father get along? Was he really going to go to med school on the East Coast? What did he think about *her*?

The questions nagged her. She needed to know. And though she tried to remind herself that Tanner was little more than a stranger—a stranger who wouldn't appreciate her probing, she couldn't stand not knowing. He was too important to her.

Tanner pulled the boat into the dark shadows of a tiny inlet and Maggie tried to tactfully broach one of the questions on her mind. Before she could speak, however, he said, "We can't water-ski today, so I thought we'd swim at Phantom's Cove."

"Can't water-ski?"

"We have no spotter. The lake patrol demands three in the boat—skier, driver and spotter—in case the skier gets in trouble without the driver knowing it."

The boat gently rocked and neither of them moved. Sunlight beat heavy and hot on Maggie's bare legs. "Could we talk, then, for a while?" she asked, almost breathlessly.

He settled himself on the red cushions, his legs stretched out in front of him. "Sure. Got something on your mind?"

She blushed. Always forthright, she seemed now to be a stranger to herself, unable to voice what she felt. "Tell me about your father," she said at length. "If you don't mind, that is. Connor alluded to things last summer and I've wondered ever since."

"About me? Why?"

"I don't know." She felt her chest tighten. "I just have."

He studied her through lazy eyes. "You're awfully young."

"I'm only a few years younger than you."

He thought that over for a long time, his gaze never far from her face. She sensed a change in the air but couldn't put her finger on it, and she waited in silence, heat prickling her scalp and sending a trickle of sweat down between her breasts.

She thought he wasn't going to answer and was searching for a new topic, when he said, "Last summer was rebellion. My father and I don't get along very well, and last summer I put him through the wringer."

"How do you mean?"

"I thwarted him every way I knew how. I never came home when I should. I snuck out in the evenings—with your brother's help," he added, grinning slyly. "I didn't help out at his clinic the way I'm doing this year. I just plain didn't give a damn. He tried grounding me, threatening me, cutting off my money. But he was so damned worried about propriety that I had the upper hand. He *had* to avoid a scandal."

Maggie leaned back, her arms on the hot fiberglass back of the boat. "Why?"

Tanner made a deprecatory noise. "Beats me. Latent puritanism, I'd say. Anyway, he wants me to become a doctor, and when he caught Connor and me with . . ." His hesitation made Maggie realize he'd suddenly remembered whom he was with.

"I won't rat on my brother, if that's what you think. I wouldn't do that."

He laughed silently. "No—I was more worried what you'd think of me."

His tawny eyes held hers and the moment spun out timelessly. Mesmerized, Maggie cleared her throat and managed to tear her gaze away, feeling a wave of heat build from her lower limbs. "I won't think anything."

He hesitated, then said, "We were with some girls, and he caught us in, um, a very compromising position. Not the worst," he put in quickly, giving her a look, "but bad enough."

Maggie didn't say anything. The thought of Tanner with a girl—any girl—filled her with a poisonous emotion she recognized as the same one she'd witnessed on Tricia's face.

"You're shocked," he said bluntly.

"No." Maggie circled her lips with her tongue. "What happened then?"

Tanner made a face. "My father was furious, but the worst thing is he blamed Connor for everything—not me. He'd never even met Con before!" He shifted, as if his thoughts made him uncomfortable, then stared out over the water. "He'd never embarrassed me before, but he embarrassed me that night. I didn't know where he was coming from. I still don't. But I was humiliated that he was my father." With a sigh he added, "Now I try to keep things straight so he won't come unglued, but it's tough."

His honesty impressed Maggie. "And med school?" she asked carefully. "Was that his idea or yours?"

His eyes swept over her again. "You're very perceptive, aren't you?"

"Connor thinks I'm nosy."

He smiled. "You're his sister," he said. "I guess he would." With a reflective soberness she was beginning to recognize, he answered, "My being a doctor was my father's idea, but it got planted in my head so young that I believed I wanted it as much as he did. Until the past few years."

"And now?"

"Now I'm not really sure…maybe…" He shrugged and his eyes narrowed thoughtfully.

The afternoon wore on and he told her other things about himself, how his mother, a quiet, artistic person who'd been stifled by his overbearing father, had died several years earlier, how he'd struggled to get over her death and be the person his father wanted him to be, how in the end he'd rebelled against everything and only his father's wish that he become a doctor had survived.

Maggie, at sixteen, was no expert on people in general—and certainly in men in particular—but she had good instincts. As she listened, she distantly sensed that Tanner Baines was a man worth fighting for. He had all the qualities she inherently prized: honesty, intelligence, a touch of self-mockery that smoothed over any arrogance and a quick, dry sense of humor that matched her own.

Shadows were lengthening when she got through answering some of his questions about her: what she wanted to do with her life, how she felt about her family, where she planned to go to school and what she planned to study. Startled at how fast the time had passed, Maggie looked at her watch and realized she'd fallen in love with Tanner Baines in one afternoon.

Just before dusk they ran out of things to say. Maggie felt the first cooling breeze as she looked across at Tanner. Sunlight was slanting into the boat, moving with gently swaying fingers across the hot red cushions and the dark skin of his legs. She'd never known she could be so happy.

"We didn't swim," Tanner observed in surprise as he glanced at his waterproof watch.

"It doesn't matter."

She smiled sleepily and stretched her arms, aware, suddenly, that his gaze had drifted lower, over the tanned skin of her neck and arms to the swell of her breasts above the one-piece red suit.

He tore his eyes away but Maggie's heart beat faster. She slowly dropped her arms, watching him. He didn't want to want her, but he did. She was woman enough to understand that much, but she wasn't brave enough to do anything about it.

With a suddenness that took her by surprise he stepped on the gunwales and dove cleanly into the dark green water, the boat lurching slightly from his thrust. Maggie let out a pent-up breath and leaned over the side, waiting for him to come up.

When he surfaced, she asked, "How's the water?"

"Try it and see." He shook water from his hair and gave her a smile.

Her own dive wasn't as powerful as his, but she knifed cleanly through the surface. Her body was shocked by the sudden chill, and when she came up she was gasping. "It's freezing!"

He laughed. "It's deep here. And cold."

"You don't say." She was treading water, moving slowly backward so she could swim around to the aft of the boat and climb up the ladder. But Tanner was between her and her objective. "I'm getting out."

"So soon?"

"It's late. I've got to get back, and I need to thaw out."

As she swam past him, she felt his hands circle her waist. She turned, curious, and felt a thrill of anticipation. She saw the grim purpose of his mouth, the sensual need in his eyes. Fascinated, she remained breathless, feeling the slight brushing of his legs against hers as he kept himself afloat.

"Maggie..." With one hand he grabbed the ladder; with the other he pulled her nearer.

She had no idea what to do. Time stretched as she watched and waited, aware of his inner torment. Hunger burned like a flame in those gold eyes. Slowly he drew her firmly against him.

His heart was a hammer, pounding against hers. Her own pulse was out of control. His face was beaded with water, droplets running ever more quickly from his hair. She focused on his lips the second before she felt them on her own, tender, needing, waiting for her to decide. Tentatively she answered, wrapping her arms around his waist, depending on his support, feeling how hot his mouth was on her cold flesh.

A fever grew between them, radiating from Tanner, burning into Maggie's passive form. He kissed her and kissed her, and she met him with weak, parted lips, drugged by the potency of desire. His breath was ragged, and she felt the convulsive way he tugged her closer.

Sensations rippled through her and she wound her arms around him, seeking the liquid muscles beneath his flesh, tasting his skin as she felt his tongue roughly lick the water from her cheek.

Instinctively she wrapped her legs around him, seeking support, and then abruptly it was over. He froze, his heart still thudding out of control, his muscles hard and poised. "My God, Maggie..." he muttered hoarsely, and before she could even blink he'd thrust himself away, leaving her scrambling for the ladder.

He swam so long underwater she became frightened, but when he finally shot upward, gasping for air, her relief was short-lived. His expression was stony and determined.

"That," he said succinctly, "can't happen again."

He was quiet on the return trip, too quiet, and Maggie, wrapped in a fluffy red-and-white beach towel, shivered with anxiety and cold.

On the long trek up the cliff to his house she had to hurry to keep up with him, her wet feet slipping in her sandals, her hair falling in front of her eyes. He waited for her on the back deck, and by the time she reached him she was out of breath—and gloriously furious.

"Thanks a—whole lot—for waiting for me," she managed to choke out. "I really—appreciate it."

"Damn it all, Maggie." He shook his head and clenched his jaw.

"I'm not a silly little girl," she said tersely. "You didn't take advantage of me. You couldn't. I wanted to kiss you."

His face registered incredulity. "I wanted to do a helluva lot more than that," he said repressively.

"You think I don't know?"

For a moment he just stared at her, then he swore beneath his breath and turned toward the house. "Come on. You've got to go home before things get totally out of control."

She had no recourse but to follow him, but at the car she hesitated, wanting something more, some kind of reassurance. "Thank you for today," she said in a small voice. "I enjoyed myself."

She heard his deep sigh and saw him lean weakly against the sunbaked hood of the car. "So did I, Maggie." He made a rueful face and almost laughed. "You're lucky this didn't happen last summer. I wasn't nearly so noble."

"Am I lucky?"

His eyes darkened. Seeing her stricken face he had to look away. "Don't . . ." he warned between his teeth, and then left before the situation could get out of hand.

In September Maggie turned seventeen, and during the following school year she started a new practice—dating. She'd never had much interest in boys, other than Tanner, but this last year of school she made a conscious effort, trying to see the boys in her class through new eyes. Beyond that she set her sights on college, worrying how she would ever amass enough money to get her through.

By school's end she'd made the decision she wanted to study something in the medical field, and that a career was more important to her than romance. Newly sophisticated, she'd given up her foolish dreams about Tanner Baines and determined she wasn't even interested in seeing him this summer.

Until Con let it be known that Tanner was having a party.

"It's a big bash to celebrate graduation. His dad's out of town so Tanner's having his friends over. He's been accepted to a Boston medical school."

Desolation settled around Maggie's heart like cold ice. Boston. Medical school. She'd been naive to think she'd gotten over Tanner. The thought of him moving away for at least four years was almost more than she could bear.

"Want to come?" Connor suddenly invited. "I don't think Tanner would care. He seems to like you."

"What makes you say that?"

"I don't know. He asks about you a lot—what you're doing, how you are, et cetera, et cetera. God, it's been two years since you climbed through the window. He still remembers."

So Tanner hadn't told Connor about last year's boat trip, about the stolen kisses they'd shared.

They went to Tanner's party together and Maggie was glad for his presence. Connor knew everyone, it appeared, and he performed introductions, never downgrading Maggie as his younger sister, which was a definite change for the better.

But he left her about a half an hour into the party and Maggie had to fend for herself. When one particularly bothersome boy kept dogging her, she was glad to hear Tanner's familiar drawl sound from somewhere behind her head. "Pardon me, Doug," he said, "but Maggie's a personal guest."

Maggie turned. Amusement gleamed from Tanner's tawny eyes.

With an apology the drunken Doug wandered off, and Maggie said, "I'm not a personal guest. I'm a party crasher."

"I told Con to bring a date."

"I am *not* my brother's date."

He laughed, that deep, sexy rumble that set her senses on fire. "Then be mine. I don't have one, either."

There was a difference in him that had been missing before, a surety, a lack of tension. Had he reconciled with his father? she wondered. Did that account for the change?

She didn't have a chance to ask him as people drifted in and out, some down to the boathouse dock, others drinking and eating in the soft June sunshine on Tanner's back deck. But he kept her right by his side, possessively, and Maggie couldn't help her spirits from soaring as she puzzled over what this might mean.

Connor noticed Tanner's attentiveness and raised his brows at his little sister. Maggie met his gaze blandly, but Con frowned. When the party came to a close he was right beside her, a proprietary move that both amused and irritated Maggie.

Somehow Tanner had managed to send everyone home except her and Con, and as the clock struck midnight they walked outside, standing awkwardly together in the front drive, as silent as the billions of stars flickering overhead.

Maggie wished Tanner would ask her to stay, but he just looked at Con. Neither of them said anything, and in the end Maggie had no choice but to leave with her brother.

She fretted anxiously over when she would get to see Tanner again, and as it turned out, she didn't have to wait long. To her utter surprise he showed up on her doorstep not two days later. Bedraggled and berry-stained from her work at the cannery, Maggie stood in shocked wonderment when she opened the door. Tanner had never been over before, not even as a friend of Con's.

It happened that her mother was at work that evening, so Tanner didn't get to meet her. Excusing herself, Maggie quickly showered and washed and blow-dried her hair, half believing he would magically disappear by the time she was through. But he was still there, seated indolently on one of the threadbare armchairs. He invited Maggie out and they took his boat across the lake to the dock of an exclusive restaurant. Within minutes they were shown to an outdoor patio table, shaded from the evening sun by an umbrella, their chairs pulled close together. They ate fish and sipped tea and fed crusts of bread to the ducks and geese that landed on the railing and waddled between the tables. They laughed. They talked. They fell in love all over again, and Tanner told her that he and his father had finally come to terms when the Boston medical school had accepted him.

It was the only spoiling moment of a wonderful evening, the realization that Tanner would be gone in a few months' time. But Maggie remained positive, and as the summer wore on they met at various places, keeping a distance from their homes by some unspoken mutual agreement. Maggie didn't want to run into Con, and Tanner, although he and his father got along better, sensed it would be better to keep his feelings for her under wraps. Dr. Baines was notorious for objecting to anything, or anyone, that might deter his son from becoming a doctor.

But they stole moments together when Maggie wasn't working at the cannery or Tanner wasn't helping out at his father's clinic. They shared kisses and touches, and desire throbbed between them, dangerous and seductive. It was Tanner who drew the line on their sexual experimentation, however, carefully making certain they didn't go too far, too fast. Maggie was too blissfully in love to care. She just wanted Tanner and she knew he wanted her. She even dared to believe there might be a place for her in his future.

Then, toward the middle of August, Dr. Gerrard Baines found out his son had a new girlfriend.

The news that his father had questioned Tanner about whom he was dating filled Maggie with dismay way out of proportion to the circumstances. She could still visualize the man glaring at Tanner's sports car, could still remember hanging from the limb outside Tanner's bedroom window, expecting discovery at any moment.

"You'll have to meet him soon," Tanner had told her. "He's not so bad."

"How come I don't believe you?"

"Because I've given you the wrong impression. Come here..."

And he'd pulled her into his arms and kissed her deeply and thoroughly, the way he had all summer; the way that left her only half-satisfied, aching for more; the way that promised more later, when the time was right.

The whole summer magic came to a head at twilight one fateful August evening. Tanner had purposely kept Maggie with him at his house, waiting for his father to come home, and they were both edgy and anxious. Meeting Dr. Baines was the acid test as far as Maggie was concerned— far worse than facing Connor with their feelings, the next unavoidable task.

She was in Tanner's arms, watching purple shadows descend from the trees over the lake, listening to the soft, evening sounds of lazy insects, when Dr. Baines's car turned into the drive.

Tanner tensed and cocked his head but didn't release her, and when his father walked down the hallway and called, "Tanner? Are you home?" he yelled in answer, "We're on the back deck."

Maggie would rather have had some space between her and Dr. Baines's only son on their first meeting, but she understood intuitively that Tanner was making a stand— and this was the way he had to do it.

Upon seeing Maggie, Dr. Baines halted at the open doorway, stunned. "I thought you were with Tricia," he said baldly.

"Not tonight."

Maggie held her breath. She knew Tanner had seen Tricia a few times this summer, more to keep his father off his back than anything else. But he'd assured her their relationship was over now, and she believed him.

Tanner's hands tightened around her. "Dad, this is Maggie Holt. Connor's sister."

"No!" The blood drained from the older man's face. *"No!"* he said with an anguish that made Maggie's blood run cold.

Even Tanner was shaken by his father's extreme reaction. "Tricia and I have quit seeing each other," he explained, giving Maggie a clue to why Gerrard Baines was so upset. "I've been with Maggie."

His chalky face turned even chalkier. "You can't have been," he said again, profoundly shocked.

The air was charged with emotion, destroying the lovely somnolent evening. Instinctively positioning himself between Maggie and his father, Tanner said evenly, "I'm in love with Maggie."

He'd never actually uttered those words to Maggie, though she'd sensed how he felt. Her head spinning, she heard him say, "and I want to marry—"

"NO!"

Tanner's father swept through the doorway like an avenging angel, as if he would forcefully keep the words from passing his son's lips. In disbelief Tanner stared him down and Maggie, torn between ecstasy over Tanner's confession and true fear at his father's reaction, stood slightly behind Tanner's left shoulder, wishing this scene could have been played out without her.

Gerrard flung out a trembling arm. "You can't marry this . . . girl. She's not right for you. You can't—" He inhaled harshly and thundered, "I forbid it! Now take her home and come back so we can talk."

Tanner flushed deep red, resentment flashing in his eyes—the same resentment that had been thinly scarred over but never completely healed. He took Maggie's hand and led her to the door, but his eyes were locked to his father's and they delivered a grim challenge: *You can't stop me!*

Tanner was deadly quiet as he drove around the lake, but instead of taking her home, he drove to the quiet, secluded stretch of wave-lapped shore they'd used as a lovers' retreat all summer. It was a piece of lakeside property primed for development; its signs extolled all the virtues of buying a home on the lake. Tanner and Maggie had spent many hours by the shoreline, hungering for each other. But on this night Tanner's mood wasn't loving, and Maggie felt a chill of premonition as she followed after him down the moonlit path.

He stopped beside a huge fir, its lower branches, bent under their own weight, brushing his shoulders. "I meant what I said, you know. I do love you, and I want to marry you. I want you to come with me to Boston."

Breath held, Maggie searched his face, anxious to believe.

"This summer's been a torture," he said on a heavy sigh. "I have to keep telling myself you're only seventeen."

"I'll be eighteen soon."

"Not soon enough...." As if some unbearable burden were finally lifted, he reached for her, winding his hands in her long hair, kissing her with a fervency that had always been held in check before.

Maggie responded eagerly, her young body as willing and ready as his. Her mind had been made up for a long time. She loved him and she wanted to be his. It wasn't a question of wrong or right, of waiting until she was older, until they were married. She wanted him now, in the heat of a summer night, and Tanner, whose defenses had been steadily crumbling and whose emotions were still at fever's pitch from the scene with his father, couldn't hold back any longer, either.

They fell to the ground together, the tempo of their breathing shallow and ragged, their mouths searching, their hands fumbling for each other's clothes. Too many months of painfully slow touching had led to a torrent of unfulfilled needs, and it wasn't long before Maggie was on her back, lying on Tanner's discarded jacket, her body naked and trembling beneath the power of his.

"I want you," he muttered, kissing her throat, her breasts, her abdomen with an abandon that made her head fall back, her hands clench into his hair.

"I—want—you," she managed, her skin hot and burning from the feel of him rubbing sensuously against her.

"Oh, Maggie..."

"I love you, Tanner. I love you."

There was no more waiting. She felt him hesitate, just for an instant, and she wrapped her legs around him. He kissed her crushingly, and entered with one, fateful thrust, her small cry of pain muffled against the hard contours of his mouth.

Then she felt him move inside her, slowly, building, changing the shock of painful initiation into a bubbling cauldron of desire. She moved with him, accommodating, and learned more about loving in those few feverish moments than she'd ever imagined.

When he slumped against her she cradled his head, hearing him say emotively, "I love you, too, Maggie. Believe me. I always will."

The breakup happened the very next morning. Maggie, knowing his father would already be at his clinic and Tanner wasn't due at work until later, stopped by his house. But Tanner had looked as if he hadn't slept at all and he'd been extremely quiet—until he took her to the back deck and told her he was marrying Tricia Wellesley.

Looking back, it was painfully apparent that Tanner had used her that evening in the dreadful game he'd played out with his father. But she'd always believed he'd loved her, at least to some degree, and she couldn't forget those beautiful summer nights spent in his arms, the closeness they'd shared before Tanner had buckled under to his father's pressure.

If indeed that's what had happened. To this day she was unsure. It could have been that he'd truly loved Tricia all along. He'd even admitted to seeing her, though he'd said it was only for appearances' sake.

Over the years Maggie had succeeded in forgiving him for hurting her so badly—but Con never had. Though he didn't know what had transpired between them, he sensed her pain. To this day Maggie couldn't bring up Tanner's name without having her brother denounce him in some way.

And so the future had unfurled without Tanner. Con had gone to law school, Maggie to college. The only further footnote on the summer was that Maggie ended up receiving a last-minute grant from the university she'd chosen—a surprise that hadn't been able to assuage the ache deep inside her.

For fourteen years her thoughts had often touched on Tanner; she'd wondered what it would be like seeing him again. Now she knew. She was still attracted to him. But this time she was bound and determined not to let him ever find out.

Chapter Four

When the phone rang in the midnight stillness, Maggie had to drag herself up from the depths of sleep. She groped for the receiver, dimly aware that her dreams had been disturbed and fragmented, filled with images from her past.

"Hello?" she murmured sleepily.

"Don't tell me you're already in bed," said a familiar male voice.

"Con." Maggie smiled and lay her head back against the pillows.

"Sorry about the late call, but I got tied up at work this afternoon, and since you didn't return my call..."

"I was busy." Maggie yawned.

"A likely story."

"I was. You're not the only one who has to work for a living y'know."

"You call telling people what to eat working?"

It was great to hear his voice, even greater to be teased like the old days. "Better than ambulance chasing," she said, hiding her amusement.

"I am not and never have been an ambulance chaser." Con paused for effect. "Although a juicy divorce now and then helps pay the phone bill."

They both laughed. Maggie's depression slowly lifted as she thought how fond she was of her brother. His irreverence had cured her blues more than once. "You'll spoil my opinion of you when you talk like that," she said softly. "How come I remember a case where you kept a family together after the kids' parents died? Wasn't that Connor Holt who did that? Fighting for right against might—might being in this case the whole state of California?"

"Luck, my dear. Foster parents wanted to adopt the whole lot of them."

"Oh, really."

"Yep."

Maggie knew differently, and sensing she was embarrassing her brother, she took the opportunity to needle him some more. "Oh, that's right, I forgot. You're just in it for the bucks."

"And the prestige."

"My materialistic older brother," she said fondly. "You don't know how good it is to hear your voice."

Sensing more in her tone than she'd expected to impart, he asked, "Oh? Any reason in particular?"

Maggie stared up at the ceiling, tracing a hairline crack with her eyes. How could she tell him about Tanner? Knowing Con, he'd probably go through the roof just hearing he was back in town. "No reason. I've just been kind of lonely lately."

"Well, be lonely no longer. Big brother's coming back to Oregon—maybe permanently."

Maggie sat up straight, reaching for her bedside lamp. She switched it on and blinked against the glare. "Really?"

"Would I lie to you?"

"Yes, as a matter of fact. And you have. Many times."

"Well, I'm telling the truth this time. Seriously, Maggie. I'm looking for a change in my life, if you know what I mean."

Indeed she did. Connor's marriage to the daughter of one of the senior partners of his law firm had broken up the year before and there had been hard feelings all around. His ex-wife, a woman raised with a silver spoon stuck firmly in her mouth, had never been a favorite of Maggie's anyway. Linda and Con had married while Con was still very much into his social climbing phase. But since Con had matured, his need for that kind of social high life had diminished, and what little he'd had in common with his wife disappeared altogether. The divorce had been inevitable. Maggie, in fact, had been surprised the marriage had lasted as long as it had, and she wondered about Con's decision to stick with the firm. A sense of misplaced allegiance, she supposed, and, thinking of her reaction to Tanner, concluded she and her brother both suffered from the same malady.

"So when's the big move?" she asked.

"Soon, hopefully. I've got a few things to wind up here and then I'm history. I'm coming to Portland tomorrow to scout around. Think you could put me up?"

"Uh . . . for how long?" she teased.

"As long as it takes, brat. Probably about a week."

"I'll see if I can juggle my heavy social schedule."

"Can you pick me up at the airport?"

"Oooh." Maggie's brows drew together. "I don't know. I've got an appointment at eleven. You'd have to arrive here by ten at the latest."

"Done. My flight leaves at seven." He gave her all the particulars on flight number and arrival time.

"Then I'll see you then," she said lightly, committing the information to memory. "Now I've got to get some rest, or I'll sleep through my alarm."

"Okay. Oh, and about that heavy social schedule you mentioned. I hope you're telling the truth."

Some of Maggie's pleasure in talking to him dissolved. Con always pushed for her to get out and meet people, though she'd never felt he'd actually approved of any of the men she'd seriously dated. His attitude was all a hangover from Tanner. He was just so afraid she would get hurt again.

"I'm managing to keep busy," she dodged. "No, don't ask me anything more," she interrupted as Con tried to drag out some specifics.

"You still seeing Chad Collins?"

"Yes," Maggie said firmly, making a face at the small fib.

"That the best you can do?"

"Oh, go to bed, Con," she said, laughing. "Good night."

"Good night, Maggie. See you tomorrow."

There was a tenderness in his tone that soothed Maggie's troubled thoughts long after she'd hung up and turned off the light. Through her open window she felt the chilly night breeze, and she inhaled deeply, wishing it could clear her head as sharply as it did her lungs. But images of Tanner and Shelley seemed to dance behind her eyes, that one flash of vulnerability she'd caught on Tanner's face almost impossible to banish.

I hope this isn't the shape of things to come, she thought fervently, then got up and took two aspirin to help her fall back asleep.

* * *

If there was ever anything guaranteed to start Maggie's morning off poorly it was getting caught in rush-hour traffic with a horn-happy driver behind her. By the time she got off the freeway to the airport she was in a bad mood, and even the sight of Connor's lean, lanky form as he dashed through the parked cars to where she was idling couldn't completely replace her glower.

"Bad night, huh?" he said, stowing his bags in the back seat and climbing in beside her. "Something must have disturbed your sleep cycle."

"If that's an apology, don't bother. I had to get up and answer the phone anyway."

Con grinned, a slash of white that had caused more than one female heart to flutter, but that only made Maggie more aware of how undone she looked in comparison. "Do you always have to be so—" she searched for the right word "—perfect?" she demanded.

"Why, Maggie. Perfect?"

Grumbling, she pulled into traffic, blasted the car in front of her with a long blare of her horn, then headed toward the city. Con, thank goodness, kept silent until they were on the last leg toward Lake Oswego.

"I'll have to drop you off and take off immediately," she said, a note of apology in her voice. "Sorry."

"That's okay. And don't worry. I'll have dinner waiting when you get home."

"I wish," she said, her mouth curving into its first smile of the day. She pulled the nose of her car into her driveway. "It is good to have you here, even though I haven't acted like it."

Con stepped from the car, grabbed his bags, then leaned his elbow on the open door and gave her a searching look.

"Why do I think there's more to this bad mood than just a sleepless night?"

Maggie leaned across and pulled the door shut. "Don't ask questions. I'm late."

"I'll demand a full accounting later," he called after her, but Maggie just blithely waved her hand as she drove off. There were just some things she couldn't discuss with her brother—and Tanner Baines was definitely one of them.

Her schedule left very little time for introspection, and on this day Maggie was glad. But several times she wondered if Shelley would show up for her next scheduled appointment. Tanner had made it clear he didn't want Maggie anywhere near him or his daughter, but Maggie sensed Shelley had strong opinions of her own. It would certainly be in character for the girl to continue seeing her just to thwart her father.

Or is that wishful thinking on your part?

With a grimace meant for life in general she dug into her work, ignoring her own self-doubts. But at the close of the day she heaved a deep sigh and glanced at her watch. Six o'clock on a Friday night. She wondered if Connor had been serious about dinner. She doubted it. His culinary skills were dismal anyway.

"I'm going home now," Karen said, looking in on Maggie.

"I'm right behind you. Is Monday's schedule still as heavy as it looked earlier?"

"Heavier. Mr. Rookheiser needs immediate attention."

Maggie snorted. "So what else is new?"

Karen smiled. "There is something, actually. That new patient . . . Shelley Baines? Her father called and canceled her appointment. I tried to reschedule, but he said he'd have to get back to us. I got the feeling we shouldn't hold our breath."

Maggie nodded, but after Karen left she stared blankly at the wall in front of her desk. So Tanner had canceled. No surprise there. But a part of her burned with injustice all the same.

"Maggie?"

She glanced up just as Chad poised his hand to rap on her door. With a twinge of conscience she smiled and said, "Well, hello. What're you doing here at this time?"

"The chief of staff's been studying possible replacements for Samuelson, and as I hear it, I'm on the list."

"That's great." No matter what Maggie's problems were with Chad, she wished him success.

"We could get the word as soon as tonight," he said. "Any minute."

"I hope you get the job," she said, meaning it. Then, thinking of her own situation with him, added, "So you're going to hang around here and see what comes down?"

"I'd like to. But you said you wanted to talk. How about if I stop by later, after dinner?"

Maggie plucked her sweater from the peg on the back of her door. Hesitating, she said more to herself than Chad, "My brother, Con, is up from Los Angeles. He's staying with me for the next few days. He said he's making dinner, but that could mean anything."

"Mmm." Chad nodded, glancing at his watch. "Maybe we should make it tomorrow, then."

Realizing she was searching for another opportunity to put off ending their relationship, Maggie shook her head. She needed to declare her feelings as soon as possible; Chad deserved that much. To wait longer would just make it that much worse. "No, come over as soon as you hear the word, and we'll eat dinner together—either Con's concoction or something I can whip up. We'll wait for you. I really do need to talk to you."

"Sounds important." Chad gave her a sideways glance, but she could see his mind was still occupied with thoughts of future glory.

"It is." Her face darkened and she seriously considered telling him right then, on the spot.

But as if understanding she was about to deal him a blow he wasn't ready for, Chad laid his hand on her arm. "Later, okay? I've just got too many things on my mind."

Maggie gave him an uncertain smile. "Sure," she said, and the moment slipped away.

They walked into the soft June evening together, and Maggie was assaulted by that same bittersweet feeling that had followed her around like an unwelcome cloud for days. She left Chad at the steps to the hospital, her mind already on another path.

What was Tanner thinking of by cutting off his daughter's medical support? What kind of father was he?

Had his decision been made solely because of her? She shook her head, inadvertently shaking loose wisps of auburn hair from her chignon. Sliding behind the wheel, she unscrewed the sunroof and vowed to herself she was going to take the short way home and not think about Tanner or his house on Skyridge Drive again.

"Your record stands on its own, Dr. Baines," the professional voice on the other end of the line went on. "We would very much like to offer you the position."

It was with an effort that Tanner didn't just slam down the phone. Feeling how tightly his teeth were clenched, he rubbed his hand over his jaw and said gruffly, "I'm sorry. I'm not interested."

"Would a little more time make the difference? We could give you until the end of the month."

In his mind he counted to five. He wanted to say no. He wanted the whole damn world to leave him alone, but he knew it would be rude, foolish and self-defeating to alienate the staff at Briar Park just because he couldn't stand the thought of accepting a high-profile job. And there was no use explaining his reasons. Only someone with his same kind of disfigurement could understand how uncomfortable it was to see people glancing at his hand, then glancing away, pity in their eyes. His few forays into the public eye had been enough to kill his zeal for more, and his mind now replayed all the whispered comments:

"Such a shame..."

"Isn't there any hope...?"

"The end to a brilliant career..."

If they only knew the half of it.

"Dr. Baines?"

"I appreciate the offer," Tanner managed in a civil voice. "Tell the chief of staff I'll get back to him."

"Wonderful, Dr. Baines. I'll tell Dr. Huffman to expect your call."

Tanner hung up, his mouth twisting in irony. He supposed he should be gratified that his reputation had preceded him, but instead he just felt weary. Weary and depressed. His days of practicing medicine were over, stolen from him by an accident that could have been avoided.

Sighing, he poured a tumbler of scotch. Maybe it was a flaw in his character, but there was no way he could work up enthusiasm over becoming a diagnostician. He was a surgeon. Period. It had been his one desire in the medical field and now it was gone.

Turning over his right hand, Tanner examined the puckered flesh. He flexed the fingers, feeling a familiar numbing tingle in his fingertips. Time would erase the sensitivity, but no amount of physical therapy would bring back his dexterity. Too much damage.

He shook his head, wondering when people would get over being shocked at the sight of it. Even Maggie...

Abruptly he pulled his thoughts back to safer ground. Better to forget about Maggie once and for all, as he should have years before. But his hand mocked him and his face grew long as he remembered how Maggie had unknowingly been a reason for its current state.

The accident that had lost him the use of his hand had been the result of an argument between him and Tricia—an argument about Maggie.

They'd been at a party at a friend's house in Boston, an elegant affair where Tricia could bask in the kind of glitter and gossip she adored. Tanner had stood on the sidelines, as usual, nursing a drink and wishing he were somewhere else. His attitude had infuriated his wife, and by the time they left, her temper was boiling and she was spoiling for a fight.

"Let me drive," Tricia had insisted, throwing off his arm as she'd reached for the car door. "I want to. I've only had two drinks."

"You've had a whole lot more than two." He'd tried to wrestle the keys from her, but for a small woman she was surprisingly strong.

She pushed him away, pulling her silver fox shawl close over her bared shoulder as she got in the car and slammed the door behind her.

"Tricia!" he called angrily.

"Stay at the party with your little girlfriend," she said with a sneer, firing the ignition until purple smoke plumed out of the tail pipe of the Mercedes. "I'll go home to our daughter."

His own anger erupted. He charged around to the passenger side, oblivious to the growing crowd on the upstairs balcony. Yanking open the door, he threw himself inside just as the tires shrieked against the pavement.

"What the hell are you talking about?" he demanded. "Slow down!"

"I saw the way you looked at her. *You* can tell your daughter you want a divorce."

"You're not making any sense," he said through his teeth.

"You don't love me. You never loved me. You just keep searching for another Maggie Holt!"

The streets were dark and wet, and a fine rain was misting all around. Tanner was more concerned with her driving than the thrust of the conversation; it was too well-worn a topic.

"I don't want a divorce and I'm not interested in any other woman," he said tersely. "Now slow down!"

His words had only goaded his wife. She slammed her foot on the accelerator and the Mercedes leaped forward. The last thing he could remember was thinking she would never make the curve. He'd woken up in the hospital, his hand a throbbing, bandaged mess—and had known instantly that his days as a surgeon were over.

Tricia, incredibly, had survived almost unscathed, but their marriage was over. As a means to justify herself, he supposed, she blamed him for the accident, as she'd blamed him for all the unhappiness in her life. In the aftermath of the crash she even tried to blame him for Shelley's diabetes, as well, though the condition ran on her side of the family. Trying to reason with her had been a vain effort, and Tanner had finally given up. What difference did it make anyway? She was right on one thing: he'd never loved her. And just hoping it would happen—as he'd wanted it to—hadn't worked, either.

Memories of Maggie had been too strong.

As Tanner took another swallow of scotch, his mouth twisted bitterly. So many mistakes. Too many to count.

He closed his eyes. And what about Shelley? How could he even bridge the gap with her again? During his recuperation period he'd been particularly apathetic toward his wife and his daughter, and that had been the worst mistake of all. Tricia had used the time to poison Shelley's opinion of him, and by the time he'd surfaced enough to notice, the damage had been done. Always a handful, Shelley had been damn near impossible since Tricia's death. Their relationship now vacillated between frigid politeness and white-hot rage. He was at a loss to know how to deal with her.

And now there was this situation with her and Maggie. God, what a mess!

Running a hand through his hair, he walked onto the back deck, staring through the trees with a grimness of purpose that reflected his state of mind. The evening heat poured over him, slow and seductive. He saw the paint-peeled boards of the deck atop the boathouse and wondered if they were as rotten as they appeared to be. Probably. There was a certain poetic justice there.

Lost in thought, he didn't hear footsteps until they were right behind him. Spinning around, he felt his heartbeat accelerate before he saw that it was his daughter. For just a minute he'd been thrown back in time, expecting Maggie—in a faded blue sundress, her hair tangled and wild, a look of hope and innocence lurking in her green eyes that was far more potent to Tanner than Tricia's blatant sexuality had ever been.

"What are you doing?" Shelley asked, and Tanner's ghosts from the past promptly vanished.

"Thinking."

"About what?"

"You, among other things." He crossed the space between them, but Shelley shifted away, her back stiff and straight. Tanner stopped short. *Some things take time.* "I wanted to talk to you about the nutritionist you were seeing," he said.

"You don't like her." She slid him a glance out of the corners of her eyes.

"I don't have an opinion about her one way or another," he said, aware that he was lying. "But I know what you're doing. You're playing the same game you did in Boston. Acting like you're sick when you're not."

"Is that what she told you?"

"You know it isn't." He met her defiant gaze squarely until her eyes slid away. "You've got her as bamboozled as you had all the others!"

"What the hell do you know about it?"

"Shelley!" Tanner was stern.

"I could lie down and die before you'd ever notice! Maybe that would make you happy. One less problem to think about!"

"This isn't a game anymore," he growled, angrily eating up the distance between them.

Shelley backed away. "No, it's not! It's not a game! You don't believe anything I say. You don't know *anything*!"

Eyes brimming with tears, she turned on her heel and ran from the deck. Tanner stood in silence for the sound of two heartbeats before taking several steps after her. But the slamming of her upstairs bedroom door stopped him cold. His shoulders slumped and he went back to his spot by the rail.

* * *

Maggie raced around the kitchen, too glad to have Con back to complain about the incredible mess he'd left her. She scraped out the burned copper-bottomed pot, then tasted the spaghetti sauce and declared it edible.

Con sat on one of the stools at the corner, his chin on his laced fingers. "See? I'm not such a bad cook."

She made a sound between a laugh and a choke.

"I'll have you know I made Château Blanc for Linda one night and she said it was great."

Maggie worked the cork on a bottle of wine and eyed her brother skeptically. "Chateaubriand, you mean. And don't tell me you don't know it."

"Château Blanc. I burned the chateaubriand and tried to cover it up with white wine. But it was good."

"I'll bet," she said with total lack of belief. The cork popped and Maggie poured them each a glass of rosé. "Do you talk to Linda much?"

"Every sixteenth Thursday whether there's a full moon or not."

"Seriously."

He shook his head.

It crossed her mind that this was the perfect time to bring up Tanner, but she couldn't seem to think how to do it. After all, how long had it been since she and Con had been together alone? Probably years. Bringing up Tanner's name would only spoil the mood and she couldn't bring herself to mention him yet.

"Here's to new acquaintances," she said, clinking her glass against his.

"What about romance? That used to be one of your favorites."

"Okay, to romance, too."

Con took a gulp of wine. "What about Chad?"

"He's a friend."

"That's all?"

"Yes." At Con's look Maggie added, "I thought maybe there could be more between us, but we're just not made for each other."

"So Chad's out of the picture."

His tone sounded as if she were doomed to be an old maid, and it irked Maggie. "I can't make myself love him."

"Is that what you've been trying to do?"

"Yes!" She glared at him, then said reluctantly, "I've got to tell him how I really feel tonight."

"Correct me if I'm wrong, little sister, but isn't this the guy you said you might get engaged to?"

Had she said that? Maggie winced. "Well, yes. It was sort of understood between us. That's why this is so hard."

"Is there someone else? Another man?"

Maggie turned down the burner of the now boiling pasta, fiddling for an extra long time over the dial. She had a sudden image of what Con would think when he found out about Tanner, and said a trifle testily, "That's not how I operate, Con."

The doorbell saved her from further explanations, but any feeling of relief was quickly doused by the thought of what was in store. She dreaded facing Chad. Talk about being thrown from the frying pan into the fire.

"Hello, sweetheart," Chad said distractedly as Maggie opened the door. He gave her a kiss as he came inside and she managed a smile. Then he shook hands with Con. The two men had met once before, and though Con had reservations about Chad, he felt the young doctor truly cared about Maggie.

"You remember Connor, Chad," Maggie said by way of introduction.

Chad nodded. "How could I forget Maggie's infamous brother?"

"That's right." Con grinned. "And believe everything you hear about me."

But Chad didn't return his smile. Instead he heaved a sigh and sank onto the couch, a scowl planted firmly on his brow. Maggie and Con exchanged a look and she shrugged. She didn't know what was wrong with him.

"Could I get you something?" she asked. "Con and I are having rosé."

"No—thanks."

"Is something wrong?"

The look that crossed his face fell somewhere between anger and hatred. "Why don't you ask me who got offered the job of head of surgery?"

Maggie's heart sank. "Oh, no. Who?"

Chad tilted back his head and closed his eyes, his mouth a white line. He seemed unable to answer.

Glancing helplessly toward Con, Maggie said quietly, "Whoever it is, he can't be as qualified as you are."

"Oh, yeah?" Chad rose to his feet, nostrils flared in outrage. "How does Dr. Tanner Baines grab you? They didn't even make him fill out an application. They called him on the phone, for God's sake, and begged him to take the job!"

Maggie gasped. She felt Con start beside her but didn't have the courage to meet his burning gaze. "Tanner Baines?" she repeated dazedly.

"That's right. They claim they don't need a practicing surgeon. 'Dr. Baines's medical expertise more than compensates for his physical limitations,'" he said in a falsetto. Then in his normal voice added disgustedly, "The whole thing makes me furious."

In the silence that followed Maggie could hear the ticking of Connor's watch. It sounded like thunder in the quiet room.

"You didn't tell me Tanner was back," Con said, his voice low and ominous.

Maggie licked her lips. "I didn't have a chance."

It was patently untrue, but Chad unwittingly saved her from further explanations. "Well, I hope he doesn't take the position," he said flatly. "I hear he's impossible to work for."

Maggie had heard just the opposite; his co-workers in Boston had raved about his skill and easy manner when they'd been questioned by the paper after the accident. But she wasn't about to say anything in Tanner's defense. Not with the dark looks on both Chad's and her brother's faces.

With a mumbled excuse, Maggie went to see about dinner. She ignored the heavy silence that had dampened the mood, and chatted like a magpie throughout the meal. But eventually she ran out of things to say. Between Chad's glum fuming and Connor's studied silence, the evening wore on intolerably and Maggie was forced to take refuge in her wineglass. By the time dinner was over she felt almost numb.

But as she followed Chad out to his car her mind cleared. There was no reason to drag on the inevitable, no matter what his frame of mind was.

Clearing her throat, she asked, "Are you ready for that talk?"

"Shoot," he said, his lips drawn.

"I've been thinking about us—about our relationship."

"Say no more." He blew out a pent-up breath. "You're going to tell me you don't want to see me anymore. The perfect ending to the perfect day," he snarled beneath his breath.

Maggie regarded him helplessly. "It's just that—"

"Save it, Maggie. You don't want to see me anymore. Fine. Don't. Just tell me what I did wrong and leave it at that."

"Nothing! You did nothing wrong. I just don't think we're really made for each other."

"That's the best you can do?"

"Chad . . ." she implored.

"Forget it." He slid into the car and slammed the door shut, turning the ignition.

A wave of depression settled over her, as deep as the gathering twilight. "Look, I didn't want it to end this way."

"You're just chock-full of comforting clichés, aren't you?"

He backed out of the driveway before she could say anything more, and she was left standing beside the street, the breeze pressing her skirt against her legs. Slowly she walked across the yard to her front porch, her steps cushioned by the dry grass. Con was waiting in the living room and Maggie sensed she'd just moved from one confrontation to another.

"Did you talk to Chad?" he asked as she started clearing their plates.

"Yes."

"How'd it go?"

"Terrible."

He stretched his shoulders and followed her into the kitchen, his expression sober. "Why didn't you tell me about Tanner, Maggie?"

"Do I have to report everything to you?" she countered lightly.

"Why did you hide it?"

She sighed, plunging her hands into the soapy dish-water. What was the use? Con was determined to play his big brother role to the hilt. "I didn't hide it," she said with a touch of defiance. "He's back in town. I don't know for how long." With a softer tone, she said, "Tricia's dead, Con. She died from a cerebral hemorrhage."

There was a moment of silence as Con digested this. He drew a shaken breath and asked, "Have you seen him?"

"Tanner?"

"Yes, Tanner."

She carefully washed off a plate. "I've seen his daughter, Shelley. She's a diabetic and she's come to me for consultation. She's got some big problems."

"What kind of problems?"

"Oh, I don't know." Maggie sighed and slipped the clean dishes into her wooden dish rack. "She doesn't take her illness seriously enough. She totally refuses to listen to advice and ignores my warnings. She's screaming for attention."

Con looked down at the toes of his shoes. "Have you talked to Tanner about it?" he asked casually.

Hanging up the dish towel, Maggie turned to face him. "Spit it out, Connor. If you want to know what it was like seeing Tanner again, I'll tell you. Horrible. That's what it was. He was cruel and unfeeling and didn't seem to give a damn about his daughter. I got caught in the middle and he told me in no uncertain terms to get out of Shelley's life. Satisfied?"

"Yeah." He grimaced. "At least for now."

"And what's that supposed to mean?" Maggie demanded. "For God's sake, Con, let it alone. Right now I'm more concerned with how Chad feels. He's devastated that the hospital chose Tanner over him, and I can't help but feel sorry for him. And then I come along and deal the final blow. I hate myself."

"Hey, Maggie . . ." he said protestingly.

"No, I mean it, Con. I can't do anything right." Squeezing past him before he could offer further comment, she unlocked the Dutch door to her backyard, giving it a hard kick to get it open.

"Don't be so hard on yourself," he said, meeting her underneath the sagging awning that protected her patio. "If it wasn't working with Chad he had to know. But Tanner's a whole other story."

"You're telling me?"

"Tanner practically destroyed you once, Maggie. I was around to pick up the pieces, remember? I'm not going to sit around and let it happen all over again."

"You're overreacting." Turning her face to the fragrant breeze, she closed her eyes and ignored him.

"Am I? Then why are you so bound and determined not to talk about him?"

Maggie's lips tightened. With difficulty she held on to her temper. What good would it do to argue anyway? Con was absolutely right. He had been around to pick up the pieces, and though he'd never known the depth of her relationship with Tanner, he'd seen the rubble left behind. It wouldn't take a genius to figure out she felt deeply betrayed because she'd given Tanner some vital part of herself—and Con was no fool anyway.

"Let's just change the subject," she said, picking up the stray tabby who spent half his time at her house. The cat purred and closed his yellow eyes.

Con dropped his hands lightly on her shoulders. "There you go again," he said softly, then turned and walked back in the house.

Maggie held the cat under her chin, feeling welling up inside her that had no right being there. She breathed deeply several times, calling herself every kind of fool. Then she set the cat down and went back inside, slammed the door shut and turned out the lights.

Chapter Five

The following Monday was crisp and cool, with the promise of heat to come in the afternoon. Maggie parked her car, stepped out on the curb, then handed Con the keys through the open window. "Don't wreck it," she admonished. "It's still new to me."

Con gave her a look that wasn't meant to inspire confidence. "What do you do with all your money anyway?" he asked as he settled into the driver's seat.

"I save it."

"For what?"

"A rainy day."

"They're all rainy here. Haven't you ever thought of buying that house you live in?"

Maggie shrugged. "Sometimes."

"It could use some fixing up."

"If I needed a business counselor, I'd go out and get one I could trust."

He shook his head. "Take a few risks, Maggie, or you'll end up becoming a wealthy, lonely old woman. Bye."

Hitching up the strap of her purse, she stared after him in bemusement as he waved out of the top of the sunroof and sped out of the parking lot. His warning hit deep. Her conservatism was something she both lauded and secretly worried about. And Con—the creep!—knew her far too well.

She walked along the brick pathway to her office, lost in thought. Maybe it was time to take a second look at herself, take a few chances. After the mistakes of her past she'd vowed never again to put herself in a position where her impulses and desires ruled her head. Yet she couldn't have gotten as far as she had without taking a few risks, and—Tanner excluded—she'd come out ahead.

She was still contemplating her future when Mr. Rookheiser showed up for his appointment. Eyeing her with his sharp blue eyes, he said, "You look like you could use some of your own advice."

"How do you mean?" Maggie asked.

"Well, you look tired, girl. No pep. Maybe your diet's got you down."

"I don't think it's my diet," she said with an ironic smile. "But thanks for the advice anyway. Now let's get back to you..."

Her session with him went surprisingly well, and as they were wrapping it up, her phone rang. Mr. Rookheiser waved, frowned suspiciously at Karen as he passed, then headed outside.

Maggie punched into her line. "Maggie Holt."

"Maggie, this is Gayle Kempwood. I got a call from Shelley Baines's father this morning about her diabetes. I'm sure you've heard of him, Dr. Tanner Baines?"

It seemed inevitable, somehow, that the call should concern Tanner. Her heart sinking, Maggie could already guess what Dr. Kempwood's call was about. "I know Dr. Baines," she answered in a careful voice.

"Do you? Well…hmm, that makes this even more odd. He requested I find a different nutritionist, Maggie. I asked him why, but he just said he wanted someone else. I'm sorry."

She sounded uncomfortable and perplexed, and Maggie, seeking to ease her mind, said, "Don't worry about it. I already knew. It's more a personality clash between us than anything else, and if he wants someone else, that's fine with me."

"He seems very, er, certain of what he wants."

"Yes." Maggie looked out her window, wondering if that was entirely true.

"I gave him the names of several other nutritionists, but none of them is around this area. Frankly, I got the impression it didn't much matter to him one way or the other. He doesn't seem to take Shelley's illness seriously."

Maggie's lips drew into a line. "I wish I knew why."

"He and Shelley are coming by my office this afternoon," Dr. Kempwood went on, "and hopefully, I can get a better handle on what he wants."

"Good luck."

Her skepticism must have come through, because Gayle asked tentatively, "Have you heard the rumors he's been asked to take over Dr. Samuelson's job? I have to say that worries me a little, given his attitude about Shelley."

"Tanner's a great doctor." Maggie was positive on that. "He was a top surgeon and I know he'd do an excellent job."

"I didn't mean to imply any less." Gayle sounded as surprised by Maggie's unexpected fervency as she was herself. "I just wish I understood him a little better."

"Maybe you can draw him out this afternoon."

"I hope so." Gayle was dubious. "Let me know if anything else develops."

Maggie sighed as she hung up, horrified by how quick she'd been to charge to Tanner's defense. What she'd said was true, but she'd certainly overreacted to some understandable criticism.

Feeling out of sorts with herself, she stood and stretched, wishing she could forget both Shelley and Tanner. But Tanner's name seemed to be on everyone's lips these days. He was a force to be reckoned with on the Briar Park Hospital staff and he wasn't even employed here—yet.

How are you going to like working with him?

The question rolled around Maggie's mind. She had no answer for it. Though she didn't doubt Tanner's expertise, she wondered about his objectivity—at least where she and Shelley were concerned.

Frowning, she thought about being under his employ. What if he decided he didn't want her around at all? Could he convince the chief of staff to affiliate a different nutritionist with Briar Park? Could he force her out of a job?

Maggie shuddered. *You're getting paranoid,* she thought. But she couldn't dismiss the idea out of hand.

Con breezed into her office at closing time. "Relax. The Bug is safe and sound and currently filled with gas. I even spent my own hard-earned cash on a wash-and-wax."

"Good." Smiling, she gathered together some papers and stuffed them in her briefcase. "I've got to drop some papers over to Dr. Kempwood," she said, holding out one file in particular. "Do you mind waiting?"

"Nope. In fact, I'll come with you. Who's Dr. Kemp-wood?"

"She's an internist at Briar Park. In fact, she's the doctor in charge of Shelley Baines's case." She held up the file. "This is Shelley's file. I have to take it back to Gayle."

"Then Tanner was serious about not wanting you to help."

"Oh, yes." Maggie was grimly positive.

Briar Park Hospital's reception area was done in dusty blue and pale yellow. A florist had just made a delivery of flowers, and baskets covered the reception area, filling the room with their scents. Maggie could smell rose and honeysuckle and felt vaguely envious of the patients receiving such extravagant arrangements.

"You were right, Con," she murmured. "I haven't taken enough risks lately. I don't even know anyone well enough—male or female—who would go to the trouble to send me flowers."

He gave her a quick glance, then put his arm around her shoulders and squeezed. "Hey, why so down in the mouth? You were straight with Chad, so don't feel bad about that. And not having to deal with Shelley—and therefore Tanner—has got to be a plus. Things are going to start looking up. I can feel it. Who knows what's right around the corner?"

As if his question were meant literally, he turned the corner to Dr. Kempwood's office with a flourish, sweeping his arm in front of her. Maggie was rolling her eyes at him as she strode past and she didn't see the couple in the hallway until she nearly ran smack into Tanner and Shelley.

For Maggie it was sheer devastation. Her first thought, curiously, was about how she looked. Wilting hair, lab coat, scuffed and sturdy shoes—her feminine pride did a steep nosedive.

Everyone stopped dead.

"Well, hello, Shelley," she said unevenly. "Tanner."

"Maggie." Tanner was as stiff as she was.

It was one of those moments when no one knows what to do. Maggie saw everything at once: the simmering hostility in Shelley's blue eyes, the spark of emotion in Tanner's tawny ones, Connor's swift intake of breath.

As if called into battle against his will, Con cleared his throat. "Hello, Tanner. It's been a long time."

The two men looked at each other with barely concealed dislike. It was a shame, Maggie thought, after the affection they'd once shared. If she hadn't been so unwrapped by this unexpected meeting she might have done something to defuse their anger, but as it was all she could do was stand in silent agony, resenting their bare civility, deeply aware that she was responsible for it.

Shelley glanced from one to the other, her gaze eventually landing on Maggie and drifting to the incriminating file she held in her hand. SHELLEY BAINES stood out clearly on the tab.

Maggie licked her lips and said, "I'm taking it back to Dr. Kempwood."

"You are?" Her voice was small and devastated. The swift glance she sent her father was full of poison.

Tanner's face darkened, but he didn't defend his position. Instead he asked Con, "Are you living in Portland?"

"Los Angeles. But I've been offered a job with Pozzer, Strikeberg and Carmen in Lake Oswego."

Maggie's ears pricked up. This was news, indeed. Realizing Con had been saving that tidbit until later, she wondered why he felt compelled to alert Tanner.

"So you're a lawyer," Tanner observed, his face relaxing a bit as he considered his old friend.

But Con wasn't interested in friendship. "So you're a doctor," he answered with a cold smile.

The gauntlet had been firmly thrown down. Panicked, Maggie stepped into the fray before it could become a full-fledged battle. "I hear you've been offered head of surgery here at the hospital," she said to Tanner.

"Administrative head of surgery," he corrected.

"Same thing." Maggie smiled disarmingly, her eyes darting nervously toward her brother. She sent him a silent warning: *Don't make a scene!*

Tanner missed nothing of the exchange. "Same thing, except I wouldn't be performing surgery."

"Why not?" Con asked, ignoring Maggie.

She almost gasped before she realized his question was totally innocent. Con really didn't know about Tanner's hand. Had he been aware of Tanner's renowned status as a surgeon and the accident that had professionally crippled him, he would have never asked such a thing. But Con had made a point of avoiding any news about Maggie's ex-lover, and Maggie herself had known better than to bring the subject up.

"Con just got here from L.A. on Friday," she said to Tanner quickly. "He's been gone a long while."

Her apology wasn't necessary; Tanner took no offense. As an answer he pulled his hand from his pocket, holding it out in front of him. "There was a lot of nerve damage," he explained.

Maggie marveled at how Con took the news in stride, feeling no need to apologize himself. "Permanent damage?" he asked.

"All my feeling hasn't come back yet. But even if I trusted myself to use it, I wonder how many of my patients would."

Tanner's faint smile was an echo of his sense of the ridiculous, which was one of the qualities that had attracted Maggie to him in the first place. Con, too, appreciated it, though only Maggie, who knew him so well, saw his annoyance pass.

"Can we go now?" Shelley asked in a bored tone.

Tanner's lips tightened fractionally before he said, "Sure." He turned to Con. "Nice to see you again, Connor." He held out his injured hand.

Con shook it without a qualm. After Tanner and Shelley left he looked after them and said quietly to Maggie, "You're much too sensitive about his hand. It gives you away."

Maggie glared at him. "And what does that mean?"

"I think you know," he said blandly, then held open the door to Dr. Kempwood's office.

The lake looked green and inviting as they drove through the tangled streets along its banks, sunlight glimmering jewellike off the windswept surface.

"I want to go for a swim," Maggie said suddenly, longing for the feel of cool water against her hot skin.

Her nose had been pressed to the window as Con drove them home, but now she turned to look at him. He was frowning and she wondered if he'd even heard her.

"Con?"

"What?"

"Let's go swimming. I feel hot and itchy."

"I know. You were on one foot and the other in Dr. Kempwood's office."

"Well, you just wanted to talk forever," she grumbled.

Con's brows lifted. "I didn't realize we had such a pressing engagement this evening."

Maggie went back to her perusal of the water. Con and Gayle Kempwood had hit it off instantly, and all it had done was make her feel more lonely and unsettled than she already was.

"Mind a question?" he asked, shifting down around a hairpin curve.

"Shoot."

"What really happened between you and Tanner way back when?"

Her heart gave a funny little kick. Con had never questioned her before. It was the unwritten rule. "Nothing much. A first crush, that's all."

"You were in love with him. I know that. But I always thought that it was one-sided. Now I don't know...."

His musings only increased her uneasiness. "It doesn't matter. It's long over now."

"It's been long over, Maggie. But if you want it back—I'd say it's there for you." His eyes narrowed and his foot hit the accelerator. "His eyes were all over you."

"You're out of your mind," she muttered angrily.

"Oh, no, I'm not." Con was cold and clear. "Why did you two break up in the first place?"

How could he be so smart and so dense at the same time? "Tricia," she said succinctly.

"Maybe."

"There's no 'maybe' about it, Con. He wanted to marry Tricia. He did. It's over. Just drop it, okay? And take me swimming."

She hunched her shoulders and refused to be goaded by any more of his questions. They changed their clothes at Maggie's cottage, then drove in silence to the swim park. But after diving into the crystal cold water, slicing through it expertly, she felt better. Spirits reviving, she purposely wiped the cobwebs of her past aside.

Heaving herself onto the dock, she shivered and waited for Con's black head to surface. When it did, she said, "Why is it you won't give up about Tanner? Good God, Con. I've lived a thousand lifetimes in between."

He hauled himself upward, and sat beside her, a pool of cold water settling around him. "No, you haven't. You've had a few aborted relationships and a career you've dug your nose into, but you're afraid to really live. You think I don't know? Get serious, Maggie."

"I've always done exactly what I wanted to do."

"And paid the price," he added dampeningly. "Whatever happened between you and Tanner shaped your life, whether you like to admit it or not. And now he's back, and I can see it happening all over again."

"After one little meeting?" she said scornfully. "You're jumping to conclusions. Better stick to the facts, counselor."

"The fact is, little sister, I'm not going to let you get hurt again. Someone's got to stay around to keep your eyes open for you."

She glared at him, but without real anger. "You haven't changed a bit. You're still as insufferable as always, and by the way, why didn't you tell me about the offer from Pozzer, Strikeberg and Carmen first?"

"The opportunity arose when we were talking to Tanner and Shelley and I took it. By the way, did you notice how much Shelley looks like Tricia?"

"Hah," Maggie said, not to be deterred. "You're still trying to impress Tanner, just as you did in the old days."

For an answer Con shoved her in the water, and after her shriek of protest, Maggie took off swimming for shore. He caught her easily and sped by her.

"We've both made mistakes striving for what we wanted, Maggie," Con muttered as he walked out of the water and snatched up his towel. Tossing one to Maggie, he added, "I mean, look at me and Linda. Just be wiser this time, okay? That's all I ask."

"I'm far wiser than you know. And besides, you're all wet—no pun intended. Tanner's not interested in me. He never was, and he still isn't."

Con followed her back to the car, keeping his counsel. He wasn't nearly so certain as she was about Tanner's feelings. With a man's instinct he'd felt the tension crackling between them, and Tanner had been as big a part of it as she had—maybe bigger. Whatever had bound them in the past was still alive today.

He just hoped Maggie was smart enough to steer clear of it this time.

Her work had always been a refuge for Maggie during times of crisis, and though right now her life seemed to be perking steadily along, she couldn't help an underlying feeling of uneasiness that made her throw herself into her job. She spent a lot of time dealing with patients, making phone calls, reading up on new research, and when that still didn't fill up her time, even stooped to reorganizing her desk—a task she detested.

Con went back to Los Angeles at the end of the week, promising to return as soon as he tied up a few last loose ends. Maggie was left with even more empty hours. Worse yet, when her mind wasn't crammed with data, it invariably turned to thoughts of Shelley and Tanner—a state of affairs Maggie didn't understand but refused to analyze too closely. Dr. Kempwood had said she hadn't discovered any reason for Tanner's apathy over Shelley's health, and Maggie, though it was no concern of hers, continually stewed and fretted about the whole situation.

One afternoon, late in the month, she'd just finished checking Mrs. Tindale's weight loss, when Karen came back from her break and gave Maggie the high sign that meant she'd heard some interesting news. After Mrs. Tindale left, Karen closed Maggie's door behind her and said, "The illustrious Dr. Baines turned down the position as head of surgery. He called the chief of staff this morning."

Maggie couldn't understand why she felt so let down. "Oh" was all she could think of to say.

"Maybe Chad will get that promotion now," Karen said, blithely unaware of Maggie's conflicting emotions.

The soft bell of the lobby door dinged and Karen went back to her desk. But she needn't have bothered. The patient walked right past her into Maggie's office and planted herself in front of the desk.

"Shelley!" Maggie said in surprise.

"Why don't you want to be my nutritionist?" the girl demanded.

Her manner, as ever, put Maggie on the defensive. "Well, it wasn't that. Your father—"

"I know about my father! He told you to quit seeing me. What does he know? He doesn't know how I feel!"

Shelley flung herself into the chair and stared mutinously at Maggie, as if all the blame had landed in her lap. She looked terrible; her dark hair was lank and stringy, her face white. She'd lost weight, and apparently any interest in her appearance at the same time.

With a feeling of getting in over her head, Maggie said, "I can't solve your problems with your father. Only you can. My function is as a diet consultant."

"But you know him," Shelley said, watching her carefully.

"We've known each other a long time," Maggie admitted.

"You could talk to him for me. He'll listen to you! I heard you that night at our house. He was listening to you."

"Shelley, as much as I would like to help, it's not a nutrition consultant you need. Maybe a family counselor could better suit—"

"No!" She stood up, her fists clenched. "He'll never pay any attention. They'll say, 'Oh, sure, Dr. Baines. Whatever you say, Dr. Baines.' But you didn't."

Uncomfortable over Shelley's eavesdropping, Maggie couldn't help wondering how much she'd overheard. Hopefully not too much.

Mentally shuddering, Maggie hardly knew what to say to her. It had been coincidence—or if she were the superstitious type, kismet—that Dr. Kempwood had sent Shelley to her in the first place. But now the girl seemed to see her as some kind of savior. She couldn't be more wrong!

"Your father must have his reasons for changing your nutritionist," Maggie said, wading through treacherous waters. "Maybe you should just talk to him."

"Oh, sure. That's so easy. He doesn't like talking to me. He doesn't like me. And I know why."

She was waiting for Maggie to take the bait, but there was no way she would. Maggie was almost afraid to hear too much about Tanner.

"He blames me for forcing him to marry my mother. Did you know that?" Shelley asked.

"Oh, Shelley. Sometimes people just don't show each other they love them," Maggie said desperately. "Maybe if you—"

"She was pregnant when they got married."

It was the kind of cold statement meant to be a bombshell, and it had the desired effect on Maggie. It took her several moments to collect herself, and by that time the damage had been done. Shelley was too shrewd not to notice how she took the news.

Not that Maggie believed it for a moment. It was just the bald delivery that had gotten her down. She knew far too well who Tanner had been with the summer Shelley had been conceived, but she couldn't very well tell the girl it was herself.

"I don't believe your father would feel that way even if it were true," she murmured. "You're his daughter."

"It is true! Ask him sometime!"

Maggie shook her head. "I don't know why you're telling me all this. It would be better if Dr. Kempwood recommended someone you could talk to."

"I don't want anyone else," Shelley said flatly. She walked to Maggie's bookshelf, fingering several leatherbound copies of medical journals. "Anyway, I've been losing weight and I'm still having dizzy spells even though I eat right."

"Plan A?"

She had the grace to flush. "No. Not every food. Look, don't you want to help me?"

Yes. But she had no authority. Tanner had forbade her to help Shelley, and the girl's problems were far more complicated than diabetes alone.

"You don't want to help me," Shelley said, answering her own question. Her mouth turned downward. "I should have guessed."

"Shelley..."

"You're just like all the rest," she flung out. "All I want you to do is talk to him, but you don't care. You're not getting paid, so it's not worth the effort, right?"

"What do you want me to talk to him about?" Maggie demanded as Shelley fled toward the door.

"I don't know!"

This time Maggie followed after her, but by the time she got to the door Shelley was across the lawn and running in the direction of the hospital. There was something about the sight of her—slim legs encased in faded jeans, long hair blowing wildly behind her, an air of dejection and unhappiness that made a mockery of her youth—that reminded Maggie of herself.

How could Tanner do this to her?

Sweeping back into her office, Maggie snatched up the phone, stabbing out Tanner's number. She thought better of it instantly and slammed down the receiver. What right did she have to demand an explanation?

Yet Shelley had pleaded with her to help. She'd begged Maggie to see him on her behalf. Tanner owed them both an explanation.

Drawing in a breath of courage, she grabbed her sweater and locked the office door behind her. Well, all right. She'd give it one shot. And she'd be damned if he would turn her away again without some answers first.

There was something imposing about the Baines house that Maggie could never quite get over. She pulled into the driveway this time instead of across the street, but she quailed a little inside at her own brazenness. Just because Tanner had seemed a bit more approachable at the hospital didn't mean he would welcome the sight of her at his house.

Her briefcase was clutched in her hand as she mounted the steps to the porch, and her body was stiff with apprehension. Blowing a wayward strand of hair out of her eyes, she straightened the line of her dress, wishing she'd taken more time with her appearance before she'd charged off on this wild impulse. Yet what good would it do to look her best? Realizing her folly, Maggie made a face and pressed her finger to the bell, hearing the familiar peal of deeptoned chimes. A shiver slid down her spine.

Mrs. Greer answered the door. "Why, Miss Holt," she said, looking flustered.

"Is Dr. Baines in?"

"Er, yes. But he's upstairs working."

Upstairs working? Maggie's eyes involuntarily turned toward the curving white banister. Working at what? "Do you think I could see him?" she asked when the housekeeper didn't offer any further information.

"Let me check."

Maggie was left waiting in the entry hall as Mrs. Greer puffed her way up the long stairway. Above her head the chandelier swayed gently from the draft caused by the closing of the front door. She remembered other times—distant times—when she and Tanner had been locked in an embrace, the chandelier slowly rocking, casting geometric patterns of light over their faces and hair.

She walked quickly across the parquet floor to the peach-and-cream Oriental carpet, her steps echoing behind her, as haunting as her memories. Why, oh, why, did her recall have to be so sharp? She knew plenty of people who could barely remember what they had for dinner the night before, yet she seemed cursed with a memory that could etch out a scene as if it had just happened.

She heard the squeak of the stairs before Mrs. Greer came into view again. "He'll be right down," she said.

"Is Shelley here?"

"No. She's visiting friends." Mrs. Greer, Maggie now saw, had her purse in hand. She was on her way home. "Why don't you wait in the kitchen?" she invited. "You might be more comfortable there." Smiling, she let herself out the front door.

Alone, Maggie stood in the hallway, looking pensively after the woman who'd once been so supportive of Tanner's and her relationship. What did Mrs. Greer think now? Maggie wondered as she walked toward the kitchen.

Forced to view another room where bittersweet memories would run rampant, Maggie inwardly braced herself. The kitchen looked out on the back deck, and it was just as she remembered it, even to the chip in the Formica where Tanner had grown impatient trying to uncork a bottle of pop and had finally broken the neck against the counter. Gerrard had nearly had a heart attack over that one!

She sat at the maple table, pinching her lower lip between her fingers. A clock ticked quietly from the wall above the refrigerator. Nothing had really changed.

She heard his tread on the floor, then the soft muffling as he strode across the Oriental carpets. She'd barely collected her thoughts when he was in the doorway, looking somber and remote and about as approachable as another galaxy. In a pair of worn and tattered jeans he reminded her of a much younger Tanner Baines. But the black T-shirt fit the toughened man before her, and she knew she had a long way to go before he would even give her the time of day.

"Hi," she said awkwardly.

"What are you doing here?"

Hardly an auspicious beginning, she thought with a sigh. "I came to see you. To talk about Shelley."

"Shelley?" He frowned. "You're not treating Shelley anymore."

"I know that." Piqued, she rose from the table but didn't attempt to walk any closer to him. His attitude rankled. Too much time had passed for him to treat her this way. "She came to see me today and I—"

"Shelley?"

"Yes. She asked for my help."

His jaw tightened. "She doesn't need a nutritionist," he said flatly. "She makes up half her symptoms. Anytime something goes wrong, Shelley starts complaining about being sick."

Maggie couldn't believe her ears. "That's so callous! I never would have thought that you, of all people—"

"Look, Maggie. You don't know anything about it. Believe me, my daughter's a master at getting what she wants."

"But you're a doctor! How can you stand there and diagnose her when you don't pay any attention to her yourself?"

She'd stepped way out of bounds. Knowing it, she still wouldn't have drawn the words back had she been able to.

Tanner's gaze narrowed on her. "I don't pay any attention to her?" he repeated softly.

"She pleaded with me to help her today," Maggie said, her hopes sinking. "Shelley wanted me to talk to you and I told her I couldn't, that she wasn't my client. She was crestfallen." Daring a glance at his stony face, she braved onward. "Then I decided it was worth the effort anyway. *She's* worth the effort. I figured I could put up with your insolence and anger if I could just get you to listen to me."

Tanner stared at her in amazement. "My God."

"She's your daughter," Maggie went on doggedly. "She needs your help."

His lips tightened and she braced herself, expecting him to blast her for her rudeness. A part of her almost hoped he would; anything was better than this terrible apathy and lack of concern. But all he did was raise his hands and run them frustratedly through his thick, silvery blond hair, his fingers tugging at the hair at his nape. It was a sensual move, one Maggie had difficulty watching. Her eyes searched the room for something—anything—else to look at.

"Shelley is my problem," he reminded her again, his tone measured.

"She's sick, Tanner."

"She's playing on your sympathies," he said tightly. "Can't you see that? Aren't you enough of a professional to tell when someone's lying to you?"

A heartbeat passed while Maggie sought to hold on to her temper. "Not always," she said in a low voice. "I've been lied to in the past and I didn't know it."

Tanner's nostrils flared in outrage, but he didn't comment. Maggie's pulse was beating so fast she could hardly breathe and she had to wait until she could control her voice before saying, "But I can tell when someone needs help."

"I know how to deal with my daughter."

"Do you?"

"Yes," he said flatly. "Now you've said your bit and eased your mind, so go away."

"Tanner!" Maggie scrambled from her chair as he strode from the room. "Don't you dare walk out on me. I want some answers. You owe me that much!"

"I don't owe you anything, lady!"

"The hell you don't." Her temper flared hotly and she threw caution to the winds. "You owe me an explanation.

But the desert could turn to ice before you'd ever give me one."

"Just what are we talking about now?" he asked coldly.

"You know." Her eyes dueled with his in silent fury, and she put a lock on the conscience that warned her to stop provoking him. "But I don't care about the past anymore. However, Shelley's health is something else again. I can't give up on her, not when she's *begging* me to help her. She's your daughter, Tanner," Maggie appealed. "All I want to do is help."

She thought she'd finally gotten through to him. He seemed torn, as if he wanted to give in but something was preventing him. Though she cursed her own temper, she could forgive herself if he would just listen to her.

"What is it, Tanner?" she asked when the moment had stretched almost to eternity. "Why can't you see what's staring you right in the face?"

"For God's sake, leave me alone!" He twisted on his heel and strode down the hallway, but Maggie was right behind him. She figured at this point she had nothing to lose.

Catching him at the door to the den, she grabbed his arm. "I can't decide if it's Shelley or me you don't want to face."

"Get the hell out of here!"

His voice thundered through the entry hall, causing the chandelier's crystal teardrops to quiver and clink together, like the soft whisper of voyeurs gossiping about the drama playing out below them.

"No," Maggie said determinedly. "I can't."

The telephone gently purred from the desk inside the den and Tanner eagerly seized the opportunity as a means to end their conversation. But Maggie had no intention of giving up. She was fighting for Shelley, but in a sense she was fighting for herself, and maybe even Tanner, as well. She paced the spacious entry hall, trying not to hover outside the door.

"Hello, Father."

Tanner's drawling tones drifted easily from the inner room and immediately the temperature of her blood seemed to drop ten degrees. Gerrard Baines! Just the thought of him still had the power to make her knees quiver.

But he didn't intimidate Tanner. "No, I'm not working at a hospital...." There was a long pause, then Tanner said, "Yes, I've heard the offer, but I have no intention of taking the job...." Another pause, then Tanner said softly, "I don't really give a damn. Try peddling your advice to someone else."

He hung up so abruptly Maggie caught her breath. She was standing stock-still, her eyes huge, when he reappeared in the doorway.

"Well?" he demanded.

"Your father," she said, still bemused.

"Yes." The faintest touch of humor played at the corners of his mouth as he saw the effect Gerrard's call had on Maggie. "You can see how far our relationship has progressed over the years."

"It's a shame, the way things are between you."

"Is it? I'd call it just deserts. He set it all up years ago."

Thinking he must mean the career Gerrard had chosen for him, Maggie said, "I thought you enjoyed being a surgeon. You said as much to me and Con."

Something flickered behind his eyes, some kind of memory or emotion that Maggie couldn't discern. "That part of my life is over," he said flatly. "Over and done with."

"You are so incredibly good at cutting off pieces of your life." Maggie shook her head. "Can't you see what you're doing? Your relationship with your father is such a prime example. You're doing the same thing to Shelley!"

"My father and I have an understanding about things you can't begin to fathom, Maggie, so quit trying so hard!"

"You didn't used to feel that way," she said recklessly. "You used to wish things were different with your father."

"Damn it all!" Tanner roared. "How many ways do I have to say it? Get out of my life. Just stay away from me and Shelley. We don't want you here!"

"*You* don't want me here," Maggie corrected in a whisper. Like a hot tide, an unwelcome wave of emotion swept through her, burning her throat. He was right. She was trying too hard and he didn't care.

"That's right," he said, pounding in the last nail. "I don't want you here. I don't want to see you again."

Her purse was still in the kitchen. Maggie swept past him, fighting back frustrated tears. Why did it matter so much? she wondered. She hadn't really expected him to react any differently, but it hurt all the same. She yanked the purse from the chair, her strap tangling. It was the last straw, and she jerked so hard the chair nearly tipped over. When she whipped around, Tanner was standing in the doorway.

"I won't bother you again," she said with a trembling voice. She wanted to kick herself for betraying her true feelings.

She walked to where he stood, then stopped short when it didn't appear he would budge. His pallor showed beneath his deep tan, but all she could think about was escape.

"You don't know what it's like," he said unevenly. "I don't want to hurt you, but you just..."

"I've got to leave," she said unsteadily. She couldn't hear this.

"It's not just because you're you that I'm moving Shelley. Believe me. There's so much more involved."

Maggie hunched her shoulders. "It doesn't matter," she murmured.

He made a sound of self-hate. "Oh, God, Maggie..."

"Look, for Shelley's sake, I hope you heard at least part of what I said." She could count the seconds until she was going to be past dealing effectively. Tears were collecting in her throat. "Goodbye, Tanner."

"Is Shelley the only reason you came?"

The words were wrested from him, uttered quickly, as if they tasted bad on his tongue. Maggie just stared at him, her green eyes moist and wounded. She didn't know how to answer. "I don't want to play this game with you. You know how I feel about Shelley."

"That's not what I asked."

Maggie turned away. "Your daughter needs help," she said unevenly. "She asked me to come. I came."

He was far too near. She could feel the heat from his body, could smell his musky and oh, so familiar male scent. She thought of his muscles, his slim hips and board-flat waist, and was swamped with emotions better left untouched.

To her dismay, she saw his scarred hand steal upward, felt it lift feathery tendrils of hair off her damp forehead. She held her breath and tried to tell her feet to move, but they seemed rooted to the floor.

His jaw worked, the muscles tightening. She expected him to say something, but he remained silent, his golden gaze fastened somewhere near her crown. He seemed mesmerized by her dark, burnished mane.

It was then that she realized she'd lied. Shelley wasn't the only reason she'd come. She'd wanted to see Tanner again, despite his objections. He was like a fever in her blood that had never truly been cured.

"Do you hate me, Tanner?" she asked, wetting her lips.

"God, no."

"Did you hate me back then? When we broke up?"

"No. Maggie . . . you don't—"

"Then why are you so anxious to have me out of your life now? If it's something I've done, I have no idea what it is. Just tell me. I can't stand this game playing."

"It's not game playing," he said roughly. "It's . . . it's . . ." He broke off and shook his head, as if the answer were either out of reach or too terrible to voice.

"Tell me," she urged, her lips parting. She was so close, so close . . .

"It's not you."

"Then what?" she asked. "Please, Tanner." In his eyes the same passion smoldered that had been alive in the past. A longing rose inside her, swift and frightening. In a moment of clarity she realized Con was right. She did still love Tanner. Loved him in a way that defied explanation.

He looked away, but when he turned back she was still gazing at him, her eyes liquid and clear. Tanner felt himself sinking into a vortex of seduction that would take him straight to hell, but he couldn't stop himself. Fingers trembling, he smoothed her cheek with his thumb.

It was the sight of his scars that brought back his senses and he pulled his hand away. But Maggie, never one to let fate's whim decide her future, clasped his hand and brought it back to her face. She curved his fingers around her jaw, loving him with fathomless eyes.

"I can't, Maggie," Tanner said, tortured.

"Why can't you?"

"Because it's wrong."

Her breath escaped on a quiver. "Oh, no. No, it's not."

There were limits to her boldness. She wasn't afraid to show her feelings, but she was woman enough to want him to make the first move. She could see his indecision, feel the weightiness with which he considered his actions. Why? she wondered. What could cause such reluctance when his breath was coming as fast as hers, his eyes were filling with the same dusky passion?

He shifted his weight, turning, and she turned, too—an emotive ballet in which every movement held a dozen different meanings. His thumb ran over her lips, insinuated itself between them. Maggie waited breathlessly, a little shiver hiding beneath her skin at the sensual, sinuous invasion. The unhealthy attraction of her past still existed: she wanted Tanner as she'd never wanted anyone else.

His hands moved to her shoulders, holding her tightly. Her heart was pounding out of control, her face flushing with heat. If he didn't kiss her she'd scream!

But whatever held him back was a powerful force indeed. His whole frame shuddered and she was amazed by the torment in his eyes. Though her hands longed to wind around his neck, burrow into his thick silvery blond hair, she refused to let them. Instead she waited.

"Maggie..."

Her name was a protest on his lips. She could only encourage him with her eyes, and though she wasn't aware of it, her feelings were only too eloquent.

With a groan he cupped her chin, tilting it upward, seeking her mouth with his.

His lips were tender at first, touching so softly and carefully that Maggie was left trembling and unfulfilled.

She wanted more and she let her mouth move against his, tempting him, urging him to explore all of her.

His body was like steel, hard and tense, as if poised for flight. What did he expect her to do? All she wanted was to love him.

He broke off abruptly, breathing hard, dropping his hands and looking away.

"Tanner." Maggie whispered softly, and when he turned to meet her gaze again, his eyes were dark and tormented. "Don't stop."

"Oh, Maggie. You don't understand!"

"I understand more than enough."

She cradled his face in her hands, loving the rough texture of his cheeks. If she could have, she would have run her hands over him, rediscovering all the planes and angles that had made her fall in love with him the first time. But she was walking a tightrope; he was looking for a reason to flee.

"Tanner." She rubbed her mouth lightly against his. When he didn't move she let her kiss deepen, tentatively, and rejoiced when passion finally broke the leash on his control. With a groan he ground his mouth down on hers, his tongue seeking an entry as he yanked her to him, his heart hammering against her breasts. Maggie responded wildly, all the pent-up desire of fourteen forgotten years singing for release. His fingers wound in her hair, imprisoning her, and she slid her arms around his neck, thrilled to feel the strength of him, lean and muscular, against her.

And then abruptly he pushed her away. Violently. So hard she stumbled and had to reach a flailing arm for the wall. Stunned, she saw him scrub the back of his hand across his mouth, his chest heaving.

Nothing could have wounded her more. No amount of name-calling, no physical injury. He'd stabbed into the core of her womanhood with one terrible gesture, and part of her love for him died.

Pulling the tattered remnants of her pride around her, Maggie straightened and turned blindly toward the front door.

"Maggie, wait." Tanner's voice was rough with emotion.

"Go to hell, Tanner Baines."

"Wait, please.... I can't tell you—"

"Right." She cut him off swiftly. "You can't tell me. Well, hear this. I don't give a damn. I don't care what your reasons are—for hating me and for neglecting your daughter. I don't care. *I just don't care!*"

His hand grabbed for her, but she spun away, eyes glittering angrily.

"Well, I care," he said, his throat working. "I care about you and Shelley. I can't help it if I seem like a monster—I just can't bear to have you around. But what you saw—it's not what you think."

"Goodbye, Tanner."

"Maggie..." he protested in agony.

His hypocrisy was the last straw. Whirling around, she leveled a finger at him and said in a furious, trembling voice, "I understand perfectly. I've felt it before. This is the same old prejudice that Con ran up against. *I'm not good enough!* Maybe you acquired some scruples over the years after all, Dr. Baines, because you warned me enough times to stay away from you. I was just too stupid and thick skulled to listen. Well, now I know. And don't worry, it's a lesson I won't soon forget."

"You don't know anything about it!"

Maggie's hand was on the door, and she was trying frantically to unhook the latch. Her nerves screamed until she finally yanked it open, a cool evening breeze whipping around her, fanning her overheated cheeks, tousling her already ravaged hair.

She gave him one last silent glance. His misery was clear, the same tortured agony she'd witnessed on his face years before. Only this time her heart was hard. This time she understood him.

She, Maggie Holt, was of a poorer class.

Fighting back a cry of pain, she raced down the cracked walkway to her car.

Chapter Six

Maggie!"

She was halfway down the cement pathway. The sound of his voice made the hairs on the back of her neck rise, but she just increased her pace.

"Damn it, Maggie, let me explain."

She kept walking.

An arm reached out and yanked her around, caught in Tanner's grip. His eyes blazed into hers. "Damn it," he muttered, "I want to talk to you."

"I'm through talking to you. We don't have anything more to talk about."

"Your pride is a terrible thing, Maggie. It blinds you. Would you just listen? I'm trying to apologize."

Maggie wrenched her arm away. "There is no apology. I don't want anything from you!"

What little was left of Tanner's control disappeared. He reacted on instinct, letting his better judgment disappear under an avalanche of suppressed need. Lunging forward, he grabbed both her shoulders, dragging her to his chest and battling her struggles with steely determination and inflexibility. Maggie twisted and turned, glaring up at him, her green eyes flashing with rage.

"I thought I could leave it like this," he said unsteadily. "It would be better if I could. But I can't. I can't have you hate me like this."

She gave up the fight and turned away. She wanted to hate him. It would be so much simpler to hate him. "Let me go, Tanner."

Lines etched unhappily on either side of his mouth. "Listen to me. You don't know how I feel. I can't even tell you."

"Then let go of me. The conversation is over."

"Maggie...I loved you..."

"I don't want to hear it!"

This time she struggled free before his grip could tighten. She couldn't listen to him now! Not after what he'd just done! Anything he said would be a lie meant to appease and she was far too susceptible to his lies.

"Maggie..."

"It's over, Tanner. You made that clear. Shelley's the only common ground between us. Goodbye."

It was in her mind just to leave. He'd been cruel and deserved no better. But as she dug through her purse for her keys she heard his rasped breaths, and even his cruelty couldn't force her to act in the same way. "I don't hate you," she said bitterly. "I wish I did, but I don't."

"If I could change the past I'd do things differently, Maggie." Tanner's face was shadowed and somber. "It would have meant a lot to me for us to be friends."

"Friends," she echoed scornfully. "You don't know what you want from me."

"Oh, yes, I do." His mouth pulled into a self-deprecating line. "Oh, yes, I do. And it keeps me awake at night."

Maggie shook her head, her hair tumbling to her shoulders. She couldn't hear this. She had to get away. "I can't talk to you any longer."

"I'm sorry. God, I'm sorry. It wasn't supposed to be like this."

Summer magic filled the air. No matter how much she wanted to ignore it, she couldn't. It had woven around her heart, ensnared her soul. "You kissed me as though you wanted me," she whispered. "Then you tossed me aside."

He grimaced and turned his eyes toward the star-studded sky. "I shouldn't have kissed you." When he glanced her way again she couldn't read his expression. "I'd rather lose my other hand than have you look at me that way. But I can't fall in love with you again."

Her will was crumbling like the gradual erosion of water against stone. But she was tired of his cryptic remarks; they did nothing but aggravate the part of herself that still itched to understand. Only her pride, as strong as Tanner had said, kept her from begging for an explanation once more.

"I'm leaving, Tanner. I've got to go." Her feet were already moving down the path toward her car, when she remembered something else. "What should I do if Shelley comes to see me again?" she asked in a low voice.

"I don't know. Maybe it's . . . not such a bad idea after all . . . her coming to see you."

"No, Tanner. I won't see her just to ease your conscience."

"That's not it. You said yourself that she begged you for help. She hasn't begged anyone for help—ever. Seeing you, well, that's progress." He clenched his teeth. "As long as we're clear on why she's seeing you."

"She needs a psychologist," Maggie said bluntly.

"She wants you."

"I'm not qualified."

"Maggie," he said impatiently, "Shelley plays games. I think that's why she went back to see you. She wants to use you somehow. But, hell, I don't know—maybe some good can come out of it." He exhaled heavily. "What do you think?"

It was a question she couldn't answer. She longed to help Tanner's daughter, yet she knew her own limitations. And she didn't want any further contact with Tanner.

"I'll see her again if she wants me to," she finally agreed. "But I'm going to tell Dr. Kempwood what's going on."

"Fine. Let's leave it at that. I'll call you later this week."

"No, Tanner. You can talk directly to Dr. Kempwood."

"I'll need to talk to you, too, Maggie."

She closed her ears and walked quickly the rest of the way to her car. Without looking back, she wheeled onto the narrow road, breathing easier only when she was miles away from his house.

What had happened back there? On the surface, his feelings were fairly clear: he didn't want to love her. Well, that made two of them: she didn't want to love him, either. Unfortunately, the attraction that had brought them together still existed. Refusing to acknowledge it wouldn't make it go away. The only way to keep things status quo was to not see Tanner again—*ever*—which was fine as far as Maggie was concerned. She would rather walk through fire than chase after Tanner Baines and bare her soul one more time!

But could his daughter be her patient? How could she avoid seeing him under those conditions?

It was the last question that kept Maggie awake most of the night.

The hospital corridors were bustling at ten o'clock in the morning as Maggie made her way to Dr. Kempwood's office. She knocked on the door, but it was locked. Making a face, she retraced her steps and was about to cross the parkway to her office building, when she ran into Sandy Francis.

"Maggie!" Sandy said, a smile stretched across her face. "We haven't seen you around much lately. Chad says you've really been busy."

"I have." Maggie returned Sandy's smile, but she'd learned to treat the surgical resident with caution. Sandy was a political player who felt Chad was her personal property in a way that had always baffled Maggie. She'd treated Maggie like a rival, though there was no reason to, and more often than not had coldly excluded her from any discussions about the hospital.

Not that Maggie cared. But she'd learned to tread carefully around the feisty, ambitious woman.

"We're all going to Maxwell's this evening. Maybe you'd like to join us?"

The invitation was a surprise and one she took with a grain of salt. "Thanks, but I've really got too much to do. Maybe next time."

"Chad'll be sorry you're not there."

Was Sandy fishing? she wondered. If Chad hadn't told her their relationship was over, he must have had his reasons, and Maggie wasn't about to rock the boat. "Chad will understand." She headed for the door.

"Oh, did you hear?"

Stifling a sigh, Maggie stopped and turned, seeing Sandy frowning down at her nails. "Hear what?"

"The news. Chad's been appointed head of surgery."

"Really? No...I didn't know," Maggie murmured.

"Didn't he tell you?" Sandy asked in all innocence. "I thought you'd be the first on his list."

So Chad had been given the position Tanner had turned down. Maggie hoped he was up to the task, and couldn't help regretting the loss to the hospital of a doctor of Tanner's caliber. "I haven't seen Chad yet today."

"He's the best man for the job," Sandy said enthusiastically. "Now we'll see some innovative decision making. Thank God Dr. Baines didn't take the job! I shudder to think what would have happened to the department!"

"Why do you say that?"

Sandy looked at her as if she were extremely dull. "At least Chad can perform an operation. I'd find it very difficult taking orders from someone who hasn't even been able to try out new techniques. Briar Park would quickly become archaic and outdated headed up by a nonpracticing surgeon like Dr. Baines. His hand is worthless."

Maggie's indrawn breath was full of reproach. She remembered Tanner's gentle touch, the way he'd lifted her dampened curls from her forehead. Her face flushed. *Not worthless, Sandy. Not worthless at all.* "I think you're being extremely shortsighted," she said evenly. "Dr. Baines's credentials speak for themselves and he doesn't strike me as the kind of man to rest on his laurels. Past achievements are just that—the past. His future is a lot more viable than you give him credit for."

"Whoa!" Sandy lifted her brows. "I didn't know we felt so strongly."

"*We* pay attention to facts. Excuse me."

Maggie gulped air as she walked into the morning sunshine. She was furious. Sandy's pigheadedness had gotten under her skin, and Maggie felt like strangling her!

So why do you always defend Tanner?

Her expression darkened. Why, indeed? She hadn't forgotten the way he'd wiped the feel and taste of her from his lips. It wasn't the kind of thing she could forget. Yet she couldn't stand by and listen to anyone denounce his ability as a doctor. She knew, because she'd made a point of knowing, just how far-reaching and important his contribution to the medical field had been. It angered her when people called him down for the count.

"You've got a patient," Karen said, jerking her head in the direction of Maggie's office as Maggie entered the reception area.

"I didn't have one scheduled."

"This one just showed up. Again," she added meaningfully.

Maggie knew it was Shelley even before she saw her slim shoulders, wrinkled shirt and tattered jeans. Hearing footsteps, Shelley whipped around, regarding Maggie with huge, suspicious eyes.

It was almost more than Maggie wanted to face so early in the morning. "Hello, Shelley. Next time I'd appreciate it if you make an appointment first," she said repressively. "I could have had another patient."

"Then I'd wait."

Maggie met her gaze. "What did you want to see me about?"

"Well . . . my diet . . . of course."

Maggie flipped through her mail, certain more than ever that she'd made a mistake by letting both Shelley and Tanner into her life. Shelley was no more interested in talking diet than Maggie was right now. Knowing where the conversation would lead, she anticipated the next question and said, "I talked to your father yesterday."

"I know. He said so."

"You talked it over with him, then. Good."

"If you can call it talking." Shelley flipped her hair over her shoulder. "He accused me of staying out all night and getting in trouble."

"Any truth to that?" Maggie inquired.

"He doesn't like my friends. He won't let me see them. The only person he lets me see is you, and that's because if I fell over dead he'd feel guilty."

Maggie blinked in amazement. So this was what Tanner had meant by her theatrics. "Now wait a minute. You were the one who wanted to see me, not your father."

"Well, he gave in, didn't he? He must want me to see you. Gotta keep Shelley's diet on track, right?" She shrugged indifferently. "What does he think you can do for me?"

"Nothing. Absolutely nothing." Maggie's tone was just short of angry. She hated being manipulated. "He doesn't expect anything out of me. He said you made up your symptoms and played games and that my treating you would be a waste of time. I'm sorry, Shelley, but so far he appears to be right."

Momentarily taken aback, Shelley came out fighting. "You're all the same. I knew it! You're listening to him, too!"

"What do you expect out of me? I'm a nutritionist. Not a psychologist, or a friend, or even a confidante! If you want to take out your anger on someone, fine. But why me?"

"Because he likes you!"

The words were out before she really knew what she was going to say, and for a moment afterward Shelley was as surprised as Maggie. But she pulled herself together quickly. "That's not true," she said, her lips compressed. "I just thought you could help me. That's all."

"Well, I can't." Maggie tightened her jaw. "Not in the way you want." *Not in the way your father wants, either.* "But if you want to talk about your diet and overall health, that I can do. How've you been feeling lately?"

"The same."

"Did you by any chance make up some of these symptoms? The dizziness for example?"

"Are you calling me a liar?"

"Are you looking for a reason to have a fight?"

Shelley's nostrils flared, her brows drawing together in a glower that suddenly reminded Maggie of her father. So there was some Tanner in Shelley.

"How long have you known my father?" Shelley asked after a lengthy pause.

"A long time. What's your insulin intake been?"

"Did you know my mother?"

Maggie regarded her frustratedly. Shelley seemed obsessed with her parents' relationship. "Yes, I knew her. We were acquaintances."

Shelley's gaze grew distant, as if she were tackling some weighty problem in her mind. "I think she used to talk about you. That's why your name was so familiar."

Maggie nearly choked. Tricia used to talk about her? Why in the world would her name be brought up? Especially to Shelley? "We spent a couple of summers at the lake," Maggie said. "We didn't know each other very well. Now are we going to get back to your diabetes, or not?"

Shelley didn't answer. In fact, she grew very moody, and while Maggie tried to draw her out she seemed to retreat farther and farther into her shell. When Maggie's next scheduled client appeared Shelley left passively. Somehow that was worse. It worried Maggie to think what might be going on in her head.

She worried all the way home, then grew tired of pacing her living room floor and did something totally against her better judgment—she joined the group at Maxwell's.

Chad was surprised to see her. "Maggie! What are you doing here?"

Sandy Francis looked as if she regretted needling Maggie earlier. "I invited her," she admitted reluctantly.

"I heard the news, Chad," said Maggie, smiling. "Congratulations."

"Here." He pulled out a chair next to his. "Come and sit down."

The evening progressed much as Maggie had anticipated, with laughter, some ribald humor and more than one toast offered up to Briar Park's new head of surgery. She was glad to think about something else beside her own problems, and seeing how happy Chad was, she regretted not being enthusiastic about his promotion. He would do a good job, she was sure. He'd wanted the position so badly.

"It is only temporary," Chad mentioned, with a surprising show of humility, toward the end of the evening. "But if all goes well, it'll become permanent."

He walked Maggie to her car, his chest still puffed out with pride. "I don't suppose your showing up tonight means you've changed your mind."

"It means I'm glad you got the job," she said softly. "I know how much you wanted it."

"After what you said to Sandy this morning, I got the impression you thought Baines was more qualified."

Maggie's conscience pricked her. In all truthfulness she did feel Tanner was more qualified, but she would never hurt Chad by telling him so. "I just didn't like Sandy denigrating him."

"Baines? Why? What did she say?"

"Oh, the same old stuff about his hand." Maggie looked away. She felt awkward, sensing how eager Chad was to pick up where they'd left off. The last thing she'd wanted to do was give him the wrong impression. "Well, congratulations again. I know you'll do a good job." She smiled and reached for the handle of her car.

"That's it? No congratulatory kiss even?"

It was the kind of moment Maggie dreaded, when she realized she'd put herself in an uncomfortable situation from which there was no easy way out. Standing on her tiptoes, she intended to give him a quick kiss on the cheek. But Chad seized the opportunity to kiss her full on the mouth, and the feel of his lips pressed tightly to hers repelled and embarrassed Maggie.

"See what you're missing?" he whispered, slowly releasing her. Swaying a bit on his feet, he gave her a twisted, half-drunken smile. Maggie was just relieved to be free of him.

"Good night, Chad."

He sighed. "G'night, Maggie."

Taking pity on him, she asked, "Do you need a ride home? You really shouldn't drive."

"Whose home? Yours or mine?"

"You to yours. Me to mine. But I'd be happy to drive you."

He waved her away. "No, thanks, Maggie," he said bitterly. "I'll catch a ride with Sandy."

She nodded, feeling worse than she had when she'd arrived. What she wanted from Chad, he couldn't give: friendship. Friendship like the kind Tanner had offered her and she'd rejected.

"Damn," she said softly, grinding the gears on the Volkswagen. Everything always ran full circle back to Tanner Baines. Would it ever be possible for her to get completely over him?

The light in the boathouse revealed a cobwebbed mausoleum of rusty equipment and junk. Tanner wiped his hand over his face and it came away covered with dust-laden pieces of web. He stood on the concrete slab that surrounded the sloop. There was no boat now. Just a muddy hole where once water had lapped in from the lake.

Overhead the boards looked worm-eaten and ready to cave in. He picked up a crowbar and tentatively touched the ceiling, loosing dirt and wood in a dust-choking stream. Coughing, he shaded his eyes, seeing dusky twilight sky through the hole he'd punched clean through the ceiling.

"This place is a disaster," he said aloud, his breath blowing the hanging gossamer threads in a wild dance.

Touching the button to the ratchet system that raised and lowered the boat, he was surprised to hear it hum and grind as it began to lift. He hadn't expected it to work.

The chain screeched through the cogs and he half feared the walls would fall down around him. Instead the chains rose slowly upward, the rusted iron pulley counterweights lowered and the boat's cradle lifted with a sucking sound from the ooze below.

It made him feel better, this testimony that some things still worked. It was like being told to have faith, and he looked at the mud-dripping chain framework for a long time before he switched out the light and headed back to the house.

There was no path anymore and he tramped over weeds and ivy until he got to the steps at the deck. These he tested carefully, searching for rot even though he'd replaced the worst of them earlier in the summer.

Once on the deck he leaned his forearms on the rail and stared downward through the trees to the top of the boat-house. In the evening light he couldn't see where he'd poked the hole through. In fact, from this view the boat-house looked eerily intact, like it had been in his youth. He could almost imagine things were just the same.

Except they weren't.

Checking his watch, he walked to the side of the deck and looked toward Shelley's upstairs window. One light shone steadily.

She was angry at him. Again. No news there, except he'd been trying harder to get through to her since his disturb-ing meeting with Maggie. But Shelley was a master at playing devil's advocate, and as usual, they'd fought, he'd gotten frustrated and furious, and that had sent her slam-ming up to her room.

Tanner sighed. He really didn't know what Shelley wanted from him. Tricia had made sure she always went to the right schools, entertained the right friends, only went out with the right boys. He'd relaxed the reins a bit since her death, but Shelley's reaction had been to rebel more, not less. She'd transferred all her fears and anger to him for some reason, but that didn't make it any easier deal-ing with her. Half the time he wanted to toss up his hands and walk out.

Only Shelley was his daughter—as Maggie had pointed out so eloquently. He couldn't leave her. He loved her. And he would be here as long as she needed him.

Thinking it was time he tried to smooth over their latest tiff, he went inside and mounted the stairs two at a time. He knocked on her door, hearing the faint music coming from her stereo. When there was no answer he twisted the knob, opening it a fraction.

"Shelley?"

No answer.

With a feeling of déjà vu he threw the door wide to find her room empty. Her bed was a mess of blankets. Magazines littered the floor. The window facing the old oak tree was wide open.

His initial reaction was rage, followed swiftly by fear. It wasn't the first time she'd taken off after a fight, and though he knew it was her escape valve, a way to blow off adolescent steam, it scared the wits out of him. What if she forgot to take her insulin? What if she forgot on purpose? How could he get to her if she needed help? *What if she went into a coma?*

Irrational thoughts, but ones he couldn't dismiss. Shelley's too smart for that, he consoled himself. There was no reason to expect the worst. She was just so damn headstrong! She was the one who refused to take her illness seriously, not he, but it was like talking to a brick wall trying to tell her so.

Tanner stared out the window at the twisted oak tree. Had she shimmied down the trunk? Now wouldn't that be ironic? More than likely, however, she'd just walked boldly out the front door.

Standing on the second-floor landing, he considered his options. This was not a new scenario. He'd searched for her other nights, but to no avail. When she was ready to come home, she would come. They would fight. She would run crying to her room and the whole cycle would begin again. He was too used to the battles to fool himself it would be different this time.

Had she taken her insulin before she left?

Curling his hand into a fist, he decided there was nothing to do but outwait her. He needed time to get his head together and be prepared when she deigned to show up anyway. *And please, God, let her show up unharmed.*

With his head full of dark demons, he walked to the end of the hall and unlocked the narrow door under the eaves. A flight of steps led upward to the attic. Mounting them, Tanner felt the hot, breathless air that had gotten trapped near the rafters envelop him in a wave of heat.

He stood at the head of the stairs, sweat trickling down his neck. A gleaming new typewriter sat on a teak stand against the far wall. Walking toward it, he picked up the neat stack of typewritten pages on the scarred end table against the corner wall. He read the first one, then crumpled it into his palm. He did the same for the next ten and then threw them all viciously into the trash, kicking the can with the toe of his boot.

Sinking onto a once glorious but now faded rose-colored love seat, he ran his hands over his face, then flung his head backward, staring at the rafters. Where had all his confidence gone? He'd had so much of it once. Buckets of it. Enough to make him believe he could live with the decisions of his youth.

But it was gone. Blown to bits. As substantial as the dust motes that flickered in the light from the overhead bulb. He didn't trust himself anymore.

He'd made a mistake with Maggie, and it had cost him more than he could measure.

Heaving a sigh, Tanner tried to forget the past. But it was a living, breathing part of him that had come back with a vengeance since he'd returned to Oregon. He'd thought the move would be a catharsis, a way to put his life with Shelley back on track after Tricia's death. But all it had done was stir his blood and make him remember things better left buried.

Oh, Maggie, Maggie.

He shuddered and clenched his teeth. There had been a time when he'd loved her more than life itself. Getting over her had been the hardest task he'd ever tackled. He'd thought he'd succeeded, too, and he'd been determined to make a good life for himself and Tricia.

He'd been satisfied at the beginning of their marriage, he realized. He'd had his work, a beautiful wife and a lovely little girl. He'd dropped Maggie from his consciousness the same way he'd dropped his father. Only Gerrard had tried to keep in touch and Tanner had refused to see him.

So much of what had happened had been his father's fault.

Far below him he heard the front door softly close. Shelley. Tanner was on his feet, down the attic stairs and at the second-floor landing before she'd even mounted two steps. Her hand on the railing, she looked up, surprised to see him waiting for her. Instantly her expression became sullen, her mouth tight.

"I'm not going to ask you where you've been since it won't do any good anyway," Tanner said without rancor. "But there are a few rules around this house and there's one in particular—if either of us leaves, he or she leaves a note for the other. Understand?"

"If I'd told you I was going, you wouldn't have let me."

Tanner met her defiant stare evenly. "You're right."

"This place is jail!"

"It's a jail of your own making."

She flounced upstairs, squeezing past him with a baleful glare that made Tanner wonder if he'd been too tough on his assessment of his father all those years ago. Parenthood was no picnic.

She slammed the door in his face.

"Shelley, I don't want to fight with you," he said to the panels. "I'm trying really hard not to. But I won't be your whipping boy just because you blame me for everything that goes wrong."

"I don't blame you!"

"Yes, you do."

"You hate me!"

"I don't hate you," Tanner said, his exasperation turning to anger. "You're my daughter. I love you."

"You don't love anyone but *Maggie Holt*!"

Her words stopped him cold. There was a telling moment of silence before he said, "What the hell does Maggie Holt have to do with this?"

The door cracked the tiniest fraction. "I went to see her today. She knew you and Mom, just like Mom said."

"I don't know what you're talking about."

"Mom always said you wanted to marry a girl named Maggie. I just didn't put it together until now. That's why we came back here, isn't it? So you could have your little girlfriend."

"Damn it, Shelley! If you don't stop this game playing once and for all I'll take you over my knee and spank you!"

"You couldn't!" Shelley was more incredulous than outraged.

"Try me."

The door cracked wider so she could get a better look at him. "You're serious."

"I'm fed up with all the nonsense. You're a diabetic. You need to be careful. But there's no reason to turn this into a drama where everyone around you has to rip his guts out to help you."

"Like Maggie Holt?"

Realizing she'd hit a nerve, Shelley was bound and determined to rub it raw. Tanner just met her questioning eyes with a cold glare that warned she'd reached the limit of his patience.

"Maybe it would be easier if I just left!" she flung out.

"There's no maybe about it. It would be."

Her gasp revealed her true feelings; her eyes showed her pain. She would have slammed the door again, but Tanner grabbed her by the forearm. "There's a Shelley I love hiding behind this adolescent I don't understand. Why don't you let me see her once in a while? She's the Shelley I love."

Her eyes were wet with unshed tears. "I hate your words!" she said tremulously. "You're so good with them. But they don't mean anything!"

She yanked her arm from his and shut her door.

He realized he'd just heard an echo of one of his wife's favorite accusations.

Tanner's temper boiled. It took all his strength not to blast Shelley for her selfishness. He strode down the stairs and out the front door, furious that she'd quoted Tricia, uneasy with the growing conviction that something had passed between his wife and daughter that he knew nothing about. Something terrible. Something that had turned his daughter away from him.

Maggie.

He stopped short. What had Tricia said about Maggie?

Tanner collapsed against the trunk of the oak tree. Shelley couldn't know the whole truth; Tricia hadn't known. But Tricia had guessed, and she'd come close enough to the right conclusion enough times to make Tanner sweat.

What lies had she planted in Shelley's young mind?

His hands were cold and clammy. For the first time in fourteen years he realized he couldn't keep his secret much longer. The principle parties had to know.

He had to tell Maggie.

And then she'd hate him as much as he hated himself.

The Portland airport was crowded with summer travelers carrying reams and reams of luggage. Several flights had been overbooked and tempers were flaring. To make matters worse, all flights from Los Angeles were running over an hour late owing to some foul-up in scheduling. The whole thing was a horrendous mess.

Maggie stood at the periphery of a crowd, consulting her watch. Con was already forty-five minutes late, with no arrival time listed on the board next to his flight number. She hadn't planned on this delay. Her meeting with Dr. Kempwood was due to start in ten minutes.

Sighing, she sank onto one of the few available chairs. She supposed she should be glad, really, since she dreaded having to go over Shelley Baines's case with the doctor. She dreaded everything to do with the Baineses! Yet she'd said she would help, and come hell or high water, she was determined not to back out now.

"Flight 541 from Los Angeles will be arriving at Gate 42 in fifteen minutes."

"Hallelujah," Maggie said beneath her breath. She gathered her purse and headed for the concourse. All around her she could hear weary passengers grumbling and complaining. She couldn't wait to meet Con and get out of there.

Watching out the window, she saw his huge silver bird touch down effortlessly and wished her own life were working as smoothly. Grimacing, she imagined how perfect Con would undoubtedly look, then was both surprised and slightly alarmed to see how rough and tumble and bleary-eyed he was when he walked off the plane.

"What's wrong with you?" she asked. "You look terrible."

"And good morning to you, too."

"Did something happen?"

Con sighed and laughed humorlessly. "Let's get my bags and get outta here. I'll tell you on the way."

It was Linda, of course, he told her later as she drove beyond the speed limit all the way to Briar Park. Linda had made life hell for him as soon as she'd learned he'd definitely accepted Pozzer, Strikeberg and Carmen's offer.

"I didn't think she gave a damn one way or the other," Con said, bewildered.

"Maybe she doesn't. It's still tough to let someone go."

"Thanks a lot."

"Well, do you want her to want you back?"

Con scratched his beard stubble and made a face. "No. But I'd like someone to want me."

Maggie smiled. "Poor baby. Self-pity doesn't suit you. Neither does your appearance. Get it together. Fast. We're going to see Gayle Kempwood."

"God, Maggie! Have a heart. Let me at least shave first. I didn't have time after the scene with Linda in the middle of the night."

Stepping on the accelerator, Maggie murmured, "Don't I remember you warning me against Tanner Baines? Sounds like you could use some of your own advice, brother dear."

At her office, Con changed clothes and managed a quick shave in record time. Even so, Maggie left ahead of him, and by the time Con rapped softly on Dr. Kempwood's door, they were already in a healthy discussion about Shelley's problems.

"I'm worried about her insulin intake," Dr. Kempwood was saying. "The blood test we did on her suggests she isn't getting enough."

"Do you think she's just neglecting to take it?" Maggie asked as Gayle answered her door.

"Maybe. Or maybe she's doing it on purpose. Hello, Connor."

Her theory put Maggie into a blue funk, and as Con and Gayle got reacquainted she tried to rationalize Shelley's behavior. A nagging voice inside her head said it was Tanner's fault. He wasn't paying attention to the signs. Yet Shelley was old enough to be a responsible person. Maybe, she rationalized, Dr. Kempwood's tests were taken on a day when Shelley just hadn't been as careful as usual. She didn't want to think they reflected the usual state of affairs.

"You're doing more tests?" Maggie asked, though she knew the answer.

"As soon as possible." Gayle shook her head. "I can't find any physical reason for what's happening other than simple lack of intake. If Shelley's injecting herself with the right amount of insulin and eating right, she should have no problem."

"I'll ask her about her diet again," Maggie said, rising. *And hopefully she'll give me a straight answer.*

"Can you talk to her father? He should be able to tell you what she's eaten. For that matter, he probably knows about her insulin. But I can't seem to get him on the phone."

Maggie felt Con's eyes on her. "He won't return your calls?"

"Worse. No one answers there at all."

Knowing Tanner's reclusiveness, Maggie found that odd. She would have said as much, but she didn't feel like it with Con in the room. "I'll do what I can," she told Gayle.

When she and Con were out in the hall she took the offensive before he could nail her to the wall over Tanner. "Looks like you and Gayle have a mutual admiration society. When are you going to ask her out?"

"I'm not. You're going to invite her over for dinner."

"Oh, and why's that?"

"Because I like Gayle. I don't want to start something I'm not ready for and end up ruining a great friendship."

Maggie gave him a long look. "You have gotten cautious."

"I've been burned."

Con took her car and left, promising the next time he came to Oregon he would drive his vintage T-Bird and make sure she had her own wheels. He expected to be completely moved by the end of July.

Maggie spent the afternoon lost in her work. She looked up only once, around four o'clock, and felt a wave of heat waft through her open window, reminding her that the summer was waxing on. Each day seemed a little bit hotter than the last, and July promised to be one of the warmest on record.

She was running her hand along the inside of her neck, feeling how sticky her skin was, when the phone buzzed.

"Maggie Holt," she said distractedly.

"Maggie, it's Tanner."

She nearly dropped her pencil, then glowered at her fingers as if it were all their fault for the way she'd overreacted. He hadn't needed to say who he was. His first few syllables stopped her heart. "Well, hello. What can I do for you?"

"I'd like to see you."

"Oh?" she said when he didn't elaborate.

She heard his frustrated expellation of breath. "I need to talk to you."

"About Shelley?" Her mouth was dry. She knew instinctively this was something else.

"If you like," he said. "But that's not why I called. I've been thinking about some things. Look, I just need to talk to you. Could you come by the house?"

Her senses were wild, mixing up the messages her brain was sending. In a basic, feminine way she understood what was coming, and it scared the wits out of her. "You want to talk about . . . us? Oh, Tanner, it's not necessary."

"There is no 'us' and there hasn't been for a long time." He was clear on that. "But I need to straighten some things out with you."

Thinking he wanted to apologize for the way he'd treated her, she said, "Look, it doesn't matter. I don't care about what happened the other night."

"Listen to me!" he said furiously. "It matters to me. And it matters to you, too. Or hell, it should."

"Con's here. In Lake Oswego. I can't come."

"Why?"

"He's my guest," she hissed through her teeth.

"You don't want to tell him," he guessed. "You don't want him to know you have anything to do with me."

"I don't have anything to do with you."

There was a heavy pause. "Yes, you do, Maggie," he said quietly.

His arrogance would have been infuriating if he hadn't been so damn right. As much as she might like to think she wasn't tied to him, she was. In ways she neither understood nor wanted.

"All right," she said. "I'll come. When?"

"Five o'clock?"

"Will Shelley be there?"

"No. She asked to stay at a friend's tonight and I said okay."

So that's why he'd called tonight. She found that faintly alarming, though rationally, if they were going to discuss anything concerning themselves or Shelley it would be better not to have her around.

"And Mrs. Greer?"

"What the hell does it matter?" he demanded. "I'm not going to attack you!"

"She won't be there, either," Maggie answered herself. She knew it.

"Are you going to make me meet you somewhere else? If that's what it takes, okay."

Because she understood Tanner, she knew how difficult it was for him to go out in public. He was too notorious, too many people wanted to stare and comment.

"Your place is fine," Maggie answered flatly. "But I can't be there until after five-thirty."

"I'll wait."

When she hung up the phone she found her hands were shaking. Annoyed, she pressed her knuckles to her mouth. So she and Tanner were going to be alone. So what? What could he do to her that he hadn't already done?

"Nothing," Maggie said aloud, sweeping up her purse. "Not a thing."

Chapter Seven

I could be seventeen again.

Maggie yanked on the emergency break, remembering the times she'd pulled in behind Tanner's souped-up car. This time the car she parked behind was a silver-blue Mercedes 350 SL. The scene had altered since she was a teenager: there was no sports car and no Tricia Wellesley. The house was all that remained. The house and Tanner.

Maggie climbed from her car, took a deep breath and headed for the front door. She would get this meeting over with and return home as quickly as possible.

Home. She made a face. Con's recriminations still crashed and echoed through her mind.

"You're going to Tanner's *tonight*?" he'd bellowed when she'd delivered the news. *"Why?"*

"Because he asked me to."

"And that's all it takes?"

"Contrary to what you think, I don't need a keeper, Con! I'll be back before you know it."

The memory faded, squeezed out purposely as Maggie pulled herself together. Con hadn't had to berate her; she already wished she'd never agreed to come. Yet she couldn't deny that excitement was growing inside her. She'd waited too long for the truth.

Shivering though the night was warm, Maggie hurried up the front steps and rang the bell. The chimes pealed through the house, but minutes went by and no one answered. She was in the act of ringing again, when the door suddenly opened inward.

"Hello, Maggie," came a familiar drawl.

He was dressed in gray: gray shirt, black jeans faded to gray, gray shoes. The shirt was silk and clung to his skin, but she knew that he hadn't dressed for her. He'd obviously been out somewhere, and belatedly she remembered Gayle Kempwood's mentioning she was going to try to get him to meet with her at the hospital.

She wished now she'd insisted on the same thing.

"I thought you might change your mind," he said, holding the door for her.

Surreptitiously she wiped her moist palms on the skirt of her white shirtwaist dress. "I did change my mind. Four times. I only came because Con told me not to."

To her surprise he threw back his head and laughed. The sound rumbled through the room, reminding Maggie of another time, another Tanner. Her arms broke out in gooseflesh.

"I thought you were different, Maggie," he said, still grinning. "But you're not."

"Yes, I am." She stepped past him into the foyer. "I'm completely different. I know the difference between truth and fiction now."

"You knew it back then," he said, his grin fading.

She looked him in the eye and said nothing. They both knew he was wrong.

"Come on into the kitchen," he said, inclining his head. "I'll get us something to drink."

She was relieved he hadn't chosen the den, though her memories were probably more acute in the kitchen. Still, bright lights and hard chairs were better than moody shadows and plush cushions. She couldn't trust herself with him. Even knowing he thought she wasn't good enough, she still couldn't trust herself.

He brought her a snifter of brandy and she lifted her eyes questioningly.

"Did you want something else?" he asked.

"No." She lowered her eyes and took a swallow. She almost never drank, only an occasional glass of wine and on special occasions, brandy. His instincts about her never ceased to amaze her.

Tanner, too, had a snifter, and now he swirled it gently, his eyes downcast. Sensing how difficult this conversation was for him, Maggie took the initiative.

"You wanted to talk to me," she reminded softly. "So talk."

His mouth quirked, and when he lifted his eyes, she could barely hold his tawny gaze. Her heart was beating in her throat, light and fast. She saw his jaw work several times, could feel the frustration and emotion rippling outward, but then he shook his head and said, disappointingly, "I'd like to tell you a few things about Shelley first. It's important to me that you should know."

Maggie slowly let out her breath. She hadn't realized she'd been holding it. "I'd like to know—about Shelley," she said.

Tanner regarded her thoughtfully. Maggie's hands were twisting in her lap and he knew how anxious she was to hear what he had to say. But it wasn't going to be easy; he needed time. And he silently thanked her for giving him that time.

"Shelley's a symptom of an old, old problem that I can't seem to resolve," he said, frowning.

"What does that mean?"

"It means she doesn't trust me. There's all this turmoil going on inside her and I can't get close enough to her to find out what it is."

Maggie settled into her chair, tugging nervously on the wide red belt around her waist. "Is there a reason she doesn't trust you?"

His smile was ironic. "Probably. I'm not very trust-worthy, y'know."

Maggie looked at him sharply. The lines of humor bracketing his mouth were very attractive. *Don't make me like you, Tanner.* "I mean, is there a specific reason?"

"If there is, I don't know what. It's all mixed up with my relationship with Tricia and it's been a thousand times worse since Tricia died." He pulled out a chair, twisted it around and straddled it, stretching his arms in front of him and holding the snifter as if he were examining it for flaws. "But it began earlier, about the time Shelley's diabetes was diagnosed."

He was directly in Maggie's line of vision. She could see the way his pants stretched over his thighs, could remember the taut, muscular skin beneath. Uncomfortably warm, she ran her hand over her throat. "How did Shelley react when you learned the truth?"

"Terrible." Tanner couldn't help watching Maggie's hand. Self-conscious, she dropped it to her lap again. "She was young—hell, she's still young—but then it was worse.

She had all the signs: frequent trips to the bathroom, embarrassment over it, a reaction right after she ate. I questioned Tricia whether diabetes ran in her family, but she wouldn't talk about it. I had no choice but to take Shelley in myself, and I think, somehow, she's always blamed me for it.''

"She doesn't seem that unfair," Maggie murmured. "She's too smart."

"Too smart," Tanner echoed grimly. "Yes, she's too smart." His tone suggested he found that a mixed blessing. "Anyway, when we learned she was going to have to give herself shots Tricia got hysterical. It didn't help."

Maggie could imagine only too clearly. A frightened child. A hysterical mother. An insistent father. "The shots are subcutaneous. It's not like finding a vein."

"Try telling an eleven-year-old that. And a mother tigress who doesn't want to hear it." He drank down the rest of the brandy with a grimace. "It colored our relationship from then on. That relationship's at an all time low, by the way."

"How much control do you have over Shelley?"

Tanner's harsh laugh was answer enough. "Not a whole helluva lot." He gave her a quick look. "Maybe that's one reason I want you involved."

"You didn't want me involved in the beginning," she reminded him quietly.

"In the beginning I didn't want you anywhere near me."

Maggie stood and walked to the open French doors that led to the back deck. No breeze blew in and the heat seemed to swell in the glassed-in room. "What do you want now, Tanner?"

She heard the scrape of his chair, then felt his breath on the back of her neck. "Since you don't want to be friends,

I guess I'll have to settle for a laying down of arms," he said. "Think that's possible?"

"I don't know." A shiver slid down her back and she walked through the doors to the deck. The evening sun slanted downward, heating her crown, making her scalp tingle. She turned her face upward and closed her eyes, wishing she had more sense than to let him get to her.

"You were a big part of my life, Maggie. It didn't just go away overnight."

"No? You could have fooled me." She tried to keep her tone light.

"Tricia never forgave me for falling in love with you. She never forgot, either. I think she even mentioned it to Shelley. That's part of the problem."

Maggie's eyes flew open. She turned to stare at him. "What do you mean?"

"Shelley brought your name up to me the other night. She accused me of being in love with you."

"*What?*"

"She thinks I brought her back to Oregon so I could begin seeing you again."

"You said she didn't know about us!"

"She doesn't. She's guessing." His mouth curved appealingly. "As you pointed out earlier—she's too smart."

The sound of faint music from the far side of the lake drifted through the still air. Maggie blindly turned in its direction, feeling oddly upset. Rationally, there was no cause for it. They were talking about a long ago love affair that could have no bearing on what Shelley was feeling today. "What's there to know anyway?" She lifted her shoulders. "We had a brief summer fling. That's all."

"It was more than that. We both know it. And Tricia knew it, too."

"It was a summer fling," Maggie repeated. A heart-beat passed. "For you."

"If you believed that, you wouldn't be here now," Tanner said impatiently.

"Wrong." Her pride consumed her. "I'm here out of curiosity. That's all. You wanted to talk to me, not the other way around."

As always when dealing with Maggie, Tanner's frustration level hit its limit. "You want me to prove you wrong?" he demanded, stepping over his own boundaries, moving toward her in a way that made Maggie shrink against the rail.

"Your arrogance is unbelievable!"

"Yeah. Like your stubbornness."

"If you touch me I'll—"

"What?"

"Scream," she hissed, glaring at him.

His anger sank as quickly as it has surfaced; he realized how dangerous it was to test her—to test himself. Leaning his forearms on the rail, he made certain there was enough space between them to make her comfortable. "So scream," he suggested with a touch of humor. "Scream away."

Even she had to recognize the ridiculousness of their situation, but her pride wouldn't let her smile. She felt angry and humiliated and hardly knew what to say to him. It didn't help that he was regarding her with amused tolerance. She didn't want him to treat her that way. She didn't know what she wanted.

He was about to say something, when the phone interrupted him. "Just a minute," he said, and went to answer it.

Alone in the heat, she felt herself relax a little. She wished he wouldn't bait her the way he did. It made her feel young and tongue-tied and totally frustrated. He did it on purpose. To strip away all her carefully erected barriers. Well, she wouldn't let it happen again, and when he reappeared from the other room she opened her mouth to tell him as much, but his first words stopped her short.

"It's for you."

"Me?"

"It's Connor."

Maggie gave Tanner an uncertain look as she went into the den. She picked up the phone, hesitating a moment, hearing Tanner's soft tread outside the door. "Con?"

"You all right?" he brother asked.

"Of course I'm all right," she answered in a furious undertone.

"Think you'll be back soon?"

"You'll be lucky if I ever come back."

"Okay, okay. Point taken. I was just going to go out but thought I'd wait if you were going to show up anytime soon."

"Go ahead and go." Maggie twisted her neck to peer out the den doors. Tanner was nowhere to be seen. "I'll be back in a while, but I don't know when."

"Take care, little sister."

"You, too."

She walked into the foyer and was about to head in the direction of the kitchen, when she heard Tanner's voice sound from somewhere above her. "Big brother's watching."

He was sitting on the stairway, about halfway up. Maggie walked to the bottom step and placed her hand on the banister. "Big brother has a thing or two to learn about privacy. What are you doing up there? Eavesdropping?"

"I want to show you something."

To Maggie's knowledge, the only rooms upstairs were bedrooms. At first she thought he was kidding, but quickly realized he was completely serious. "Look, Tanner, maybe I ought to go now...."

"Give me a little more time, Maggie. Please."

He disappeared at the landing and she heard his long footsteps recede down the hallway. She hesitated, wondering which of them had lost their mind—herself, for certain—then, sighing, began mounting the stairs after him.

"Tanner, I—"

Maggie stopped. He was standing beside an open doorway that led to another flight of stairs, this one extremely narrow. "You want to show me something in the attic?" she asked incredulously.

He flashed her a quick grin. "That's right. I saved all my old cadavers from med school and stored them upstairs."

"I ought to be able to smell them," Maggie said dryly.

"They're frozen."

"Did anyone ever tell you you have a penchant for lying?"

"Yes, as a matter of fact." He pushed the door open further, beckoning her nearer. "You did."

She was standing beside him now, aware of his familiar scent and the dusty heat that drifted from the attic. "I'm not going up there, y'know. I don't care what you want to show me."

"What happened to the adventurous girl who climbed up my oak tree?"

"She met with an untimely death years ago."

"Let's resurrect her."

She shook her head, her gaze never leaving his, but Tanner's eyes said he wasn't giving up. Did he know he was touching that part of her she didn't want to believe still existed? "Maybe Shelley learned her game playing from a master."

"No. My game playing's different. Come on."

His hand encircled her upper arm and he tugged her after him. Reluctantly Maggie took the first few steps. It was then that she remembered Mrs. Greer's saying that Tanner had been upstairs working. On the heels of that thought came another: Gayle Kempwood's comment that he hadn't answered his phone.

"You're doing something," Maggie said in dawning comprehension. She stopped in her tracks. "You're working on something."

He nodded, giving her arm another tug. "I want your opinion on something."

"Why mine?"

"Because you understand," he said simply.

She continued mounting the stairs and eventually they reached the top. Not knowing what to expect, Maggie had allowed her imagination to take flight. To say the sight of a typewriter, stand and old furniture was a letdown couldn't come close to expressing her feelings.

"You're writing?" she asked.

For once in his life, Tanner seemed unsure of himself. "Yeah."

"You've literally locked yourself in a garret and are writing? What? What are you writing?"

"A book. And I haven't locked myself in."

"As good as," Maggie said, walking toward the thin pile of pages on the table under the window. "You don't answer your phone when you're working."

"How do you know?"

"Gayle Kempwood's tried to call you."

She picked up the pages, scanning them, sensing him close behind her. It took her a second or two to realize what she was reading. This was no medical journal; this was a novel.

Her heart lurched. "What are you writing about?" She twisted around to look in his eyes, her own wide and worried.

"Be serious, Maggie. Do you think I'd write about us?" He shook his head, his nostrils flared. "You have no idea..."

"No, I..." She made a sound of self-condemnation. "I don't know what I'm thinking. You just—you just make me crazy!"

Tanner smiled. "It's a thriller. A medical thriller." He gestured to the overflowing wastebasket. "I've had a few false starts."

"You want me to read it?"

On this he hesitated, grimacing. "Yes."

"Now?"

"Whenever."

"But I thought..." Maggie left her sentence unfinished. Hadn't he called her over to talk about the past? She cleared her throat. "I guess I mixed up the signals. I thought you wanted to straighten a few things out between us."

Her words seemed to bring him back to the present. He inhaled slowly, then silently let out his breath. "I do. I want to tell you why I married Tricia."

"I don't care why you married her. I just want to know why you used me and now feel like you've got to make it up—"

"Maggie," he interrupted impatiently. "I wanted to marry you! I *asked* you to marry me. But circumstances happened and I couldn't do it."

"What circumstances?"

He gritted his teeth. "My father."

"Oh." Her disappointment was too great to measure. So he'd buckled under to Gerrard's pressure after all. A part of her had always known.

"Maggie, sit down." He clasped her shoulders and slowly led her to the couch, forcing her to take a seat. Then he sat down beside her.

"You don't have to say any more."

He made a sound of self-condemnation. "Oh, yes, I do."

"We were kids, Tanner. You did what you had to do. It's no big mystery." Her words were light and brittle, covering up the betrayal she'd always felt. Because she loved him she'd always hoped there was something more, some other, deeper reason that would help alleviate her loss. Now she wanted to hear no more.

"I wanted you to see this—" he gestured to the pages in her hand "—because I wanted to be close to you. We were close once."

"Look, it's okay."

He sighed. "I wanted to be friends again, but you said that's impossible. And after the truth comes out, you may be right."

"What," she said evenly, "are you talking about?"

"Maggie..." The emotion swimming in his eyes was terrible to see.

"Tanner," she said, alarmed. Instinctively she placed her hand on the side of his face, reassuring him. He closed his eyes, a shudder passing through his lean frame.

She'd never been able to think straight where he was concerned; she'd always acted on impulse, on some deeper, stronger emotion than reason. He needed her now, she could tell that, so she reacted in the only way she knew how, by forgetting all the advice she'd given her tender heart and putting her arms around him, holding him, pressing her face compassionately against his hollowed cheek.

"Don't, Maggie. I'm weak."

"You are not weak." She felt his stubble grate against her softer flesh. Tanner's emotions were clearly involved and that meant more to Maggie than anything. She finally understood that he cared about her, maybe even loved her. But something was holding him back.

As far as she was concerned, whatever it was he felt was so wrong could be conquered, as long as they had each other.

Pulling back, she looked into his eyes. Knowing she would probably regret it later, she gambled with her future. "I love you, Tanner," she said quietly. "I always have. You can hurt me over and over again, but you can't stop me loving you."

His breath expelled sharply, but he didn't move.

Needing to know his feelings, she delved into the gold depths of his eyes. Shadows lurked there. So did passion. Because she didn't have anything to lose but the last tattered remnants of her pride she kissed him, her mouth touching his, her soft lips blending with his hardened ones.

He still didn't move, but his heart was pounding so hard she could hear it.

He put his hands on her shoulders to push her away, but his fingers held there, tense and shaking. Maggie kissed him again, this time feeling his lips quiver under her passionate assault. He shifted restlessly and she let her hands slide down his sides to his waist, reveling in the taut muscles she could feel beneath his shirt.

"Love me, Tanner," she breathed. "I want to make love to you."

His groan was one of anguish, but Maggie cut it off with another kiss. Her tongue teased his lips, stroking and touching. She could sense the changes in him though the rein on his emotions was like an iron vise. Almost achingly slow, his hand came around her back and drew her closer, close enough for Maggie to realize he was no more immune to what was between them than she was.

"Tanner," she whispered, frightened and elated.

His hand twisted in her hair, his mouth all over hers in a devastating kiss that drew a moan from deep within her. She wound herself around him, arms around his waist, legs entangled with his, her body stretching, reaching, trying to become one flesh.

And he complied, pushing her down on the couch with hard, hurried hands. Maggie lay beneath him, her hair a wild curtain, her eyes glazed. Lips trembling, she brought his mouth back to hers, his body moving anxiously, as if he couldn't allow himself time to think.

Feverishly he unbuttoned her dress, pressing his mouth to the creamy smoothness of her skin. His groan was one of anguish, but Maggie held him tight, her hands buried in his tangled, sun-streaked hair. She closed her eyes, arching, feeling the hurried wetness of his tongue as it tasted her and loved her. "Please, Tanner," she moaned. "Please..."

"Damn it all, Maggie!"

Abruptly he twisted away, his breaths rasping. He stood, hands clenched, his back bowed inward as he threw back his head and made a strangled sound that frightened her.

"My God, Tanner. What is it?"

"You're my sister, Maggie. My half sister. My father had an affair with your mother!"

Chapter Eight

Sunlight fell in uneven streaks through the tiny dirt-smeared window above his head. Maggie's first thought, because her mind was a void, was that he really ought to let Mrs. Greer up here to clean once in a while.

"You're out of your mind," she said calmly.

"No." He half turned to look at her, but her dress was still open, her chest still covered with a fine sheen of perspiration. He dragged his eyes away. "It's the truth."

"My mother would never have an affair with anyone."

"I asked her myself, Maggie. She told me."

"You must have misunderstood."

"My father—and your mother—both told me the same thing," he said distinctly.

She stared at him blankly. "It's a mistake," she answered, perplexed.

"Don't you think I wanted it to be a mistake?" he said through his teeth. "Don't you think after what we did that I moved heaven and earth to prove them wrong?"

"No..." Maggie put up a trembling palm, warding his words away. The edges of her world had somehow blurred, but she doggedly hung on to her conviction.

"Didn't you ever wonder why my father was so hysterical about you and Con? He didn't want me anywhere near either one of you. He was afraid I would learn the truth." Tanner's breath expelled harshly. "When he found out I was seeing you he went berserk. He told me everything when I got home that night."

"It's a lie. They lied. My mother would never, ever—" Maggie got to her feet, her knees shaking uncontrollably. "You're trying to hurt me again. You're doing this."

"Maggie. Oh, God, Maggie," he groaned, tortured. "I never wanted you to know. No one ever wanted you to know. But now Shelley—"

"Shelley knows? You told Shelley this—this—story?"

"No." Tanner moved toward her, but Maggie backed up so fast she nearly hit her head on the rafters. "I don't know what's going on with Shelley. But there's something from the past, something Tricia told her, that makes me think she suspects you and I are—"

"Tricia?" Maggie interrupted, the blood draining from her face. "It's a lie. It's all a lie!"

"Tricia only knew that I loved you," Tanner said quickly. "That I loved you, but that I married her. But she was fairly close to my father and I can't be certain what was said between them. I wouldn't think he would tell her, but he and I are barely on speaking terms."

She was so hot she felt she might faint. Her face was moist. Suddenly she remembered her unbuttoned dress, and with shaking fingers she buttoned it back up, each movement so slow as to be a ritual. Tightening her belt, she smoothed her skirt, feeling as torn apart as the scattered, forgotten pages of Tanner's manuscript that lay at her feet.

"You are either making this up or are mistaken," she said unevenly. "It is *not* the truth."

"Do you think I would make this up?" he said in angry disbelief.

For the first time since he'd delivered his fatal blow she looked at his face. Haggard lines were carved into his cheeks. Fury and self-hate and yes, frustrated desire, too, glittered from between gold-tipped lashes. Maggie swallowed and stared past him.

"No," she said softly.

"God, Maggie." He ran his hands through his hair. "I only wanted to tell you. I didn't mean to kiss you again."

"You didn't kiss me. I kissed you. Just like always." Her tone was bitter.

"I should have told you sooner. It was a mistake keeping it from you."

Tanner her half brother? Maggie just wouldn't believe it. But she accepted that *he* believed it. Slowly she sank back down on to the couch. "Tell me everything," she said hoarsely. "All the facts." Her lips twisted. "Since my mother's dead I can't ask her for the truth."

Tanner looked out the window, his mouth grim. "If you need verification you can ask my father. He'll tell you."

"I wouldn't talk to Gerrard Baines if he were the last man on earth!" Maggie spat out, surprised by her emotion.

"Believe me, I don't blame you. But he's your father, Maggie."

"No!" She sprang up again, anguished tears building in her eyes. "I won't listen to you. I don't believe you! It's all

a lie your father made up to keep you from marrying below your class!''

"Your mother told me, Maggie. I had to drag it out of her, but she admitted it in the end. I don't know which of us was sicker, her or me!''

A choked sound rose in her throat. She wouldn't believe. Wouldn't! But his logic was too terrible, his facts too clear. Tanner regarded her helplessly, wishing there were something he could do to soften the pain, knowing there wasn't.

"What did my mother say?'' she asked in a tight, trembling voice.

"She told me how she met my father.'' Wiping the sweat off his palms, he walked the length of the room and back to keep from taking Maggie in his arms and comforting her. "Let me start at the beginning. The last night you and I were together. The night we . . .''

"Made love,'' she said dully.

"Yes. Made love.'' He shot her a quick look to see how she was taking that. It was the idea of incest that had worried him more than anything else, the way she would ultimately deal with it. There was no guilt involved; they were both innocent and he wanted to make sure she understood that. But Maggie was too overwhelmed by the news to react. Later, maybe. He hoped she would let him be there then, to help her through it.

"After I took you home I went back to the house, spoiling for a fight with my father. I wasn't prepared for what came next.'' Tanner sighed. "He took me out on the back deck and sat me in a chair. All I wanted to do was argue, so he finally just yelled it out to me.

"I wouldn't believe him. Naturally. I denied it as much as you're doing now. I grabbed him by the throat, intent on making him swallow his lies." He shook his head. "Maybe I wanted to kill him. I felt like killing him."

Maggie wiped her palm across her forehead. She closed her eyes, but pinpoints of light danced behind her lids. *Stop, Tanner. I don't want to hear any more.*

"We struggled until the news finally sank in, and then I just went limp. I could barely make it to bed. I was sicker than I've ever been in my life." He stopped in the center of the room, his hands thrust in his back pockets. "But I couldn't sleep. I waited until my dad went to bed. It was after one o'clock. Then I climbed down the tree and walked all the way to your house."

"My house?" she repeated blankly.

"The walk cleared my head. But I needed to know the truth, Maggie."

He'd gone to see her mother. With a sinking sensation she finally realized he hadn't misunderstood or built a story out of his father's lies. He'd heard the truth from her own mother.

Tanner was her half brother.

The room spun in front of her eyes; heat swelled around her, suffocating her. She didn't recognize the animal sounds issuing from her own throat.

"Maggie..." Tanner was beside her in an instant.

"Don't touch me. Please." She feinted backward, closer to the wall, her hair brushing the dusty rafters. Her fingers shook as they felt behind her for support. Her thighs quaked. Giving in, she slowly wilted to the floor, leaning back against the rough wall.

Tanner understood how she felt. He'd experienced the same emotions himself, the same soul-searching disbelief and anger and guilt. "I'll get you a glass of water," he said, twisting on his heel.

"No, I want to hear it all. Now."

He hesitated, torn.

"Tell me about my mother."

With a tightening of his mouth that expressed his own helpless fury at the fates, he sank onto the couch, hunched forward, his hands hanging limp between his knees. "She was awake that night. Sitting on your back porch. I'd never met her before."

No, he'd never met her. Maggie had made a point of keeping Tanner as far away from her home as possible, partly because of Con, partly because she'd instinctively known her mother wouldn't approve of her dating someone whose social stratum was so different from her own.

"I startled her," Tanner went on. "And then...I just blurted out who I was, furiously, because I hated them both for hurting us. I told her I loved you."

Maggie's hands were at her cheeks. Her quiet, long-suffering mother had never told her about that meeting. She'd never even hinted about it.

"She shrank into the chair. It was dark out, but I could see how upset she was. She asked me how far our relationship had gone."

Maggie drew a swift breath. She stared at the manuscript pages unseeingly, her mind in turmoil.

"I said I'd made love to you."

"Oh, no." Pain ripped through her. Pain for her mother, for herself. She struggled upward, but Tanner dropped to his knees in front of her, imprisoning her wrists with his hands.

"I had to. I wanted to make her admit it was all a lie. But she didn't. She just started sobbing and saying it was all her fault, and I thought I would die.

"Maggie, her husband had left her," Tanner said, his voice breaking. "She was a single mother, raising Con, and she met my father in the park. It was just that simple. It wasn't supposed to happen the way it did."

She stared at him. "You've forgiven them."

"They both had a terrible life," he said flatly. "The affair made them miserable. That I know. And then right afterward your mother reconciled with her husband and my father tried to forget her." He looked down at his hands, holding on tightly to her wrists. "You came along the following September."

Silence filled the room. Maggie could feel it like a third presence, oppressive, heavy, weighing her down. She couldn't think. "She never told me," she said in a stranger's voice.

"I think she was probably afraid to."

"She never told Con, either."

"Maggie, she wouldn't have told me, either, if the situation hadn't been so critical."

"I've got to leave," she said suddenly. She felt dirty, hot and sweaty, soiled both inside and out. Tanner, understanding, tried to talk her out of it.

"Stay awhile. Just until the worst is over."

When she met his gaze her eyes were filled with bitterness. "The worst is never over, Tanner. It's just right out there, waiting to find us."

"Don't go. Look, I won't touch you. I won't even come near you. But let me get you something to drink—tea, alcohol, anything. I don't want you to be alone."

It was exactly what Maggie wanted, however. To be alone. Away from Tanner and all the terrible truths he'd planted in her brain. "I can't—be with you right now," she struggled to say. "Please. I need you to understand."

She rose slowly and his hands fell away. Walking out of the attic was one of the hardest things she'd ever had to do.

Tanner had knocked away all the supports she'd spent a lifetime building. Now she was headed for the unknown.

He was right behind her. Following her down the stairs, true to his promise about not touching her. But at the door he put his palm on the panels, forcing her to wait.

"I've thought about telling you a dozen different times since I got back. I didn't expect to still—" he clenched his teeth "—feel this way about you."

"Why did you come back?" she demanded.

Sighing, he said, "I don't know. Everything got so awful after Tricia died that—"

"You came because Tricia was gone. You wanted to test yourself, didn't you?"

His facial muscles were stiff. He wanted to deny her, but she had a way of looking into his soul. "Yes."

"And you failed," she whispered.

Tanner looked straight at her, in a way that dangerously liquefied her insides. "Yes."

"You married Tricia to get away from me. It's been the barrier between us all these years. Damn it, Tanner. *You should have told me before!*"

It was an echo of the same accusation she'd flung at him when she'd thought he'd used her. She felt used again. Pushing his hand away, she yanked open the door. Hot air rushed inward, striking her like a wave.

"I want to find a way for us to deal with each other," Tanner said. "I can't change what is, but neither can I bear the thought of a future without you."

"Tanner..." she said warningly.

"You're my sister. I just don't want to think I'll never see you again."

For Maggie, his words sounded like the death knell. "You are not my brother, Tanner. I have a brother. Con.

I know how I feel about him and it's not the same way I feel about you!''

"You think I don't know?" Frustration turned his mouth to a flat line.

"I don't believe any of this. I really don't. I'm going to wake up tomorrow and find it's all been a bad dream. What I'm *not* going to do is face the day accepting I have another brother. Can you really look at me as your sister?"

"I've been trying for fourteen years," he said quietly.

There was nothing left to say. Though his case was strong, Maggie wouldn't allow herself to believe. There was a tiny bit of hope inside her, almost an expectation, that if she just tried harder she could prove him wrong.

"Let me take you home," he said, following her to her car.

"No, I need to drive."

"Then let me go with you."

"No." She unlatched the door and the interior light went on, making her see the smudges of dirt on her white dress.

"Is Connor there?"

"Stop it, Tanner. I can handle myself better than either you or my brother give me credit for."

My brother. She climbed into the car, wishing everything she said to him wasn't filled with innuendos and double meanings. She stepped on the accelerator and reversed with more speed than necessary. He was still standing in the yard when she rounded the corner.

The lights were on at the cottage and Maggie realized Con was home. A whimper stole past her lips. Con. Her brother. Her real brother.

He was at the kitchen counter, poring over some briefs. The sight of him filled her throat with tears. She made a beeline for him, throwing herself at him in a way she hadn't since she was a child.

"Hey, Maggie. What the hell—?"

Sobs shook her, torn from deep inside her. She buried her face in his neck and crumpled his shirt in her fists.

It took him about two seconds to react.

"What did he do to you?" he demanded in a low voice. "What in God's name did he do to you?"

Maggie inhaled on a short gulp of anguish. "Nothing. Nothing."

"Damn it!" Con roared. "It's the last time. I can't stand to see you like this. I'm going over there and taking care of him once and for all." He practically pushed her off his lap, and she stumbled backward.

"No, Con." Maggie wiped her eyes with the back of her hand, frightened out of tears. "You can't. He didn't do anything. He just told me why—what the reasons were— and I just came straight to you."

Con's neck was a dull brick red. He barely heard her, so intent was he on evening the score with Tanner.

"Listen to me, Con! Please! I'm in love with Tanner and I can't be! Just leave it alone. Please."

"You're not in love with him. You just think you are."

Maggie's eyes were windows to her soul. She'd spoken the truth; she did love Tanner. As a woman loves a man. As a wife loves her husband. And that was the biggest sin of all.

"Ahh, Maggie." Connor sighed. He put his arms around her and led her back to the kitchen, helping her onto one of the barstools.

"I'll be okay, Con. Don't worry. I'm going to get over him and everything will be fine...."

* * *

It was no use expecting her world to return to the same order it had been before Tanner had dropped his bomb. Everything was changed. Nothing was the same. She woke up feeling terrible, then went to bed feeling worse. Her sickness was of the soul and it had no cure. There was nothing to do but accept what Tanner had said, but she could never accept it. She loved him too much.

Maggie walked through the days like an automaton; it felt as if she'd acquired someone else's body. Each task seemed to need extra thought. Every movement had to be planned out. Nothing, nothing, could be expected to work as it once had.

About a week after her confrontation with Tanner, Con invited Gayle Kempwood over for dinner, and though the evening was pleasant and full of lively conversation, Maggie felt detached, as if she were playing a part rather than being the person she truly was. Neither Con nor Gayle seemed to notice, however, so she concluded she gave an effective performance. She wished she could fool herself the same way.

Tanner tried to call several times, but he never caught her in. Realizing he wanted to talk to her, Maggie made a point of never answering the phone on her own. She couldn't face him yet. Couldn't face what he represented. Though she knew she was just putting off the inevitable, she didn't care. Her very being had been ripped out and she needed time to become a new person.

As each day passed, however, she began to reject his theories more and more rather than accept them. She couldn't feel the way she did and be related to him. It was against nature, all she believed in.

By the time two weeks had come and gone she'd found her footing again in a shaky world. She'd also concluded that Tanner was wrong.

Screwing up her courage, she called his house, intending to have her say. The phone rang on and on. Reflectively she replaced the receiver, picturing Tanner in the attic, diligently working on his manuscript. What did he think about when he was working? she wondered. Had breaking the lock on his secret been a release for him? Had it made it easier for him to write?

It had turned her world into a nightmare.

Friday evening after work, Maggie was unloading groceries from her car when another vehicle unexpectedly pulled in behind hers. *Tanner.* She jerked around, her heart in her throat, until she recognized the driver as Gayle Kempwood.

"Gayle," she said in surprise.

"Hi, Maggie. Have you got a minute?"

"Sure." As the real reason for Gayle's visit sank in, Maggie said, "I'm sorry, Con's not here right now. He's still at Pozzer, Strikeberg and Carmen's. Then he's heading back to L.A. in the morning to make his final move."

Gayle looked amused. "Actually, I came by to talk to you. I tried to stop by your office today, but the time just got away from me." She sighed. "It's Shelley Baines. For some reason she really worries me and I wanted to tell you a few things."

"Oh?" Maggie hefted up a bag, sweeping Gayle with a considering look. "Come on in."

Gayle sat down on a kitchen barstool after Maggie insisted she could unload the groceries herself. "I feel like I'm gossiping, but I wanted to let you know that Shelley's scheduled to see Dr. Gaver. Apparently her father called and set it up."

"Dr. Gaver?" Maggie was surprised. Dr. Gaver was Briar Park's leading psychologist. So Tanner had finally been convinced that Shelley's problems were deeper than he'd first thought. "I'm glad," she said. "I'd like to see her straighten herself out."

"She's not taking to the idea very well," Gayle said ruefully. "One thing about Shelley, she doesn't suffer in silence."

"Have you talked to her about it?"

"I talked to her father."

The egg Maggie was carefully putting into the refrigerator bin slipped from her hand, fell to the floor and broke. She mopped it up with a sponge while Gayle went on.

"Apparently Dr. Baines feels there's something eating away at her she won't tell anyone about. She's pulled some stunts in the past—forcing her parents to take her to the hospital when she wasn't ill, faking unconsciousness—that made him believe she didn't need help. He thought she was acting again this time. But now he's not sure. The bottom line is he wants Dr. Gaver to have a few sessions with her, and I'm all for it."

"You and me both," Maggie said.

"You said you know Dr. Baines. Do you have any feel for this situation?"

Maggie kept her face carefully expressionless. Inside she was cracking in two, but one thing she'd learned, and learned well, was to accept whatever blows life dealt you and go on, no matter what. "I know he loves his daughter, but—he's had some personal problems that may have eclipsed some of Shelley's."

"The end of his surgical career and the death of his wife." Gayle nodded. "I know."

Maggie's smile was faint. She hadn't been thinking of either of those two issues. As much as the accident and Tricia's death had affected Tanner, finding out he was still attracted to Maggie was the worst, most insidious, soul destroyer of all. She herself couldn't assimilate all the horrible facets of her relationship with Tanner, and so she'd conveniently blocked them out, denied them, refused to give them credence. It just couldn't be true!

"If Dr. Gaver's successful we may both lose a patient," Gayle said. "Wouldn't that be great?"

"It would be worth a lot to see Shelley stable and secure," Maggie agreed.

"Underneath that tough exterior is a frightened little girl."

"I know. I'm glad Tanner finally sees it, too."

"Tanner? You know Dr. Baines fairly well, then." Gayle slid off the stool, preparing to leave.

"I knew him when I was a kid. He was a friend of Con's."

"Really?" Gayle smiled. "It's a small world, isn't it?"

Maggie followed her outside and waved as Gayle's car backed out of the drive. Yes, it was a small world. Too small.

But I am not Tanner's sister.

That conviction grew with each passing day. If it was a form of denial, well, fine; her feelings remained the same. She believed with all her heart that if Tanner were her brother, she would know it.

But how, *how*, could she prove to him that he was wrong?

Con came home with a bottle of champagne. Maggie had made a salad and was grilling halibut steaks, when he suddenly burst through the door, holding the bottle and two glasses high in the air.

"Congratulate your brilliant sibling, Maggie." He set the bottle and glasses down and swept her away in an impromptu dance. "I've got my first case."

"Let go of me. You're stepping on my toes. What first case?"

"Well..." He grinned, so pleased with himself it was almost disgusting. "My client's got lots and lots of money. She just can't wait to throw it away."

"She?"

"Bette Granger. Do you remember her? She was a friend of Tricia's."

"Oh...yes..." Maggie slipped out of his arms and turned back to the grill.

"She wants to save this old dilapidated building from the ruins of progress and wants me to represent her."

"Wonderful, Con."

"Well, where's all the cheering and clapping, then? Don't I even get a brotherly kiss or something?"

It was the déjà vu of it all that got under Maggie's skin. Here was Con, trying once again to step into the elite social sphere that had led to heartbreak for both of them. With a lack of enthusiasm predicated on other reasons, Maggie gave him a light kiss on the cheek. A brotherly kiss. She thought of Tanner kissing her, remembered the way he'd wiped his lips, and felt a wave of revulsion sweep through her. But it was revulsion at the idea, not the man. She understood now why Tanner had wiped the taste of her from his lips that day.

"Hey, what's bothering you?" Con asked.

"Nothing. I'm glad for you. Honestly. I want you to get everything you want."

"Uh-oh. That sounds suspiciously negative." He watched while Maggie finished setting the table, her silence an oppressive accusation in itself.

When she still hadn't elaborated by the end of the meal, Con asked, "What is it?"

"It's you," she said angrily. Then, knowing she was being unfair, said, "No, it's both of us. We can't try to be something we're not."

"What are you talking about?"

"You're still trying to do the same thing—like a kid with his nose pressed against the candy-store window. Con, we don't belong with the crowd of people that Bette Granger does."

"She's a client, for God's sake."

"She was Tricia Wellesley's friend."

Connor regarded her silently, accusingly, for so long that Maggie had to get up and start washing the dishes just to find a way to escape his eyes.

"She was Tanner's friend, too," he said, untwisting the wire across the champagne top with extra fervor. His anger spilled into his tone. "I'm a lawyer, Maggie. You're a registered dietician. Doesn't that give us any credibility? Or do you just like wallowing in these memories of us being 'not good enough'—or maybe it's 'not rich enough.' Is that why you save every dime you make?"

"I hate seeing you try to be something you're not!"

"Well, then, what am I?" he demanded. "What are you?"

"I'm . . . I'm . . ." Maggie slammed a pan into the sink, anger and frustration bubbling to the surface. "I'm miserable," she said, and burst into tears.

"Maggie." Con was surprised and concerned. "Hey, Maggie." He pulled her to his chest, comforting her. "If it's Tanner, just say so. I'll do my best to understand."

She hated herself for crying, but she couldn't seem to stop. Tanner's terrible truth echoed over and over again in her mind. "It's Tanner," she admitted unevenly. "He said—he said—that—he and I were—"

"Yes . . . ?"

The words refused to come. She clenched her teeth, shaking all over.

"What, Maggie? What did he say?"

"He said that he's my brother. That we're half brother and sister."

She was holding on to Con as if to life itself. She felt him stiffen, then his utter silence made her look upward to anxiously scan his face.

"He what?" Con asked in a quiet, deadly voice.

Pulling herself away from him, she saw bewilderment and checked fury playing in equal measure across his face. As coherently and logically as possible, she told him about Tanner, Gerrard and their mother. When she was finished Con just stared at her as if he couldn't believe his ears.

He poured them each a glass of champagne, wrapping her trembling fingers around the stem of hers, keeping his grip tight over hers. "Maggie," he said. "There is no way our mother had an affair with his father. It's all an elaborate lie."

"He wouldn't lie like that. No matter what you think of Tanner, he would never make up such an outrageous lie."

"Well, it's simply not true," Connor said flatly.

"Our mother said it was."

Con swore and shook his head. "He's making it all up."

"He believes it, Con."

"Do you?"

Maggie sank onto the couch in the living room, plucking at the fabric of the cushion. "No. I can't believe it. It's all a terrible mistake. But . . ."

Con downed his drink in a single gulp, wiping his mouth with the back of his hand. He poured himself another, waiting.

"But I believe our mother had an affair with his father."

"*No.*"

"You should have heard him, Con. If you'd heard him, the way he told it." She drew a tight breath. "He didn't make that up."

"Damn it, Maggie. Tanner's been nothing but trouble for you! I wish you'd never met him. I wish I'd never met him."

"There were moments that were wonderful," she said, looking into her glass.

"I'm going to tell you something—something you don't know, or at least refuse to see. Tanner broke off with you because he *had* to marry Tricia. That's all there was to it. No big mystery. She was pregnant and his family and hers forced him to marry her."

"He wasn't having an affair with Tricia."

"Yes, he was, Maggie. He slept with her at least once. And not just that summer. Every summer. Don't you remember shimmying up the tree? Why do you think his father kept such a tight rein on him? Tanner and Tricia's relationship was hot and heavy for years."

"Not that summer." Maggie swallowed some champagne. If it was confession time, fine. No matter what had happened, she knew who Tanner had been with, and it hadn't been Tricia.

"Yes, that summer." Con sat down beside her, the corners of his mouth drawing downward. "Believe me, I know. Maybe he was seeing you, too. But Shelley was conceived that same summer and she's Tanner's child. You just won't see the truth, Maggie."

Distantly she remembered another voice. Shelley's voice. *I know why he doesn't like me. He blames me for forcing him to marry my mother.*

"He married Tricia because of me," she said dully.

"No, Maggie. He married Tricia because of Shelley."

She inhaled shakily. Closing her ears, she tried not to let Con convince her of something that just wasn't true. Yet did it matter? Was it any worse than believing Tanner's story about being her brother? No! It was a thousand times easier to accept.

Then why did she hurt so badly, so deeply in her heart?

"If it makes you feel any better, their relationship was mainly one-sided," Con said gently. "Tricia was the chaser. Half the time he was trying to get away from her. And I think he honestly cared about you."

"Oh, please." Maggie was bitter. "Tanner doesn't care about anyone but Tanner. You said so yourself."

"I just don't believe this sick lie about his being your half brother. You've got to see him for what he is, that's all. And then forget him."

His last words rang with finality. Maggie supposed that should be the way things stood. For whatever reason he gave, Tanner was not available. He'd wrapped himself in layer upon layer of lies, purposely making himself inaccessible. It was her folly to try to dig through to the man she wanted him to be. She'd only gotten what she deserved.

"Let's not talk about him any more tonight," Maggie said. "I don't want to talk about anything."

Con filled up her glass. "Okay, then. I'll talk—you listen. You never gave me a chance to really brag about myself and I'm great at bragging."

"Brag away," Maggie said, sinking farther into the cushions. She wanted him to talk forever and keep her from thinking about Tanner. Anything would be better than thinking.

A late July thunderstorm cut through the muggy heat that had settled over the area like a pall. Lightning flashed, followed by thunder, then a frantic burst of rain and hail. It was unusual weather for Oregon, and Maggie, Karen and the patients either being helped by Maggie or waiting in her reception room stood by the windows to watch.

Through a thick sheet of rain Maggie could see a small figure running madly from the hospital to the office complex. "It's Shelley!" she whispered, practically running to the front door, only to find the waif wasn't Shelley at all. She was one of the assistant lab technicians who'd gotten caught in the rain.

"Thanks," the girl said, shaking water from her hair onto the reception room floor. "Wow, what a storm! I'm soaked and I just ran from the hospital."

With a sense of disappointment way out of proportion to the circumstances, Maggie went back to her office. She'd wanted the girl to be Shelley. She'd wanted some connection to Tanner.

The storm slowly played itself out and by five o'clock the only remnants were the shrinking puddles in the parking lot and a freshness to the air that had been missing for weeks.

Maggie's phone rang just as she was locking her door. She hesitated, half-inclined not to answer it, then, muttering under her breath about people who waited until the last minute, she snatched up the receiver. "Maggie Holt."

"Still working? I thought you'd be on your way home by now."

Tanner's voice sent a shiver down her spine. Irked at her susceptibility, she said, "Then why did you call?"

"Because I wanted to talk to you and I forgot to call earlier." He hesitated, then asked, "How are you?"

Her feelings for Tanner were hard to describe. Angry. Hostile. Frustrated. She harbored a deep-seated resentment where he was concerned that she didn't quite understand. "How do you expect me to be?"

"Have you . . . accepted what I told you?"

Maggie's laugh was harsh. "No. And neither have you."

"I was hoping that by now . . ." In lieu of finishing, his voice trailed off resignedly.

"What were you hoping? That I would come to my senses? That I would accept you as my brother?"

He sighed. "Shelley's been seeing Dr. Gaver," he said, trying another tack. "On Wednesday I'm having a meeting with him and I wanted you to go with me."

"Why?" She didn't try to hide her suspiciousness.

"I don't know why!" Tanner volleyed back explosively. "I just want you with me."

"No." To her dismay she felt her lips begin to quiver and she was furious all over again that he could affect her this way. "You can tell me about it later," she added. "I'd like to know."

"I'll remember to do that, Maggie." His own anger surfaced as readily as her emotions. "Keep in touch."

She pressed her finger to the receiver. The line went dead. For a moment she just assessed her feelings, wondering why her heart was beating so hard, why her throat was hot and aching.

"Damn it all," she whispered, then tore out of the office before she could dissolve into useless tears.

Dr. Gaver reminded Tanner of his father—at least in appearance. He was tall, slim and serious. But Gerrard Baines had always had a sense of right and wrong that allowed for no gray areas in between. Dr. Gaver looked like a man who could accept just about anything.

"Sit down, Dr. Baines," he said, gesturing to a chair.

With a feeling of being back in medical school and not really having yet earned the title of doctor, Tanner did as he was bidden. He waited in silence.

Dr. Gaver wasted no time. "Shelley's got all the problems associated with adolescence, plus a few extra. She's doubly insecure—in a way I usually associate with the loss of a parent."

"Her mother died less than a year ago."

"I know. But she feels as if she's lost you, too."

Tanner frowned. He didn't like the sound of that. "Because I brought her to Oregon with me? Uprooted her from her friends?"

"Maybe. But her fear runs very deep and I can't get to it. Is there anything else you can think of that would make her believe you're leaving her?"

"Leaving her," he repeated, nonplussed. After a moment's thought he lifted up his right hand for the doctor's inspection. "I'm not a surgeon anymore. I've had a change of life-style and spend most of my time at home, but I've never even intimated that I'm leaving her."

"It could be a combination of things," Dr. Gaver said thoughtfully. "The source is a big question mark. The results, however, are clear. She's being as impossible as she can to make sure she gets the choice to leave before you throw her out."

"That's ridiculous," Tanner muttered, truly worried.

Dr. Gaver cleared his throat. "After you called, I talked to Dr. Kempwood, Shelley's doctor. She said you've had trouble with Shelley in the past. Shelley's apparently cried wolf a number of times."

Tanner leaped to his feet, pacing the small room, lifting his shoulders to ease the tension that cramped his muscles. "I know what you're going to say. I should have listened to her from the start, taken her seriously."

"I don't know that it would have mattered much in the long run. She feels she's not worthy somehow. Unless she clears the air with you, you can expect more of the same."

Tanner was consumed with guilt. He'd been so angry with Shelley for playing games, for involving the hospital and Maggie and anyone else she could. He'd thought, he realized now, that his daughter was a carbon copy of his wife—achieving attention in the most self-destructive way possible. A certain amount of that was true, but he hadn't given her the support she needed.

"I'll see what I can do," he muttered, but Dr. Gaver handed him one last piece of advice.

"Don't try too hard. She doesn't trust you already. Until she works out whatever it is that's troubling her, easy does it. Believe me, Dr. Baines, at this point with your daughter, you're damned if you do and you're damned if you don't."

Tanner's smile was sardonic. He thought of Shelley, the way she treated him and everyone else, the heartbreak she seemed compelled to cause. He thought of Tricia, how over and over again she'd stridently accused him of ruining her life. But most of all he thought of Maggie. Beautiful Maggie, who was more lost to him than his dead wife.

"That, Dr. Gaver," he said at the door, "I already knew."

Chapter Nine

It had never been in Maggie's nature to be rude or cruel to anyone. Her last conversation with Tanner preyed upon her mind and she was filled with self-recriminations, knowing she should have handled it a different way. A battle waged inside her head, one side certain he'd deserved every dart of fury she'd thrown at him, the other sorry she'd tried to wound him the same way he'd wounded her.

It wasn't his fault.

After nearly a week of stewing she finally came to a decision. Reaching for her office phone, she stabbed out his number and impatiently counted the rings on the other end. No answer. She hung up, wishing Mrs. Greer were there, since Tanner was obviously ignoring the phone. And where was Shelley, anyway?

"Has Dr. Baines called yet and scheduled an appointment for Shelley?" Maggie asked Karen.

"Uh-huh. She's coming in next week. On Thursday. He wanted to talk to you, but you weren't in the office. I put the note on your desk."

Maggie had seen the note but ignored it. Now she felt doubly embarrassed. She should have called Tanner back for Shelley's sake if nothing else.

"I don't have any appointments scheduled for this afternoon, so I'm going to cut out a little early," she said, picking up her purse. "There's something I have to do."

"Hmm. Sounds mysterious," Karen said.

Maggie smiled but didn't elaborate. Hardly mysterious—more like taxing, she thought as she drove toward Tanner's house.

There was no answer to her knock and she stood on the porch, stymied. She'd concluded there was no one home after all, when she heard an echoed hammering coming from behind the house. Wiping her hair from her brow, Maggie crossed the yard and pushed open the side gate to the backyard, following the source of the sound. The gate creaked on rusted hinges and the steps beyond led downward into a jungle of overgrown hedges and forgotten rosebushes. Spindly weeds thrust skyward, some waist high, and Maggie carefully picked her way through, pushing them aside as she tramped toward the ivy-choked backyard.

Shading her eyes against the glare off the lake, she looked down the hillside toward the boathouse. She could just make out the top of Tanner's head. He must be on the boathouse deck, she thought. Was he the one doing the hammering?

Curiosity urged her forward and as she pushed past the last bushes she saw he was kneeling carefully on the edge of the deck, nailing in new boards over a gaping hole where once planks had been.

He was shirtless and she could see the sweat on his back, the way his muscles glided beneath taut flesh each time he lifted the hammer. He was balanced so precariously she hated to call out to him, so instead she just continued through the ivy.

He heard her just as she reached the boathouse corner. Twisting sharply, he frowned down at her, his expression changing quickly to surprise. "Maggie," he said, resting his elbows on the rail.

"I tried to phone, but no one answered."

Tanner swiped at a rivulet of sweat running down his temple. His smile was self-deprecating. "I don't try to be a recluse, y'know. It just comes naturally."

Squinting, Maggie looked across the shimmering water. "I wanted to apologize," she explained.

"No need." He shrugged and picked up the hammer again.

The even beat of his hammering began again and Maggie slid him an oblique look, watching as he fit in another two-by-four, admiring the swift way he nailed it down. His hand was tight on the hammer, the scars white against his tanned flesh.

Feeling her stare, Tanner looked at the object of her gaze and flexed his fingers. "It has its functions," he said lightly. "No surgery, but I can still nail and type."

Maggie drew in her shoulders. He could make her hurt with a few careless words. "You called and made an appointment for Shelley."

"Yep." Tanner inclined his head and pulled some more nails from his pocket, slipping them between his lips as he proceeded to systematically pound them into the decking.

"Karen said you wanted to talk to me."

"I just wanted to confirm the appointment with you, that's all."

"How did your meeting with Dr. Gaver go?"

"Okay," he mumbled.

"Just okay?"

The hammering continued, an even pattern that echoed across the still waters of Lake Oswego. Maggie felt the heat on her scalp and breathed deeply, a treacherous serenity seeping into her. This was her dream, she realized ruefully. To live on the lake with Tanner and recapture that brief moment of pure happiness she'd shared with him so long ago.

He stopped and pushed back his hair, leaving a streak of dirt across his forehead, then stood up and stretched, his jeans dipping dangerously low in the front, revealing paler skin where his bathing suit never reached. Then he grabbed the edge of the railing and swung down the ladder, landing at Maggie's feet.

She stepped back instinctively, her eyes unknowingly revealing her feelings as no words ever could. She just couldn't help loving him.

Tanner's mouth was knife-blade thin. "Don't look at me like that."

Maggie felt her throat tighten. "I can't help it. You're not my brother."

"I am." He strode away from her to the boathouse door.

"I don't believe it. And neither does Con."

She followed behind him, stopping at the doorway, her hand on the casing. Feeling the grime, she made a face and pulled her hand back, wiping cobwebs from her fingers. Tanner had disappeared into the dark bowels of the room.

Then suddenly he reappeared, startling Maggie. She stepped backward, stumbled, and her hand swept upward, her fingers accidentally brushing across his bare stomach. He inhaled harshly.

"I'm sorry," she said, automatically reaching forward to wipe off the trace of dirt now covering his sweat-dampened skin. But when she touched him again she felt the tremor that ran through his muscles.

He grabbed her wrist so hard and fast she caught her breath.

"Why did you come here, Maggie?" he grated.

"I don't know. I wanted to apologize. You asked me to go with you to Dr. Gaver's and I was rude."

He let her go as swiftly as he'd grabbed her. "It's just as well you didn't go. I was crazy to call you."

"Because you don't trust yourself around me?"

The tightening of his lips was answer enough, but when he looked her way, she found she couldn't hold that stripping, tawny gaze.

"Maybe there's a reason for it," she said unevenly. "I'll never believe I'm related to you. It's just too bizarre!"

"Then you're too dangerous to be around, Maggie," he said softly. "Because you're right—I don't trust myself."

He went back inside the boathouse again and this time he was gone so long she wondered if he was waiting for her to leave. Then a grinding cacophony from within told her he was raising the chain cradle.

Stepping inside the doorway, she let her eyes adjust to the gloom. "Can I ask what you're doing?"

"Fixing things." His voice sounded from the corner. "I'm thinking about buying a boat."

"Really?"

Tanner flipped on the light. "I grew up on the lake, swimming and waterskiing. I'd like the same for Shelley if she wants it."

How could any teenager not? Maggie wondered. Her own memories of days on the lake were sun-sparkled jewels against the plain background of her youth. "I take back what I said about you," she said.

He was examining part of the chain. "You've said a lot of things, Maggie. What exactly are you taking back?"

"That you're a lousy father. I said that, didn't I? Or at least implied it. You're not. You're a loving father."

The grinding began again, so abruptly that Maggie jumped. Tanner glanced at her, irony gleaming richly in his eyes. "You're as nervous as a cat."

"Why shouldn't I be? You make it very difficult to talk to you."

"Then why bother?"

"Because I—" She tightened her jaw and met his gaze deliberately. "Because I can't help myself. I've been in love with you for a long time, Tanner. It's just not going to disappear overnight, no matter what lies you tell me."

He emitted a harsh sound of disbelief. "Your honesty frightens me sometimes."

"Maybe you ought to try it yourself."

"You think I haven't been honest? Good God, Maggie, the other day in the attic I think my feelings were pretty clear." He ducked under a low-hanging beam, putting distance between them.

"But you're trying to push me away."

"Because you're my sister!"

"No!"

He swore so violently that Maggie quailed inside. "Damn you, Maggie, for pushing me to the limit," he said between his teeth. "I thought it would be better now that you know the truth, but you're making it worse!"

"And damn you, Tanner, for believing something you know in your heart can't be true. Open your mind a little. All you've heard is two people's viewpoints. It's not fact until it's proven."

"Your mother and my father concurred. They ought to know," he said cuttingly.

"Maybe they're wrong!"

"Is that why you came over here?" he demanded. "To browbeat me into believing you?"

Maggie drew herself up, ready to deny him. But in point of fact that was one of the main reasons she'd come to see him. She wanted to refute everything he said about their being related. And she needed him to believe her, not his father, or the misguided truths of her mother.

"Has anyone done blood tests, Tanner?"

He regarded her with faintly concealed hostility. "Given the evidence, it would hardly seem necessary."

"But if they haven't been done, there's a chance my father—"

"No," he cut in harshly. "The man you think of as your father didn't reconcile with your mother until after you were conceived."

"According to whom?"

"Your mother!" he ground out.

"Maybe my mother just thought that," Maggie went on heedlessly. "Maybe her guilt forced her to believe your father was mine, too."

"You can't pin all your hopes on this!" Tanner came to her then, skirting the edge of the mudhole with catlike grace and putting his palms on her shoulders, shaking her. "Do you hear yourself? It's scary, Maggie."

"But isn't it worth the effort?" she asked in a small voice, her eyes huge.

Tanner wanted to deny her. He was too afraid of letting his desires and needs overrule his intellect. He'd lived with believing Maggie was his sister too long to harbor any false hope. But she was offering him the faintest glimmer of light at the end of a long and dark tunnel, and because his emotions were never steady where she was concerned, his heart leaped at the dream of having her again.

"No," he said, scared by his weakness.

"Do you know your father's blood type?"

"Maggie." His hands gripped her so tightly it hurt, but she suffered silently, heart pounding. "Blood typing can't prove who the father is."

"But it can prove who he isn't," she countered, trying to bank her eagerness. "Do you know Gerrard's type?"

His jaw worked. "Yes."

"Well?"

"It's B. So's mine."

From far off Maggie heard the sound of ducks squawking at one another, battling over territorial rights. A longing for their kind of uncomplicated freedom welled inside her, choking her.

"What's yours, Maggie?" Tanner asked, watching her closely.

"It's B."

He released her. "There's your proof, Maggie," he rasped, his face hardening as hope turned to dashed dreams.

"It could be coincidence. I don't know what my father's type was."

"Your father's type was B," he reminded her harshly.

"*Your* father's. Not mine. And anyway it's not proof!"

He snorted. "Isn't it? It's too damn close to be coincidence. Do you know what the chances are that you and my father would both have type B?"

"About fifteen percent."

"Right. Fifteen people out of a hundred. But the chances of all three of us—you, me and my father—being among that fifteen are very slim."

"Unless we were related," Maggie said woodenly.

Tanner nodded. "It's impossible for you to have B unless one of your parents has B or AB. Do you know your mother's type?"

She shook her head. "But I could find out from her medical records. She used to see Dr. Katzen. His offices are near the south end of the lake."

"Find out, then. It'll answer all your questions."

"Unless my real father was B, too. It's possible," she said stubbornly. "I don't know what he was and I don't have any way of knowing."

"Maggie. Your real father is my father, Gerrard Baines. He's alive and well and living in New York."

She felt destroyed, as if someone had ripped out all the pieces that made her whole. Yet she couldn't believe. Wouldn't believe! It wasn't as impossible as Tanner made it sound. He was just convinced they were related and chose to look at the evidence in the worst possible light.

"What's your father's Rh factor?" she asked.

It was the last straw as far as Tanner was concerned. She was dangling a carrot in front of him that tantalized his most vulnerable part. "Get out of here, Maggie," he growled, brushing roughly past her as he headed into the sun-baked afternoon.

"Do you know what it is?" she demanded, following him from the boathouse and blinking rapidly against the incredible brightness.

"No!" he roared. "And it doesn't matter one iota! My father is your father. It's final."

His words resounded across the still waters of the lake. Had Maggie been in a less emotional state she might have worried about who could hear. As it was she just felt dried up and lost. Lost forever in a sin she could neither accept nor understand.

"Tanner..."

"Go away, Maggie," he said hoarsely, stalking toward the house. "Go away and don't come back until you can accept me as your brother!"

"Dr. Katzen's busy with a patient," the voice on the other end of the line intoned. "Could I have him call you back?"

Maggie pinched the bridge of her nose, her mind turning. "This is Maggie Holt," she said briskly. "Maybe it would be better if I came to see him in person. He used to be my family doctor when I was a child. Would it be possible for me to see him later this afternoon? Or tomorrow?"

"Let me check."

She could hear the woman flipping through pages and her hopes sank. It seemed imperative that she learn the truth about her mother's blood type right away. Somehow she felt that if she couldn't produce results for Tanner immediately he would cease to listen to her at all.

"Dr. Katzen's semiretired," the woman said now. "He doesn't work a full forty-hour week anymore. I don't see where he can fit you in until the end of next week."

Maggie sighed. "Then could he just call me back? I need to know some medical information about my mother. She died several years ago and the only way I can find out is through her records."

Something in her voice, some evidence of her desperation, must have come through, because it finally moved the unbending receptionist. "Just a minute," she said, and put Maggie on hold. After what seemed an interminably long period of time she clicked back on. "If you can get to our offices by four o'clock, Dr. Katzen will wait."

"Thank you!" Maggie was jubilant. "I'll be there."

She hung up in better spirits. Now all she had to do was get through the rest of the day and hope she would find that her mother's blood type was either B or AB. Then her father's wouldn't have to be.

But what if it's something else? she asked herself. What if it's type O or A—one of the two most common types? Biting her lip Maggie hung on to her convictions. She wouldn't let herself think of other possibilities.

Shelley Baines's appointment was for two-thirty, but when the clock rolled around to half past two, the girl still wasn't there. Maggie paced her office restlessly, part of her worried about Shelley, part of her already out of the office on a crusade to prove Tanner wrong.

At ten before three Shelley breezed in. Defiance was still painted on her young face, but Maggie noticed immediately that she was taking better care of herself. It was a step in the right direction.

"How are you doing, Shelley?" she asked.

"I'm seeing another doctor now." She sniffed. "That makes three."

"Dr. Gaver. I know." Maggie's demeanor softened. "But I'm not a doctor. I'm a nutritionist."

"Same thing. You're all trying to find out what's wrong with me, but there's nothing wrong with me."

"That's not what you said in the beginning. You complained of dizzy spells."

"Well, I don't have them anymore, okay?" she shot back. "I don't have anything!"

As if the outburst had drained her, she sank into her chair and pulled her hair back, closing her eyes and sighing. So the change was more than cosmetic, Maggie realized with hope. Shelley, too, appeared to be growing tired of all the nonsense and hype she had been creating.

"How's your diet going?"

"Better." She shrugged. "It's fine," she said, then shook her head. "I don't even know what I'm doing here. I'm fine."

Regarding her consideringly, Maggie said, "Do you not want to come see me anymore? If you truly believe you've stabilized, we could reduce your meetings with me to say, every few months. What do you think?"

A frown tightened her brow. "You're asking me?"

"Who better?"

"My father, for one."

"Look, Shelley—" Maggie got up from her chair and came around to the front of her desk, leaning a hip on the corner, "—I think you're an intelligent young woman. I just think you're going through a tough period. You don't know what you want. For some reason you've fixated on your diabetes as a way to get extra attention." Shelley stiffened, but Maggie put up a hand, forestalling her. "But something's changed, obviously, because your attitude has. What is it? Is it because you're seeing Dr. Gaver? Or has your father been paying more attention to you?"

Anger glittered in Shelley's blue eyes. "You're all so smart, aren't you?" Maggie just regarded her silently, and finally Shelley's gaze slid away. "I'm just tired of all of it," she said flatly. "That's all."

Well, hallelujah for that. "Then what do you think about your diabetes?"

"I think I'm a freak. I think I—oh, I don't know. I just hate it." She refused to meet Maggie's eyes. "But I'm okay," she added resignedly.

"You are not a freak." Maggie was firm. "Are you ready to talk diet now? I mean, seriously?"

Shelley hesitated, as if she were afraid to take this last step toward responsibility, and she lifted her shoulders as if she found the whole concept of diet and health boring nd unimportant. But she scooted her chair closer, and for he first time Maggie had a productive meeting with her where she felt something was finally accomplished.

When Shelley got up to leave, it was without the need to blast Maggie and then run from her office. She left quitly, in the most adultlike manner she'd exhibited to date, but the depth of her insecurity showed in the way she hung her head and the unhappy slant of her mouth.

"Well?" Karen asked, watching Shelley head across the parking lot toward the unflappable Mrs. Greer.

"Progress," Maggie said. "I don't know why. Dr. Gaver must be a soothing influence. Either that or Shelley's finally beginning to believe her father loves her whether he's flawed or not. She thinks her diabetes makes her a freak," she added by way of explanation.

"I'm so glad I'm not a teenager anymore," Karen said fervently.

"You and me both."

Maggie left the offices and drove as fast as she dared to keep her appointment with Dr. Katzen. His offices were on the south side of Lake Oswego and about a twenty-minute drive from Briar Park Medical Center. When Maggie wheeled into the lot she was relieved to see several cars still in front. The doctor hadn't left yet.

As it was she was forced to wait, and she spent the time nervously flipping through magazine after magazine. Finally the tiny reception room cleared and her name was called. She was ushered into the white-haired doctor's office.

"Maggie Holt," he said, clasping her hand warmly. "It's been a long time."

"A long, long time," she agreed, smiling. "I need a favor from you and I hope you can grant it."

His brows raised. "I hope so, too."

Clasping her hands together, Maggie heaved a sigh and plunged into her story. "It's a question of paternity," she admitted. "I need to know my mother's blood type and hopefully it can tell me something about myself."

"What about your father's type? In a question of paternity, his would be more helpful."

"I know." Her smile was faint. "But my father was not the type of man to go to a doctor. He was a 'rolling stone,' as my mother used to say. I don't know anything about him, and he died years ago."

Unless my father's Dr. Gerrard Baines.

The idea was so repugnant to Maggie she banished the thought outright. She didn't believe Tanner's father was also hers. She would never believe it.

"Well, then, let's see..." Dr. Katzen rubbed his jaw and headed for the door. "My old files are in the back room. It'll take me a while to blow the dust off them and then go through them."

"May I help? I'm a registered dietitian at Briar Park Medical Center. I have access to all the hospital records."

"Then come along."

She was glad he was being so cooperative. Anxious to have the task completed, she watched the clock as they sifted through Dr. Katzen's assorted file cabinets. If he had to leave before they found it...

"Here it is," he said, pulling a dog-eared folder from a file box against the far wall. "'Mrs. Margaret Holt.'"

Maggie's fingers were shaking as she accepted the file. *It's not proof,* she reminded herself. *But it's a step in the right direction.* Opening the folder, she read quickly, turning several pages until she found what she was looking for.

Her mother's blood type was O negative.

She stared in anguish and disbelief, her heart thumping furiously. Her mother's type was O. That meant her father's type had to be B or AB.

The chances of Gerrard being her father were increasing.

She stood on the end of the public dock, staring sightlessly across the restless dark green waters. The swim park was full. All around her there was noise and chatter, but Maggie could have been alone on the planet, for all she noticed.

She couldn't begin to conceive of Gerrard Baines being her father.

Closing her eyes, she tried to steady herself, but her heart still beat too fast, her skin still felt clammy and cold. There was no one she could turn to. No one to tell. Con was hauling his belongings up from Los Angeles and wouldn't be back until the end of the week. She couldn't face Tanner with the news.

It was late July and sweltering. Maggie felt the heat penetrate her flesh, but she still felt cold. Her spirit was broken. *It can't be true!*

When she finally drove back to the house the sun was setting, painting the sky with brilliant orange and fuchsia hues. Its beauty made her bitter. Summertime. Heady, seductive summertime. Its treachery had fooled her more than once.

So absorbed was she in her own private hell she nearly ran into the back of the idling car in her driveway. A Mercedes 350 SL.

Tanner's car.

Her strength left her in a rush as he killed the engine and stepped from the driver's side, walking toward her car. When she made no move to do the same he looked in her window, his expression hard to read. Then he opened he door. "Are you coming out?" he asked.

"What are you doing here?" She licked her lips. He voice was barely above a whisper.

"Facing you again. Trying to make some sense of ou relationship—whatever the hell it is." His gold eyes looke closely into hers. "Something wrong?"

How could he even ask her? Maggie cut the engine an thrust her way out of the car. She tried to answer him, the just shook her head and walked toward the cottage. Afte several moments Tanner followed.

"What is it?" he demanded as she jerkily searche through her purse for the key.

Her laugh was hollow. "I learned my mother's bloo type today. It's O negative."

Tanner's breath whistled between his teeth. "Well, okay It's no surprise," he said quietly.

"It doesn't mean anything. It doesn't prove anything It's just—just—oh, damn!" The key slipped through he fingers, fell to the porch and slid between one of th cracks. Maggie stared after it, tears falling silently dow her cheeks.

"Come here." Tanner put his arm around her, gentl turning her in the direction of his car. "Let me take yo somewhere. Somewhere we can talk."

"My car . . . my key . . ." She gestured vaguely.

"You've still got your car keys, haven't you? Let m move your car and we'll take mine."

He guided her toward the Mercedes, took her purs from her unresisting fingers, found her car keys, reverse the Volkswagen, parked it, then slid into the driver's sea of his car.

"All set?" he asked.

She tried to answer but managed only a listless lift of her hand. She was dying inside. All she wanted to do was go to sleep for a year.

He took her to a small restaurant near the center of Lake Oswego. She'd never been there before and now she walked unseeingly through the pleasant airy rooms, past the bar to the deck that jutted over the water. The maître d' indicated a table set for two and Maggie felt Tanner's hand at her elbow as he pulled out a chair and guided her into it.

Dusk had fallen and a small sliver of a moon hung low on the horizon. Maggie fixed her eyes on it and concentrated on pulling herself together.

"The worst is over, Maggie," he said quietly. "Now it's a matter of making the best of what we've got."

She swallowed, hard. "I don't think I can."

"Try."

Hurting inside, she said lightly, "You're the doctor," but the words fell flat.

"I love you, Maggie," Tanner said soberly. "I have for a long time, but I couldn't admit it, even to myself. But if I don't face it, I'll never be able to deal with it."

Her lips trembled and she pressed them together. "You're cruel. You don't tell me what I've ached to hear until it's too late."

"That's exactly why I waited," he said, his mouth a taut line. "I've never trusted myself to admit the truth. I've never trusted myself with you."

"And now you do?" Maggie couldn't look at him.

"I trust you."

"How convenient," she said bitterly. "Lay it all on my head. Well, I won't be your conscience, because I still don't believe it!"

The waiter appeared at their table, and Tanner, after a moment of recovery, ordered them both seafood. Maggie kept her eyes focused on the lake's dancing ribbon of moonlight.

"What's it going to take for you to accept the truth?" he asked intensely.

"I want to know whether your father's Rh negative or positive. My mother was negative and I'm positive. That means my father has to be positive, too."

She could feel his disbelief. "You want to call him?" he asked tightly. "Fine. Okay. I'll give you the number."

The thought of actually talking to Gerrard Baines filled Maggie with alarm. She would be reluctant to speak to him at the best of times, but to ask him this? "You call him," she said. "Ask him. Find out the truth."

"Oh, Maggie..." He turned away, his jaw working, his eyes narrowed to slits.

"If Gerrard's blood type is negative, he's not my father. It's simple. The quest is over."

"And if he's positive? What will you do then?"

"If he's positive it doesn't definitely prove he is my father," Maggie said.

Tanner leaned back in his chair. "To what lengths will you go to prove we're not related, Maggie?"

"To the ends of the earth," she said simply.

Tanner stared at her, half angry, half incredulous. "We've been there and back, Maggie."

"You haven't called your father."

It was hopeless trying to change her mind. All he could do was work with her and time and trial would eventually lead her to the truth. But, oh, damn. Given enough time she might even have *him* believing the impossible!

"If I agree to call him, can we drop the subject for now?" Tanner asked, glad to notice her color was slowly returning.

"Yes."

"Then I agree." Privately he began to brace himself mentally for that phone call; discussing anything with Gerrard was a chore, let alone a subject as touchy as Maggie Holt.

The smile of relief she sent him was so brilliant Tanner swallowed his misgivings. He'd made the right decision. Whatever the outcome of the call, seeing her smile like that was worth it.

"What made you decide to bring me here?" she murmured, surfacing at last from her self-absorption. "I thought you were the recluse."

"I am. But you needed saving. It was the least I could do." Tanner had ordered a bottle of wine and they'd ignored it for the most part, but now he poured them each a glass. "Besides, my recluse days are over. Let people pity me. I can't stop them."

Maggie glanced at his hand. Maybe she was accepting a little, she thought, because she could look at his injury now without that all-consuming ache. But she still felt twinges of pain, bittersweet memories of a lost past.

"Did you turn down the job as head of surgery because of your hand?" Maggie asked frankly.

"Partially. Mainly because I didn't want it. Or I thought I didn't want it."

"Have you changed your mind?" Her brows lifted.

"I don't know. It doesn't matter anyway. The decision was made."

"Chad—Dr. Chad Collins—was only given the position temporarily. If you really want that job, I'm sure it's still there for you."

Tanner grimaced. "I don't know what I want, as I'm sure you're fully aware. Or maybe it's—I can't have what I do want. Either way, I'd hardly be any good in that kind of high-powered capacity."

"Oh, I don't know," Maggie murmured.

A comfortable silence fell between them, the first one she could remember since their long-ago affair. Their meals came and they ate companionably, neither making comments about anything more important than the weather and the quality of the food.

Slowly Maggie began to feel better. Tanner had the capacity, when he chose to use it, to soothe her feelings, to make her accept, at least to some small degree, the unacceptable. She let the pain of the moment slide away and refused to think about anything.

When the wine and food were removed and cups of Irish coffee placed in their stead, Maggie roused herself from her lethargy and said, "With everything else, I almost forgot to tell you about Shelley. She came to my office today and she was, well, different."

"In what way?"

"Less hostile. Not exactly accepting, but more approachable."

Tanner smiled faintly. "So you noticed it, too. Dr. Gaver said she'd trying harder. I could tell by the way she reacts to me. She's not really friendly, but she seems to want to get along more."

"Have you changed at all? In your attitude toward her?"

His pause was so lengthy she wondered if she'd touched on some point she shouldn't have. Eventually he said, "Since I told you about us—about our being related—I've been less frustrated. Maybe it shows. It certainly has in my writing."

Licking whipped cream from her lips, Maggie ignored the remark about their being related. She would accept that only when the last hope was extinguished. "How is the novel coming along?"

"It's coming." He gave her a quick look. "I'd still like you to read it."

"Maybe I can someday."

It was a strange coexistence between them; as if they were on opposite sides of a war, continually testing the battle lines. But there was less hostility, more opportunity for peaceful negotiations. Yet if Maggie seriously let herself believe this was all that could be between them, she would crumble to dust. It just couldn't be.

He took her home under a clear, starlit sky. The windows were down and Maggie's hair blew around her face. She had to keep pulling the strands away. At her house he parked in the driveway and stood beside her in the still night air, but he made no attempt to come inside and Maggie didn't offer an invitation. Instead he leaned against the Mercedes's hood and said quietly, "I'll call my father."

"Let me know what he says."

He nodded. "Maggie...?"

"Hmm?"

Whatever he was about to utter was cut off when a car came fast around the corner and braked to make her driveway. At the squeal of tires Maggie involuntarily leaned closer to Tanner.

A vintage T-bird came to a quick, shuddering halt behind the Mercedes. Con's car. And Con stepped into the warm summer night, slamming the door behind him.

"Hello, Tanner," he said evenly. "What lies have you been telling my little sister now?"

Chapter Ten

Connor don't," Maggie implored, stepping toward him.

"Don't what? Keep you from making another mistake?"

Tanner, who hadn't moved a muscle, spoke up calmly, "Hello, Con. Maggie was just going in the house and I was leaving."

"Then get the hell out," Con said coldly, taking a threatening step nearer.

"Con," Maggie pleaded, but Tanner rose to his full height, meeting Con's furious glare evenly.

"I can handle my own battles," he said.

"Is that right?" Con was unrelenting. "Is that why you came up with this whole sick story? What are you doing now, Baines? Telling her it 'ain't so' after all? How long are you going to hide behind lies?"

Tanner bristled, but Maggie didn't give him time to move before she'd squeezed herself in the small space between them. "Stop it! Both of you!" she declared angrily. "For God's sake, Con. I am not a child!"

Their war was a silent one, neither man backing down. Infuriated, Maggie pushed against her brother's chest until Con was forced to take a step backward. "Don't make a scene," she begged. "Tanner and I went out to dinner to clear the air. Please. Just let him go."

Con's glare would have frightened most men, but Tanner was unmoved. His expression was carved in stone while he let Con make up his mind, and when Con finally lifted a palm in surrender and turned toward the house, only then did he relax.

"I'm sorry," Maggie apologized helplessly.

Tanner stared after him. "His intentions are honorable. I can hardly blame him."

"He's a pain in the neck. He big-brothers me to death."

She wished she could have snatched the words back, but apart from a sidelong look that pointed out the terrible irony of their relationship, Tanner said nothing more. With a wave he got into his car, managed to squeeze past Con's and drove away, his taillights slowly disappearing down the narrow two-lane road.

Marching to the house, Maggie threw the door open. "Where do you get off?" she demanded.

Con was sitting on the couch, his head resting on the cushions, his eyes focused on the ceiling. "Okay, I plead guilty. I'm sorry. It's your life. You know your own mind."

"You don't sound very repentant."

"Well, give me time, all right? When I think of Baines— and you—"

"You know what your problem is?" Maggie declared, standing furiously in front of him, one fist propped on her hip. "Your life's too easy and you feel compelled to tinker in mine. Now I'm glad you're moving back to Oregon—no, let me finish—'' the determined light in her eyes forced Con to close his mouth ''—but don't judge Tanner too harshly. This whole thing hasn't been easy for him, either.''

''Is it my turn to talk?'' Con asked meekly.

''No.'' Maggie hid a smile. ''If you want something to eat you're relegated to peanut-butter-and-jelly sandwiches. I'll make up the couch while you go search under the porch for my house key.''

''You don't need to make up the couch. I've rented a condominium on the lake with an option to buy. That's why I'm back so soon. The moving van's bringing my stuff from L.A. next week, but I brought up some clothes. I just came by to tell you.''

''A condominium on the lake?''

''That's right.'' When Maggie didn't reply, he asked, ''What? No lecture about trying to climb out of my social class?''

''Go get the key,'' she said, the corners of her mouth softening. It was hard to stay mad at Con. ''And if you don't bring up any more of my faults, I'll try not to bring up yours.''

''It's a deal,'' Con said with relief, and for the moment the fight over Tanner was forgotten.

''The mud's being dredged out tomorrow,'' Tanner said to Mark Jenning at Jenning's Boats and Marina. ''I'd like to pick up the Chris-Craft sometime after the first of the week.''

''The boat'll be ready on Monday, Dr. Baines.''

''Perfect. Thanks.''

Tanner hung up but kept his hand on the phone. He checked off what he had to do in his mind: the boat, Shelley's next appointment, the call to his father....

Sighing, he made a face. New York time was three hours later so his father was probably already off work. What did Gerrard do when he got home from the hospital? he wondered. How did he spend his free time? Tanner had spent the greater part of his adult life blocking his father from his mind and he had no insight to the heart of the man. What motivated him? he asked himself. What did he think of day in and day out?

With a feeling of fatalism, he looked up his father's telephone number and dialed the phone. It rang three times before Gerrard's deep voice answered.

"Hello, Dad," Tanner said, wincing. He'd never been comfortable addressing him as "Father," or "Gerrard," but "Dad" was almost worse. It implied a familiarity he didn't feel.

"Tanner?" Gerrard didn't try to hide his surprise.

"There's something I have to talk to you about. It's important."

"It must be," his father said dryly. "I can't imagine why else you'd call."

"I want to discuss Maggie Holt."

Tanner didn't have to strain his ears to hear the rush of air that left Gerrard's lungs. "What about her?" he asked coolly.

"I told her she was my half sister. She doesn't believe me."

"You mean you've seen her?" There was a distinct edge of horror to his voice.

"Yes, I've seen her," Tanner answered testily. "She was at the house a few weeks ago when you called."

"What kind of relationship have you got going with her?" he demanded in a changed voice.

"Nothing like what you think. If she's my sister, she's—"

"If?"

With difficulty, he hung on to his patience. "She wants to know your Rh factor, Dad. And so do I."

In disbelief Tanner listened to the decisive click at the other end of the line. Then he heard a dial tone.

A strange feeling overcame him. His heart pounded so hard it almost hurt. His father had hung up on him. After years of trying to bridge the rift, Gerrard had cut him down when he'd made his first voluntary effort to approach him.

Why? His father cherished whatever contact they had; it was Tanner who had difficulty being with him. Gerrard would never cut him off unless... unless...

What if Maggie's right!

Tanner backed away from the phone, dazed. *Don't jump to conclusions just because you want it to be true. Gerrard would never make up that terrible of a lie. The facts are too obvious. Maggie's own mother concurred. It can't be a mistake. It can't.*

But wasn't truth sometimes stranger than fiction?

"Mrs. Greer!" Tanner bellowed as he strode into the entry hall. "Mrs. Greer!"

Her bulky form puffed from around the corner of the second-floor hallway to the landing at the top of the stairs.

"Could you stay with Shelley for a few days? I'll pay you triple your wages. There's something I have to do out of town."

"You pay me the regular rate and I'll do it," she said with a sniff, drawing herself up straight.

"Done." Tanner's smile was lopsided, as if his mouth, like the rest of him, were being pulled in two opposite directions.

Taking the stairs two at a time, he strode to his bedroom, yanked down a suitcase and began randomly tossing clothes into it.

If he caught the next flight out he could be in New York by morning.

Dawn was breaking gray and overcast over the city as Tanner's plane began its descent. He watched through bleary, tired eyes, but his mind was racing. Throughout the night he'd concocted a dozen different approaches to get his father to admit that he and Maggie were not brother and sister. He'd been so sure after his father had hung up on him. But now, with a new day dawning, he found himself less convinced of Gerrard's culpability. After all, Maggie's mother had backed him up years before, and from what he knew of that lady she would never lie about something that would hurt so many people, especially her daughter.

The taxi drive only made his doubts grow larger. By the time they were pulling up in front of his father's Manhattan apartment building, Tanner was berating himself for this impetuous, probably fruitless journey.

Standing on the front stoop for long moments, he fought an internal battle. He didn't want to face his father. They'd never really liked each other. He, Tanner, was too much like his mother, and his parents had never seen eye to eye. Gerrard was an implacable, unforgiving man.

Setting his jaw, Tanner made up his mind. "I'm here to see Gerrard Baines," he told the security guard inside the building.

Gerrard's apartment was called, and after a quick conversation, the guard motioned Tanner to go on up. He took the stairs rather than the elevator, needing to work off some energy, needing some time.

As Tanner opened the door from the fourth floor stair-well, he saw his father's apartment door was already thrown wide. Gerrard stood in the opening, clad in a bathrobe and slippers, his expression as stern as Tanner remembered, his stance as unrelenting.

"I didn't expect you to come," he said. "I think you've only been here once before, when Tricia insisted."

Tanner walked to the doorway. "You took from me the only part of my life that mattered. I've never forgiven you for that."

Father and son met each other's eyes, silently asking questions that had never been fully answered. "Come in-side," Gerrard said, and the sigh of regret in his voice was the first one Tanner had ever heard.

In the spacious living room, Tanner ignored his fa-ther's offer of a seat and stood by the fireplace, leaning one arm tensely against the mantel. "I want to know everything. Everything about Maggie Holt."

Gerrard stared at the Manhattan skyline for long mo-ments before settling into a familiar easy chair, his face suddenly looking far older than his sixty-two years. "Maggie Holt," he said, his lips tightening. "You'd bet-ter sit down, son. This may take awhile...."

Yawning, Maggie checked her watch and realized it was almost time to go home. She was tired from the restless night she'd spent. Until nearly dawn she'd run the fact that her father was likely to be Gerrard Baines over and over again in her mind, yet she still hadn't accepted it. She felt too intensely about the man. He'd ruined so much for her that she couldn't begin to believe he was her father. *Her father.* Shuddering a little, she shook off her thoughts and phoned Gayle Kempwood.

"Shelley's blood-sugar levels were nearly normal this time," Dr. Kempwood told her after she asked. "Either she's paying closer attention to her health or her father is. That last test may have been on a particularly off day. I think she even looks better now."

"You don't know how glad I am to hear that."

"Barring any unforeseen complications, I think we can safely say she's out of the danger zone. It's all a question of attitude now."

Maggie hung up in a better frame of mind. Shelley was trying harder. Tanner was trying harder. With Dr. Gavir's help the root of Shelley's insecurities might yet be discovered and then the battle would be won.

Breathing deeply, she walked outside, enjoying the late-July stillness. August was just around the corner. Another summer nearly over.

Feeling herself growing melancholy again, Maggie decided to stop by Gayle's office and invite her for dinner again. Con had hardly had time to keep up on their relationship so Maggie figured she would offer a helping hand.

Walking across the parkway, she concentrated on what was good in her life. There was Shelley's progress. And there was Con's move back to Oregon. On a lesser level, there was the understanding of why Tanner had treated her the way he had.

She was so lost in thought she didn't pay any attention to the squeal of tires in the parking lot.

"Maggie! Maggie, wait up!"

Her hand was on the hospital door. Craning her neck, she was amazed to see Tanner's lithe form weaving between the cars, then running in her direction.

Her heart leaped. "Tanner," she whispered, sensing instantly that something had changed.

As he neared she noticed he hadn't shaved and hi
clothes looked as if he'd slept in them. She was already re
leasing the door, when it suddenly pushed outward and
Chad, a glower darkening his face, strode into the late
afternoon sunshine. Sandy Francis was at his heels.

"Damn it," Chad grated furiously, turning on Sandy a
if she were the cause of his ill humor. "I'm through with
all their platitudes! What does it take to get recognized
around here?"

Maggie hesitated, glancing at the pair and wishing she
didn't have to be a part of this conversation. Tanner
hearing the exchange, had slowed his steps to a brisk walk
but was still hurrying to meet her.

"You're the best doctor for the job," Sandy said
shooting Maggie a baleful glance. "Just give the board
time to appoint you permanently. You've already got one
shoe in the door. There's no one as qualified as you ever
in the running."

"Oh, no?" Chad asked, turning instinctively toward
Tanner.

As if he'd spoken aloud, Tanner felt three pairs of eye
look his way. Maggie's were reflective, a bit proud and
glowing with expectation. Sandy's were narrowed and
suspicious. And Chad's glittered with outright hostility.

"Dr. Baines," Chad greeted him curtly. He looked as i
he would have liked to say a lot more, but he didn't. Un
beknownst to Tanner, Chad, who had always been an ex
cellent political player, was intelligent enough not to
overplay his hand. He would never chance blowing his ca
reer for the satisfaction of speaking his mind.

But Sandy Francis's loyalty had always been her blind
spot. She couldn't let Chad suffer the agony of not know
ing. "Dr. Baines, I'm Dr. Francis," she said, introducing
herself. "Forgive me for my bluntness, but have you

anged your mind about taking over as head of sur-
ry?"

Tanner felt a surge of impatience that other people's
oblems had interrupted his meeting with Maggie. He had
talk to her alone. "That's not why I'm here," he said,
s sense of honesty forcing him to add, "although I ad-
it I've had second thoughts."

Chad's expression was hard to describe. It hovered be-
veen anger and impotency and crushing disappoint-
ent. He clenched his jaw and released it several times,
rusting out his hand and saying with an effort, "In that
se, I understand the board's decision to wait."

"Thank you," Tanner said, surprised by his compli-
ent. He shook hands with Chad, wondering about the
unger man.

Chad turned to Maggie. "Sandy and Jeff and I have
ade some plans tonight," he said, unknowingly paint-
g a clear picture for Tanner. "I'd like you to come,
aggie."

The way Sandy turned her head to hide her feelings and
e quick flash of guilt that crossed Maggie's face ex-
ained more to Tanner than he'd expected to learn. His
sides twisted. She'd been engaged when he'd first come
ck to Oregon. He'd never asked her about it, assuming
was over. And now, for an instant, he felt real fear.

But then Maggie said gently, "I can't, Chad. I have an
portant meeting scheduled."

"A meeting?" Chad repeated. "With whom?"

"With me."

Tanner hadn't planned to speak up. There was too much
discuss with Maggie first before he could start staking
aims. But he knew where her heart stood, and his own
elings had been clear for over fourteen years.

His right hand cupped her elbow, guiding her away fro
the staring eyes of Chad and Sandy. Before they were thr
steps across the parkway he'd forgotten them. "I just g
off a flight from New York," he said softly, unwilling
waste time with preliminaries.

"New York?" Maggie's eyes were large and luminous

"I saw my father. He's Rh negative, Maggie. You we
right. He's not your father and he's known the truth sin
your mother died!"

The wind whipped wildly through the open windows
the Mercedes. Maggie lay limply in the seat, too ove
whelmed to do more than offer a trembling, ragged smi
and wipe away the tiny tears that kept slowly forming i
the corners of her eyes. It had happened so quickly sl
wasn't prepared to shift gears. "My God," she whispere
over and over again, her fingers pressed to her lips. "M
God."

Tanner drove with a free abandon he hadn't felt since h
youth. He was drunk with exhilaration. Drugged with tl
heady sense of being unchained. It didn't matter that he'
barely slept in thirty-six hours. The impossible had b
come possible. The possible true. *Maggie. His lover. H*
woman. His very existence....

"Do you know how much I love you?" he asked in a
unsteady voice.

She drew a quaking breath. "Tell me everything. Wh
happened? How are you so sure?"

"He told me all of it. Every lie, every reason. Most
it's not his fault, but that hardly excuses him...."

In painstaking detail Tanner told her about phoning h
father, about the strange impression he'd gotten, about h
hurried trip to New York. "When I got there, he didn
even fight me," he went on. "He just said sit down and

egan to talk. I almost think he was glad to bring it all
ut."

Tanner drew a breath, then plunged in. "He'd told me
he truth that night on the back deck. He believed, as did
our mother, that you were his daughter. The possibility
xisted that you were your real father's daughter—your
other's husband—but to Gerrard and your mother, it
eemed unlikely."

Maggie shook her head, barely able to cope. Her head
as spinning.

"Maybe they almost wanted it to be true," Tanner
used. "A kind of secret that bonded them. Or maybe it
as just guilt. In your mother's eyes they'd committed a
n and therefore you had to be Gerrard's daughter." He
eaved a sigh. "In either case, they never questioned the
uth."

He reached across for her hand and Maggie squeezed his
ngers. "But the night I told them about you and me," he
aid softly, "it rocked the very foundation of their lives.
My father called your mother several days later. They
alked about both of us."

It seemed so strange to hear it now. Almost as if it were
tale about two other star-crossed lovers, not themselves.

"Your mother was sick with self-reproach," Tanner
ent on, "and nearly hysterical that you should never find
ut you'd slept with your half brother."

"Oh, no..." Maggie moaned, covering her face and
ching with empathy for the lonely, tortured woman her
other had been. She'd never learned the truth.

"She wasn't the only one whose guilt ate her up inside.
My father procured the grant you received for college. He
uly thought you were his daughter. He wanted you to
ave an education."

Maggie looked up blankly, reeling under this shocking bit of news. "My grant? My education? Your father?"

"Unbelievable, isn't it?" Tanner said tautly. "But before you start thinking he's kinder than he seems, let me tell you this. When your mother died he decided he wanted to become a real father to you. God knows why. Maybe his reasons were completely unselfish, but I can't trust him. Before he approached you, however, he did some blood type checking on his own. Lo and behold, he learned the truth—you're not his daughter.

"But did he tell anyone?" Tanner's hands flexed on the wheel. "Oh, no. His son, the eminent Dr. Tanner Baines, had already made a name for himself in Boston. He had a socially acceptable wife and a small, beautiful daughter. What good would it do to tell him that one Maggie Holt was no relation?"

Maggie's throat hurt. She tried to find it in her heart to forgive Gerrard Baines for playing God with her life, but she couldn't. That would come with time. For now she would just be grateful for her future.

"So he never told me," Tanner said flatly. "Not even after Tricia died. He never told me."

"I wasn't good enough," Maggie said softly.

"I don't think that was really his objection." Then Tanner pulled himself up short. "Hell, I don't know. Maybe it was. He's not exactly the unbending type," he added grimly.

"Neither Con nor myself was good enough." She looked at the rapidly passing landscape, seeing glimmers of the lake between the trees. "That's why we tried so hard."

"Forget about his self-serving egotism. None of that matters now," Tanner said harshly. "The truth is out. God! I can hardly believe it. Maggie, Maggie..." He

ughed shakily. "We can love each other. The way it
ould have been. The way it can be now."

At her silence he glanced her way. "What's wrong?" he
sked intuitively.

"I just can't absorb it all. I've been trying to look at you
s a brother and failing utterly. Now to think..." Her voice
ailed off. How could she tell him she was frightened?
rightened of not living up to the expectations they'd both
uilt out of that long-ago love?

They were driving down a narrow road to the water-
ront, winding down a hill. When Maggie understood
here they were going she gave him a searching look.
You realize it's all different down here now?"

"I just want to see it."

They drove past a row of huge stately homes built next
) the water's edge, their backyards sweeping down to
aborate decks, boathouses and docks. Tanner eased the
ar to a stop beneath the drooping limbs of a huge willow,
en turned to look at Maggie.

"I told you I loved you the first time right over there,
here we made love," he said soberly.

Maggie felt breathless. Memories floated between them,
s soft and sultry as the warm summer air. She stared at the
ree-storied gray house that stood behind the willow.
everal bicycles were strewn across the yard and an
nderground sprinkler system was watering the recently
lipped grass.

"It's different now," she said.

"Not so different. Not if we don't want it to be."

His finger gently pulled her chin around until she was
orced to meet his eyes. "I still love you, Maggie. I always
ave."

If she'd had any remaining doubts, they disappeared at
e emotion that throbbed in his voice. Her lips trembled

and this time she waited while Tanner's hands cradled her chin, while his mouth came down on hers. There was so much longing in his kiss, so much tenderness, but beneath it all was the dangerous, seductive passion that had ruled their lives for so many years.

"Let's get out of here," he growled. "We've waited too damn long for each other."

He was in the act of driving to her place, when he remembered what he looked like. Rubbing a hand over his jaw, he said, "This is hardly the way to start a new relationship. I need a shave."

"No. I don't want to wait."

He gave her an amused, sidelong look. "A woman after my own heart."

"I want to be with you alone. I want to believe this is real," Maggie said, her cheeks a faint red. "I don't want to wake up tomorrow and find this is all a dream."

If he found her insecurities silly at this point, he didn't say so. Silently, because their minds were both filled with feverish thoughts, Tanner drove to Maggie's cottage. He waited behind her as she found her key and inserted it in the lock, twisting the knob.

In the living room they stared at each other, memorizing each other's features. They had known each other so long, yet they were still strangers in many ways. Slowly, so slowly that it made the back of her throat hurt, Tanner pulled her into his arms, fitting her softer curves against his harder angles. "You make me crazy," he whispered, his heart pounding against hers.

Maggie closed her eyes. He made her breathless.

"I don't even want to think about all the time we've wasted."

"Neither do I."

"Maggie..."

She looked up at him expectantly.

With a groan he pressed his lips down on hers, hard, with the same pent-up passion that had heated her blood so many times this summer without any satisfaction. But now that was in the past. He kissed her everywhere, across her eyes, down the line of her chin, over the bridge of her nose. She was liquid to his touch, a moving pliable entity that only lived to be loved by him.

Scooping her into his arms, Tanner carried her to the bedroom. He lay her down, his eyes still searching hers with so many questions. Knowing he needed reassurance as much as she did, Maggie looped her arms around his neck and pulled his body atop hers. "I love you," she whispered.

"Marry me," he said. "Tomorrow."

"Too far away. Let's go tonight," Maggie murmured.

He pulled back a second to see if she was serious, then seeing the teasing light in her eyes, smiled. "Don't make fun. I'm serious."

Then he was kissing her again, his hands shaking as they undid the buttons of her blouse, unhooked the tiny fastener on her skirt. Maggie trembled on the bed as he finished undressing her and himself. A longing, deep and profound, filled her as she saw the way the fading light glinted on his lean, hard hips.

Then he was beside her, touching her in ways that lit tiny fires inside her, kissing her with a tender abandonment that left her quivering on the brink of a desire that had been staved off for too many years.

"Tanner," she whispered. "Love me."

She wanted more, so much more. Her hands wound into his hair; her arms pulled his mouth down to hers; her legs wrapped themselves around him. The misery of empty years was forgotten in the searching, scorching penetration of his kiss, and when he raised his sinewy body over hers, she held him tightly, anxiously.

"I love you," he murmured, then pushed himself into her in a way that blew her childhood memories to bits.

Perhaps if Maggie had had more experience she wouldn't have been so overwhelmed, but as it was, making love to Tanner was more exquisite the second time, placing on the shelf the dog-eared memory of their first time together that she'd found such comfort in over the years.

But this was so immediate. So fresh and exciting. Each movement was breath catching, and she found herself hurrying, arching toward that unnamed need that only he could fulfill.

Then it came, an explosion of pure sensation that left Maggie gasping for breath, soft moans issuing from her own throat. She writhed beneath him and Tanner's release followed swiftly, almost simultaneously. He collapsed upon her, heart thudding in tandem with hers, the shudders that went through him a secret delight to Maggie.

"Tomorrow," he whispered, and she knew then that this was no dream.

Chapter Eleven

So what's the situation between you and Chad?" Tanner asked lazily.

Maggie looked at him through the moonlight, tugging the sheet over her bare shoulder. "What do you mean?"

"I'm not blind. The guy's in love with you."

His finger moved down her arm, starting a shiver beneath her skin. Maggie propped herself on one elbow, her auburn hair tumbling over her face. Pulling it back, she said, "Chad and I were semiengaged, but it was over even before you came back."

"Semi?"

"I lied to you that first night. I just didn't want you to think I might be..." She sighed, having trouble expressing her feelings. "I don't know. That I might be available."

"I was dying for you."

His words, spoken so softly from the shadows, had a deadly impact on Maggie's senses. She placed her hand on his cheek and kissed him. "It's been worse for you. You believed I was your sister for so long."

"It was hell. But if I had to do it all over again to get to where we are now, I'd do it." His arms reached for her. "God, I love you," he murmured against her hair.

He pulled her atop him, refusing to let her drag her red-tinged mane away as his hands tangled in it. "I'm only sorry about Tricia. She always knew, I think, that there was part of me she could never reach. I even wanted her to reach it, but it just didn't happen. You were in the way."

The low timbre of his voice and the feel of his taut body beneath her sent Maggie's mind to dangerous corners. "I can only feel so sorry for Tricia," she murmured. "She stole you from me. She had almost fourteen years of your life."

"I made her life miserable. She thought everything I said was just words, no meaning. Shelley accused me of the same thing a few weeks ago."

"I know better," Maggie whispered with a seductive smile, folding her arms on top of his chest and looking at him through loving eyes. "You have a great way of showing what you mean even without words."

In the darkness his teeth flashed. "So do you," he said against her lips, his hand stealing around her nape, his limbs entrapping hers. "So do you...."

"We're so glad you've reconsidered, Dr. Baines," the voice gushed on the other end of the line. "No one else has been able to meet your qualifications. We've been in a kind of holding pattern with our temporary head of surgery, but we were really hoping that you would take the position.

Our chief of staff, Dr. Huffman, will be contacting you soon and I hope..."

The voice droned on and on. Tanner put in an appropriate grunt of acknowledgment here and there, but his mind and eyes were on Maggie. She was making breakfast in the kitchen, wearing only a knee-length sweatshirt that revealed enticing glimpses of tanned thigh whenever she bent over. Her hair was still damp and artificially darkened from the shower they'd just had together and it lay in wet strands on the fine skin at the back of her neck.

"Before Dr. Huffman can make the announcement of your appointment we'll need you to come in and meet with other staff and board members and fill out the proper forms...."

"Uh-huh."

"The other contenders for the position will be notified right away. Your duties as administrative head of surgery are quite extensive. We're especially glad to have you join our staff now that we've gotten the funding for our new obstetrics wing. I'm sure you'll find Briar Park a friendly, cooperative and progressive facility...."

"I'm sure."

Amusement lit Maggie's green eyes as she heard his end of the conversation. Tanner pointed to the receiver and shook his head. If it hadn't been that he really wanted the position, he certainly wouldn't have chosen this time to notify the hospital of his decision.

"Thank you. I'll be glad to talk to Dr. Huffman," Tanner cut in on the voice, seizing the first opportunity he could to get off the phone. "Have him call me at home on Monday. Thank you."

He cut the connection with one deft finger. "Good Lord. How does anything get done at Briar Park?"

"Very efficiently, I'll have you know. But adding Dr. Baines to our staff is a definite coup."

Tanner came into the kitchen, watching as Maggie stirred up eggs with a whisk. "How will your friend Chad feel when he finds he's been replaced—in more ways than one?"

Maggie stood on tiptoe to look in her spice cabinet. The sweatshirt sneaked up to just below her derriere. "He'll bounce back. Chad knows what he wants. He just hasn't learned to put out the extra effort yet to achieve it."

"A philosopher." The sight of those long, bare limbs was too much for Tanner. He came up behind her, circling her tiny waist with his arms. "What about my marriage proposal? Think we can get married before four o'clock?"

Maggie half turned, smiling. "I believe there's a three-day wait."

"Wouldn't you know it?" he grumbled, burying his face in her soap-scented tresses. Ignoring her protests, he turned off the stove and pushed her ahead of him down the hall. "Well, fine, if we have to wait three days we might as well do it in bed," he explained, and Maggie, whose own happiness was a fever in her blood, complied willingly.

Hours later, while they rocked gently on Maggie's old porch swing and drank wine and ate cheese and French bread, Maggie said softly, "I'm worried about tomorrow."

"Why? We're going to be together." He refilled her glass, then proceeded to drink straight from the bottle.

Maggie smiled. She loved him so much. But reality was a weight on her shoulders. "Tomorrow's Sunday and then that's it. The weekend will be over and we'll have to make plans."

"Is that so bad?"

"I've got to face Con and you've got to face Shelley."

Tanner drew a deep breath, his hand stealing upward to meditatively rub strands of her hair between his fingers. "I'm not looking forward to it, either, but they'll understand."

"Listen to you," Maggie said, shaking her head. "I just wish it were that simple."

"It'll work out. You'll see."

He leaned over to give her a kiss, his lips tasting of wine. There was a thread of desperation in the way he constantly touched her, kissed her, loved her. Maggie understood implicitly. She felt the same way—as if they could lose everything if they didn't hold on tight to each other.

"Come on," Tanner said, tugging her up from the chair.

The old swing squeaked and groaned as Maggie got to her feet. She was barefoot, and though not a small woman, her head seemed barely to reach his shoulders. "What's on your mind?" she asked softly.

His fingers strayed to the zipper on the back of her sundress. "I was thinking about playing doctor."

Maggie's brows lifted. "Really."

"Mmm-hmm."

"What about the rest of our dinner?" She gestured toward the fat wedge of cheese and the torn loaf of bread.

"At the risk of repeating a cliché—I think it's time for dessert."

"That *is* bad," Maggie said with a laugh.

He swept her into his arms before she could offer further protests, and she locked her hands behind his head, smiling up at him. It seemed inconceivable to Maggie that this glorious happiness could continue, but at the same time, she couldn't imagine life without him.

Tanner tried to maneuver her through the Dutch door, swearing beneath his breath as he tried to unlatch the lock, balance Maggie and keep his lips on hers while she laughed uproariously. "You're not making this easy, y'know," he muttered.

"I know. That's what you get for trying to be such a romantic."

"If you don't like it I can drop you right here."

"I love it." She grinned. "But maybe we're too old for this kind of nonsense."

"Too old? My God, Maggie, you're a sad case. Ah-hah!" he said with male satisfaction, flipping the bolt. "Too old, my foot."

Tanner was in the act of carrying her down the hall to the bedroom, when the phone rang. "Don't answer it," he said.

"It could be important. It might even be for you."

"Mrs. Greer and Shelley still think I'm out of town, so it's definitely for you."

The phone rang again and Maggie bit her lip. "It could be Con," she said.

Seeing her expression, Tanner slowly put her on her feet. Maggie hesitated, shooting him a look of apprehension, before she picked up the kitchen extension. "Hello?"

"Maggie, it's Con. Are you busy right now? I need to see you."

"Oh, Connor," she said, and Tanner silently motioned that he would be out on the porch. But she shook her head, reaching for him. He sat down on one of the kitchen stools and clasped her hand. "I don't know if I can make it right now."

"Okay, how about later, then? I'm getting my condominium together and I need a few of the things I left at our place. Why don't you swing by, drop them off, and we'll catch dinner somewhere?''

Maggie swallowed and glanced at Tanner. "I can't tonight, Con, really. I'm busy." She thought about telling him straight out about Tanner, but the words lodged in her throat.

"Oh, ho. A big date?" She heard the grin enter his voice.

"In a manner of speaking. Do you mind if I tell you about it later?''

"Heck, no. But I demand a full accounting later. Oh, and Maggie, they say it's just as easy to fall in love with someone rich. Check his bank balance, okay?''

"That's your fantasy, not mine," she said with a smile, but Con's good humor only served to depress her.

"You didn't tell him about us," Tanner observed after he hung up.

"I just don't want the battle yet. I want to put it off until next week."

"I understand." He came around the counter and put his arms around her.

"On Monday. We'll tell them both Monday, okay?''

"Okay." There was a soberness to his words they could both understand. There were still a few battles left to fight.

With a soft sigh Tanner leaned down to kiss her forehead, then her eyes, then his lips drifted downward to her mouth. "Let's put this out of our minds until Monday. Now where were we . . . ?''

Carrying a secret had never been one of Maggie's strong points, and throughout the weekend with Tanner she had the urge to shout the news from the rafters. On Monday she could barely contain herself, but she didn't want to tip her hand to anyone before she had a chance to speak to

Con and Shelley, and consequently Monday was one of th
longest days she could recall.

By the time Mr. Rookheiser came for his three o'cloc
appointment she was so restless and fidgety he made
comment on her attitude.

"What's your problem, girl?" he complained.

"Pardon?" Maggie asked, bringing her attention bac
to the present.

"I said, what's your problem? You're as nervous as
long-tailed cat in a room of rockers."

"I've just got things on my mind," Maggie said, smil
ing. Knowing Mr. Rookheiser's opinion of Tanner, sh
couldn't resist adding, "Did you know Dr. Baines ma
soon be Briar Park's head of surgery?"

"I heard rumblings to that effect." He sniffed. "If yo
ask me, he should take care of things closer to home. Tha
girl of his needs some supervision."

Remembering Mr. Rookheiser's mention of Shelley'
late-night activities with boys twice her age, Maggie trie
to pin him down on what he meant. But the older man ca
gily sidestepped any direct questions. As usual, he was of
fering his opinion without facts to back him up, but sh
made a mental note to ask Tanner about it anyway.

As soon as she was off work she made a beeline to th
Baines home. Butterflies had taken flight in her stomach
Today they would tell Shelley, and Con, too, if he deigne
to accept Tanner's invitation to come to his house for din
ner, about their pending marriage. She crossed her finger
and hoped for the best.

"They're down with the new boat," Mrs. Greer sai
with a wide grin when she met Maggie at the door. "Go o
down there. And congratulations."

So Tanner had told her. Impulsively Maggie gave the kindly housekeeper a bear hug. "Thank you," she whispered, tears threatening the corners of her eyes.

"It's about time is all I can say," the woman answered, her own eyes looking suspiciously moist. "Now go on. Dr. Baines and Shelley are waiting for you."

The August sun was beastly and Maggie wished she'd taken the time to put on something cooler. Unbuttoning the top buttons of her blouse, she ran a hand inside her collar and carefully picked her way down to the boathouse.

A gleaming white-and-blue boat was docked alongside the boathouse, rocking gently. Tanner was inside it, his dark shoulders bent over some gear beneath the steering wheel. Shelley sat beside him, her slim frame clad in a bright red one-piece suit, the color beautifully showing off her dark hair.

Hearing her approach, Tanner looked up and grinned. "Maggie!"

"Hi. Looks like I should have gone home and changed first."

"Don't worry. We'll just go for a quick ride. Hop in. I'm just about ready."

Diffidently Maggie took his hand and climbed into the back. Shelley's gaze was dark and direct. She regarded Maggie suspiciously.

"I thought we'd drive to the other end of the lake and maybe get some iced coffee," Tanner said, his eyes on Shelley.

"I don't like coffee," she answered, her own gaze directed to Maggie. Then she turned to stare into the sun-sparkled water, and Maggie, after appealing silently to Tanner for help, sat down on one of the royal blue vinyl cushions.

"Everything'll be fine," Tanner said in a general way. The engine started with a roar that quickly became a purr as Tanner adjusted the throttle. "Ready?" he asked.

"Ready," Maggie answered.

Shelley was purposely quiet.

They cruised slowly out past the safety margin, then Tanner pushed the throttle forward. The boat leaped ahead and soon they were racing over the slightly choppy water, the wind screaming past their ears.

It was the final déjà vu for Maggie: riding in a high-flying boat on Lake Oswego with Tanner. He half turned and slashed her a grin, his blond hair pulled back by the wind. Maggie grinned back.

"Wanna drive?" Tanner yelled.

"No, thanks. I'll just enjoy this!"

They drove to the other end of Lake Oswego, and Tanner quickly slowed as the boat neared the bobbing red buoy that marked the safety zone. Maggie pulled her fingers through her hair and Shelley did the same thing. The two women looked at each other and Maggie smiled. Shelley swallowed hard and Maggie read fear in her blue eyes.

She knows what's coming.

With an inward wince, Maggie realized her decision to marry Tanner would only add to the girl's insecurities. She dreaded having to tell her.

They pulled up to the dock outside one of the small bistros that lined the town side of the lake and ordered iced coffee and soft drinks. Tanner did most of the talking, and Maggie's mouth was dry with apprehension, but it didn't matter. Shelley looked as if she'd rather be anywhere than where she was.

At length Tanner cleared his throat. "Shelley, I'm sure you've wondered all day why I insisted you come with Maggie and me this afternoon."

Shelley stiffened. Darting a look at Maggie, she drew her mouth into a compromising line. She couldn't meet her father's eyes.

"Maggie and I have known each other a long time."

She hunched her shoulders. "I know." Her voice was small and full of dread. Maggie ached for her, wishing there were something she could do to relieve the poor girl's anxiety.

"We once thought about marriage," he went on, "but the timing wasn't right and it all kind of got away from us. I married your mother and moved to Boston and Maggie went to college to become a nutritionist." He glanced warmly at Maggie, and whether he knew it or not, everything he felt was in his eyes. "Now the timing's right."

The color drained from Shelley's face. "What do you mean?"

"I've asked Maggie to marry me and she's accepted."

There was a moment of intense silence. Maggie half expected Shelley to leap up and start screaming, but instead she just sat speechless in her chair, her eyes wide and lost.

"I'm not trying to take your mother's place," Maggie interjected quickly. "I would just like to be friends, if you think that's possible."

"It doesn't matter much what I think, does it?" she said with a trace of her old bite, but after that, though Tanner and Maggie both tried to engage her in conversation, Shelley was ominously quiet.

It was twilight by the time they took the boat back across the lake. At the boathouse Tanner carefully maneuvered the boat into the newly dredged slip. He helped Shelley, then Maggie onto the concrete apron, jumped out, then pressed the button to raise the cradle. Clanking and grinding, the chains slowly rose, encircling the bottom of the boat and lifting it from the water.

"It's nice to know some things work," Tanner said, and Maggie understood completely how he felt.

They walked up the hillside, Tanner lagging back to talk to Shelley. "Don't worry so much," he advised gently. When that still elicited no response, he said, "Do you want to learn how to drive the boat? By the time you get your license you could be an expert."

She seemed nonplussed by his adult treatment of her. "You'll teach me?"

"Uh-huh."

"When?"

"Tomorrow if you like."

"But what about . . . ?"

She didn't finish the question, but Maggie could feel Shelley's eyes burning into her back.

"Unlike you and me, Maggie's got to work tomorrow," he said. "Do you mind if it's just the two of us?"

Shelley didn't seem to know what to say to that. Maggie held her breath, hoping Shelley would realize her father was trying to tell her that loving someone else didn't mean he loved her any less. But Shelley didn't offer any insight to her thoughts.

Once at the house Shelley went directly to her room and Maggie held Tanner's arm at the foyer, preventing him from following.

"What do you think?" Maggie asked.

"It could be worse." He drew her into his arms beneath the tinkling chandelier. "She didn't slam the door this time."

"But she's so insecure already. Maybe we should wait—"

"No." Tanner was adamant. "I've waited all my life. I'm not going to wait any longer. Dr. Gaver even admits that Shelley's working out her problems slowly. If this is a setback, it'll only be a minor one."

Maggie was unconvinced, but her worries over Shelley were soon replaced by new ones as Con's T-bird turned into Tanner's drive. She inhaled and exhaled several times, earning a sardonic glance from Tanner.

"He's your brother," he said. "Don't worry so much. He cares about you. It'll take some getting used to for him to accept me, but it'll happen because he loves you."

"When did you become such an optimist?" Maggie muttered, then walked onto the porch with Tanner to meet Con.

Con came up the pathway, his expression difficult to read in the dying light. "Well, well, well," he said, stopping in front of them. "This brings back a few memories, doesn't it?" He looked around the yard. "God. I thought I'd gotten over them."

"Come on in, Con," Tanner invited.

He inclined his head. "I have this strange feeling I know what's coming," he answered grimly, but followed after Tanner and Maggie.

Mrs. Greer had spent the greater part of the afternoon preparing a crisp green salad, a fruit salad and some special French bread layered with melted cheese and scallions. A white metal table with a glass top was on the deck, with four blue canvas deck chairs surrounding it. Silver and crystal glinted in the overhead light and the scent of pork roast wafted from the barbecue, while the drippings sizzled onto the coals.

"You've pulled out all the stops for this, haven't you?" Con was cynical. "Don't tell me—let me guess. No more brother-sister lies. You two are back together again. Better yet, you want to move in together."

"We're getting married," said Tanner.

"Ahh." Con walked toward the barbecue, his shoulders tense.

"Would you like a drink?" Tanner asked, placing a reassuring hand on Maggie's arm as he passed by her.

"Yeah. Anything. And make it strong, would you?" He met Maggie's imploring eyes. "I'm going to need it."

"Con," Maggie pleaded when Tanner was out of earshot. "Give us a chance to explain. Tanner just found out the other night that his father had kept the truth from him about us."

"Really."

"Look, I don't blame you for being skeptical, but don't make a scene. He and I aren't related. Please. I love him. I always have and I always will. You used to like him, too."

"I could like him again if he'd leave you alone." Con's lips flattened. "Maggie, this marriage thing—well, I'll believe it when I see it."

Her fists clenched. "You've never understood about Tanner and me!" she said in a harsh whisper.

"I understand that he's used you in the past and he's lied to you. He'll use you again."

Tanner came back with a scotch for Con and a bottle of wine for him and Maggie. If he'd overheard Con's last remark he made no mention of it. But Con downed his drink fairly quickly and Tanner went to get him another.

When he returned Con was sitting in one of the deck chairs, his legs stretched in front of him, his ankles crossed negligently. "Maybe we should get a few home truths out," he said. "Seeing as you're going to be my brother-in-law."

Tanner regarded him squarely. "Maybe we should."

"I don't like the way you've treated Maggie. You lied to her when we were kids and you still haven't told her the truth."

"What truth?" Maggie demanded, infuriated by his high-handedness. "Con, for Pete's sake—"

"Let him finish," Tanner interrupted. "I'd like to hear what he has to say."

"Oh, no, you won't." Con wagged his head. "I'm talking about Tricia now."

"Tricia?" For a moment Maggie was confused, and then she remembered Con's claim that Tanner had been seeing Tricia that same summer he'd been seeing her. Uneasiness crept over her. "Let's not go into all that now."

"What better time?" Con pressed his palms on the arms of the chair and lifted himself up, glaring at Tanner. "If you were so in love with Maggie, why did you sleep with Tricia? You never told Maggie about that, did you? But I knew."

Tanner frowned and opened his mouth to speak, but Con swept on. "Oh, I know Tricia was more than willing. She would have done anything to hook Tanner Baines."

Tanner measured him with his eyes. His mind traveled backward, and a memory, long forgotten, came to him. "You were in love with Tricia back then, too," he said on a note of discovery.

"Love?" Con was scornful. "Well, maybe your kind of love. I'd call it infatuation. I wanted her because of what she represented—wealth, prestige, respectability." He swept an arm over the beautiful appointments and surroundings of Tanner's house. "All those things that were so important to me and seemed within reach if I could just have Tricia." A humorless smile tightened his lips. "She was the biggest tease. But she only wanted you—and she finally got you."

"Look, Con," Maggie said uncomfortably, "all that was a long time ago, and we've all grown up."

"Damn it, Maggie! He slept with Tricia that summer. He had to marry her. And yet you say he was vowing never-ending love to you! I don't believe people change that much." Con turned on Tanner. "It would be a whole lot easier for me to believe that you met as adults and fell in love now, for the first time. Tell her, Baines. Tell her the truth."

Tanner looked at Maggie. Her eyes begged him to make this right, to prove her brother wrong. It seemed incomprehensible to him that an old mistake from the past made for all the right reasons could rise up and cut him down now. "I did sleep with Tricia that summer," he admitted flatly. "When she found out she was pregnant both our families wanted us to get married."

Con's brows lifted. "Well, well, well, I didn't know you had it in you."

Maggie stood in silence, despair filling her up inside. Tanner, seeing her white face, grew impatient with the whole situation. "I loved you even then, Maggie. But you were so young. Tricia was just there—eager—and you and I had spent a very frustrating summer together. Half the time I wanted to quit seeing you. I couldn't cope with how I felt about you. And Tricia and I had been together off and on for years."

"You don't have to explain this." Maggie backed up, her thigh hitting the railing. "It's all past history."

"It's not in the past if it still affects us," Tanner said with rising anger. "I would have never married Tricia just to please my father. I wanted you. I found out about the pregnancy the same night my father told me you and I were supposedly related. Tricia's parents had told Gerrard and he gave me the good news as an afterthought." He uttered a short humorless, laugh. "God, Maggie. I was a mess. Everyone wanted me to marry Tricia and so I did. It seemed *safe*."

When she didn't answer his mouth curved bitterly. "You can believe what you like, but the only lie I ever told you was that I wanted to marry Tricia, not you."

"You've got a helluva nerve," Con growled.

"Don't, Con." With difficulty Maggie pulled herself together. "I don't want any more of this."

"Maggie..." Feeling her slipping away from him, Tanner stepped forward, but she shook her head.

"It's the lie of omission you're guilty of," she whispered. *"Again."*

"I love you," Tanner said, enunciating firmly. "I've always loved you."

"Con." Maggie turned to her brother with eyes wide with pain. "I need to go home. Would you please take me?"

"You got it. We'll pick up your car later." He started to guide her to the door, but Tanner grabbed her arm.

"You know how I feel," he said intensely. "You know how we both feel. Don't leave."

But Maggie, whose relationship with Tanner had always been a roller-coaster ride of emotions, couldn't think straight. She needed to be alone. To sort out things. "Give me...tonight," she said unsteadily, licking her lips. "Just tonight, to think. I need that much."

He would have liked to force her to stay. How could she leave now, when their future stood before them, free and uncluttered? And he would have liked to shove his fist in

Con's triumphant face. Except that right now Con was looking more pensive than triumphant.

Inwardly furious, Tanner stalked down the hall to the front door, throwing it open. As Maggie passed through he said evenly, "I won't wait long, Maggie. If you soul-search this to death I'll come after you. I'll fight you until you give in. I want you too much to let you throw it all away."

He shut the door softly behind them, but his fingers curled into a fist. Con's car roared to life, and Tanner, who'd had about all he could take, strode back to the rear deck, stared for several moments at the glittering moon glow on the lake, then swept the crystal and silver from the table with a furious crash.

Chapter Twelve

Maggie stared at her reflection in the mirror. She was thirty-one years old. She'd spent most of her adult life searching for something she couldn't even name, and then Tanner had come back this summer and put what she wanted within reach.

She was a fool to turn him away.

In a haze of self-doubts, Maggie finished going through her morning routine. Sunlight streamed through the blinds over her living room window, and she checked the clock, realizing she'd overslept. Hearing a faint meowing and scratching at the back door, she opened the latch, smiling at the sight of the yellow cat sneaking inside.

"Hello, Cat. You're going to think this is your home before long," she said picking him up. She looked into his inscrutable gold eyes. "Got any advice for me this morning? Hmm? Am I being foolish?"

The cat just closed his eyes and purred.

Maggie was putting him back down again, when the front doorbell rang. The hairs on the back of her neck rose. *If you soul-search this to death I'll come after you,* Tanner had said.

But it wasn't Tanner at the door—it was Con.

"Got a minute?"

"No way. Get out of here," she said, reaching for a smile and failing. But she opened the door wider and Con came inside.

"I've been thinking all night about what Tanner said."

"You, too, huh?" Maggie went back to the kitchen and poured him a cup of coffee.

"Yeah." Con sighed. "After I got home I called Linda."

If she hadn't been so absorbed in her own problems she would have been amazed by this confession, but she was too upset to do more than look at him through empty, hollow eyes.

"For crying out loud, Maggie. Don't look at me like that. I realized some things last night—some things I've never wanted to face. I mean, I can only blame Linda so much for the way our marriage fell apart. I was at fault, too.

"Look, what I'm trying to say is, it's your life. None of us are kids anymore. Tanner made mistakes. You made mistakes. I made mistakes." Con raked his fingers through his hair. "Hell, I realized last night I've carried a grudge all these years about Tricia."

Maggie shook her head. "Do you mind? I don't want to talk about Tricia."

"Well, she's not the issue anyway. The truth is, Tanner's not a bad guy. If you love him, if you really love him—which I'm beginning to believe you do—then you ought to go back to him. I mean, it's better than ending up like me. I married Linda for all the wrong reasons. You could marry Tanner for all the right ones.''

Regarding her brother incredulously, Maggie slid his cup across the counter to him. ''Your talk with Linda did all this?''

''It put things in perspective.'' Con's smile was self-deprecatory. ''Here I've accused you of being the one who couldn't get over thinking we weren't 'good enough,' but I've been carrying the same thing around right here.'' He pointed to his shoulder. ''See that big chip? It wouldn't let me accept that Tanner really loves you, but he does. Deep down I think I've known it since that first meeting at the hospital this summer. The way he looked at you. I did some major rethinking last night and I realized I've tried to keep you from him for reasons I can't even explain.''

He didn't have to go on. She understood him better than she understood herself and she knew he'd been looking out for her in the only way he knew how. But hearing him talk about Tanner with less acrimony lifted her spirits. She smiled at him affectionately. ''Oh, I think you're explaining pretty well. You know, I never say it, but I do love you.''

''Please.'' He warded her off with his hands. ''I can only handle so much at one time.''

''I'm going to call Tanner,'' she decided. ''Right now.''

Con shrugged. ''Who knows? Maybe we can even all go to dinner some night. Me and Gayle and you and Tanner. God!'' He shook his head. ''Given time, I might even be able to deal with my ex-wife.''

Maggie almost laughed, but before she could pick up the receiver the phone rang beneath her hand. ''Hello?'' she answered.

''Maggie. Oh, Maggie. I need help.''

It was Tanner and the tremor in his voice sent a cold shiver down her spine. "What is it? What's happened?"

"It's Shelley. She's gone. She's been gone all night, and she's never done that before. I think she overheard our conversation on the deck."

Maggie's heart plummeted to her stomach. *Overheard!* Their voices had been raised. She'd been so upset she hadn't even considered that Shelley might be eavesdropping. Quickly she ran the conversation over again in her mind and she inwardly winced as she remembered the things that had been said about Tricia.

"I'll be right over," she said. "Don't go anywhere. I'll be right there."

"What's wrong?" Con asked as she dashed around the house.

"Shelley's missing. Tanner thinks she must have overheard our conversation last night."

"Oh, God." He blinked in remembrance. "I'm coming with you."

"No, Con, it's not necessary."

"Yes, it is. I caused that scene last night. I owe Tanner."

There was no changing his mind, so Maggie just let him come. She called her office and explained to Karen that an emergency had sprung up and that she needed to reschedule her appointments. Then she drove like wildfire around the twisting roads to Tanner's house.

He was in the study, on the phone, pacing. "I know it hasn't been twenty-four hours," he said tersely, "but she's a diabetic." He signaled for both Maggie and Con to come inside. "She gives herself insulin shots twice a day. If she doesn't show up soon, her health may be in danger. And she's only thirteen!" He listened for a moment, then said,

"All right, you've got my number. Someone will be here at all times."

"Tanner," Maggie said when he'd hung up. She went straight into his arms and held him, wordlessly letting him know her decision.

He buried his face in her hair for several seconds, then pulled back, lines grooved alongside his mouth. "That was missing persons." He shook his head, looking dazed. "Shelley's never done this before. She's left before, sure. But not for all night."

Remembering Mr. Rookheiser's gossip, Maggie asked tentatively, "Could she be with friends? Friends who are old enough to drive?"

"She doesn't have any friends old enough to drive. She hasn't made that many friends yet. She just knows a few lake kids."

Realizing this was no time to skirt issues, Maggie told him what Mr. Rookheiser had intimated, but Tanner shook his head. "Maybe he saw her with one of her friends' older brothers, but as far as I know, Shelley's out there on her own power. Old man Rookheiser, as we used to call him—" Tanner half smiled and shot a look at Con "—has a tendency to exaggerate."

"That guy's still alive? He used to give us so much trouble." Con stepped forward and offered his hand. "I'd like to start over, Tanner."

Surprised by Con's capitulation, Tanner shook his hand. "I would, too, Con. Sincerely." Then he ran a hand over his stubbled chin, more pressing matters weighing on his mind. "I've searched the grounds and she's not here."

"What about the boat?" Maggie asked anxiously.

"It's still in the boathouse. She's on foot or with friends." Tanner then explained how he'd called every one of her friends that he knew. No one had seen her. "I

checked her insulin supply, but I can't tell if she's got som
with her. If she's not found by tonight..." His jaw worked

"She wouldn't be that foolish," Maggie declared firmly
"She knows better."

"I'm going to do some searching around the lake
Maybe she's at the swim park or someone's seen her. Th
police have been alerted, but I don't know how much I ca
depend on them. I just feel so damn helpless!"

"I'll take the south and west side of the lake," Con sai
soberly. "You take the north and east. Maggie, stay her
by the phone."

She looked at Tanner's taut face and said, "I want to b
with you."

"I'll come back for you. Mrs. Greer gets here abou
eleven. I'll be back then."

Maggie had spent some long hours in her life. The da
Tanner had told her he was marrying Tricia the minute
had dragged by, each one an eternity. The day he'd told he
she was his sister had been a forever all on its own. But thi
day, with Shelley's life on the line, was the longest of then
all. Maggie paced and watched the clock and worried un
til she felt nauseous.

True to his word, Tanner came back at eleven. He too
Maggie with him and they drove endlessly, stopping and
asking people who lived around the lake if they'd seer
Shelley, showing them her picture. But always the answe
was no.

"It could be that she's nowhere near the lake," Tanne
said later that evening. "She could be anywhere."

"But she doesn't even know the area," Maggie argued
"Is there anywhere, anywhere you can think of, that she
would go?"

He shook his head, drawing a blank.

At seven-thirty Con showed up. He didn't have to tell
em his search had been fruitless; it was in his eyes.

Once again Tanner called the people he knew who were
helley's friends, and once again everyone expressed re-
et but no one knew where to find her.

The hours dragged by. Con fell asleep in a chair and
Maggie dozed on the couch, but Tanner lived on coffee
d nerves. He knew better than anyone that Shelley's time
as running out. The fear that quivered in his gut was that
e'd already gone into a diabetic coma. He prayed she'd
ken her insulin with her, but a part of him already knew
e hadn't.

When the phone rang at eight o'clock the following
orning, Tanner snatched it up eagerly. But it was just
issing persons, asking if she'd been located yet. "That's
ur job," Tanner snapped, then ran a hand around the
ack of his neck and squeezed hard. "I'm sorry," he said
efore he hung up. "Just find her, please."

He felt Maggie come up behind him and he turned,
olding her into his arms. "What can I do?" she whis-
ered.

"Just be here with me," Tanner said. "Stay right here."
Maggie held on to him tightly.

Con and Tanner went out searching again, but they re-
rned around noon, beaten and tired. By two o'clock
anner was already preparing himself for the worst. "If
helley hasn't taken her insulin by now she's probably in
coma."

"You don't know that," Maggie said quickly.

"Yes, I do." He was utterly grim and serious.

Con looked at the ceiling. "This is my fault. I should
ave never said those things."

"Let's not start blaming each other. It's no one's fault."
anner raked his hair back. "I'll call the Harrisons and

talk to their daughter again. Maybe there's somethin we've overlooked.''

Tanner was on the phone in the other room a long tim and when he returned he looked different, more hopefu "Lisa Harrison gave me a lead. There's a boy—she doesn know his name—who's a friend of Shelley's. He's not lake kid—he lives somewhere south of here. But he's dow at the swim park a lot. He and Shelley are pretty tight, guess.''

Con made a face. "Sounds like Connor Holt.''

"What's his name?'' Maggie asked.

"David. She didn't know his last name. He's about fi teen, has dark hair and wears cutoffs. That's all she coul tell me.''

"What are we waiting for?'' Con was already halfwa to the door.

"Please, Connor. Stay here and man the phone,'' Mag gie begged. "Let me go with Tanner.''

It was against his nature to be the inactive partner, bu seeing his sister's white face, Con banked his need to leav and nodded. "Just find her,'' he said.

Tanner drove to the swim park at record speed. Ther was hardly a place to park. Cars lined the roadway an people were everywhere. As he jockeyed his car half in an half out of a ditch, the news announcer cheerily said th mercury was going to climb over a hundred before the da was over.

"Great,'' Tanner muttered.

They wandered through the benches of people picnic ing, searching for anyone with David's description. Ther were so many dark heads in the water it was impossible t tell.

Wiping sweat off his temple, Tanner asked anxiousl "See anyone who looks like him?''

"A couple of kids. Maybe." Maggie wasn't sure. "Let's
tart asking around."

At first their questions were met with suspicion. No one
anted to say anything. Then finally a young man with
lack hair and vivid blue eyes came up to them. "My
ame's David," he said. "You lookin' for me?"

He could have been Con, Maggie thought in wonder.
he way he looked, the insolence that made his chin jut
orward. With a pang she realized how some things never
id change; like her brother he was trying to be accepted
y the "lake crowd." She wished she could warn him
bout trying to be something he wasn't before he found out
he hard way.

"I'm Shelley Baines's father," Tanner said quickly.
"I'm looking for her. I heard you were a friend of hers."

"Oh. Yeah, well..." He crossed his arms over his skinny
are chest.

"She's been missing for nearly two days, David. She's
diabetic. I need to find her, just to make sure she's all
ight. She could die."

Tanner's fear was so deep that it ran through his voice,
tremor that made even David take note. He squinted up
t Tanner, thought for a moment, then seemed to come to
decision. "There's a house for sale down on the north
ide," he said reluctantly. "There's no one there, and the
ock on the boathouse is broken. I go there sometimes and
showed it to Shelley. Maybe she's..."

"Thanks. Thanks a lot." Tanner was already half run-
ing toward the car. "What's the address?" he yelled.

"I don't know. But it's just past the second bridge. You
now, the one with the white painted rails?"

Maggie ran after Tanner. She was panting when she
eached the car, but he already had it in gear, the engine
evving.

"White painted rails," he muttered, reversing out of the ditch.

Horns blared as he pulled in front of passing motorists, but Tanner didn't notice. "I know which one he meant," Maggie said. "It used to be stained dark brown years ago and now it's—"

"Ah. I know."

He drove with a concentration that Maggie applauded. Her own thoughts and fears were scattered fragments that tossed around her mind and she wouldn't have trusted herself behind the wheel.

They found the bridge and Tanner parked. He walked straight down to the water's edge and crossed private property without a qualm, searching for the house David meant.

Maggie went the other way, down the road until she found the house with its For Sale sign slumped over in the yard. She tried to get through the gate, but it was locked. Reaching upward, she clasped the top of the fence and scrambled over, dropping onto the ground just as Tanner appeared from the next property.

Hurrying after him, she reached the boathouse just after he did. The lock was indeed broken. Tanner opened the door and called, "Shelley?" as he stepped inside. "Oh, my God..." was his next breath.

"Is she there?"

"Yes. Quick. Call an ambulance. Have them meet us at the road."

Maggie turned to do his bidding, but not before she'd seen Shelley's inert form sprawled on the floor and Tanner's capable hands slipping a needle into a vial of insulin.

* * *

If there was anything designed to make one feel mortal
was a hospital waiting room. Maggie, who'd thought she
was inured to the drama that went on within its walls,
found herself feeling helpless and weak. Her hands
constantly trembled and she kept pacing the floor, even
though she knew the best thing to do was sit and rest.

Tanner was with Shelley. The girl's blood sugar levels
had been dangerously high. There was a question of
whether or not she would pull through.

Con broke through the doors several moments later,
having answered Maggie's call by coming straight to the
hospital. "Shelley?" he asked, and Maggie lifted her
shoulders, tears welling in her eyes.

He put his arms around her. "She's going to be all right.
I just know it."

"Tanner's with her," Maggie choked out. "Oh, God, I
hope... I hope..."

"Shh."

He urged her gently into one of the chairs, holding on
to her hand. Maggie swallowed and pulled herself together. The minutes dragged by.

A florist walked in with a huge spray of red roses and
Maggie looked away. It reminded her too much of all the
sadness she'd felt in her loneliness. Now that very loneliness seemed selfish while Shelley fought for her life in the
next room.

"Want anything to eat?" Con asked.

"No."

"Coffee?"

She shook her head.

She was just about at the point where she couldn't stand
it anymore, when Tanner came into the waiting room. One
look at his face and she knew Shelley was out of danger.
With a cry of relief she threw herself into his arms.

"God, it was close," he said, wiping the back of hi hand across his eyes. "But she's going to be okay."

"Thank God," Con murmured.

"Oh, Tanner. I feel so guilty," Maggie said.

"Don't." He smoothed her hair with his hand an smiled. "I'm going to talk to her when she wakes up. want this whole mess straightened out once and for all."

"You think she'll talk to you?"

"I'm going to try my damnedest," he said with a con viction that made even Maggie think he just might suc ceed.

It was later that afternoon that Tanner got his wish Shelley, upon wakening and realizing where she was, wa frightened. Tanner was sitting by her bed and he reache over and quickly grabbed her hand. When she saw him sh started to cry, and he kissed her on the forehead. "We'r going to talk, Shelley," he said gently. "And you're goin to tell me everything that's wrong. Okay? Because I al most lost you and I can't bear the thought of goin through that again."

His daughter closed her eyes, her mouth tightening "I'm just afraid you'll leave me," she whispered.

"Never. I'm right here. I'll always be right here for you I promise."

Maggie would have liked to stay at the hospital wit Tanner and Shelley, but she couldn't let her work pile u unattended forever. While Tanner and Dr. Gaver tried t get to the bottom of Shelley's insecurities, Maggie saw al the patients that Karen had had to reschedule over the pas three days.

She and Tanner talked on the phone and visited each other for a few minutes at night, but he was too con

:erned with Shelley to stay away from the hospital for very
:ong and Maggie was swamped with work.

By the end of the week, however, she'd gotten her
:chedule back on track. Mrs. Tindale came in and found
:he had only six more pounds to lose before she reached
:er ideal weight for surgery. Maggie offered congratula-
:ions, thrilled her patient was being so successful. Then she
:repared herself for her last appointment of the day: the
:ver-taxing Mr. Rookheiser.

Their session went pretty much as always, but toward
:he end of it, he caught Maggie glancing at her watch. "In
: hurry?" he demanded. "Aren't you getting paid for
:his?"

"A friend of mine just got out of hospital today and I
:vant to go see her," she said with a smile. "Maybe I am a
:ittle anxious."

"Oh? Which friend?"

She didn't even mind his nosiness. "Shelley Baines."

"Shelley Baines? Dr. Baines's girl?"

"Yes."

Mr. Rookheiser opened his mouth to impart yet more
:lurs upon the Baines name, Maggie was sure, when there
:vas a knock on her door and, to Maggie's surprise, Tan-
:er stuck his head inside. "You're busy," he said.

"We're just finishing. It'll only be a few more min-
:tes."

"No, no." Mr. Rookheiser waved her away. "I'm done.
:Iello, Dr. Baines," he added stiffly, drawing himself up
:s straight as he could.

Tanner eyed the older man. "It's Mr. Rookheiser, isn't
:?" he asked, accepting his hand.

Maggie's eyes swept over Tanner hungrily. With Shel-
:ey's crisis coming so quickly on the heels of the recogni-
:ion of their love, they'd hardly had any time to see each

other. She hadn't realized how hard that was for her until just this moment.

He looked more relaxed than he'd been in a long time, and when Mr. Rookheiser frowned down at his injured hand, Tanner didn't even notice. *He's healing inside and out,* Maggie realized, and it warmed her heart.

How's Shelley? she asked with her eyes, and Tanner gave her a thumbs-up sign that Mr. Rookheiser didn't see.

"I hear you've taken a position here," the older man said.

"Yes, that's right. Administrative head of surgery."

"Hmm." He gave Maggie a considering look, as if he wondered what her relationship was with this young man he'd always considered a "hooligan."

Tanner's mouth twitched. "Maggie and I are getting married. Just as soon as my daughter's well enough to attend the wedding."

A gleam entered the white-haired man's eye. "So this is why you've been so anxious," he said to Maggie. "Well, congratulations." He shook Tanner's hand and gave Maggie a wink on his way out.

"Looks like you've passed the test," she said, amused.

Tanner shut the door and leaned against it. "About time," he drawled. "Tell me I was right about our wedding plans?" He came over to the desk and perched himself on a corner, looking down at her.

"I don't know. Let me think about it."

She laughed when he suddenly swung around the desk, pulling her from her chair. "You've got exactly one second, otherwise the answer's yes," he growled in her ear. "Too late. You've got to marry me."

"Okay, I'll marry you," she said happily. "Now don't keep me in suspense. Tell me about Shelley."

He gave her a long kiss that promised even more than it gave. "Shelley," he said, shaking his head. "Where do I begin? I don't know all of it yet, but Tricia apparently planted a lot of unhealthy ideas in her head. She told Shelley I was forced into the marriage, that I hadn't wanted either Shelley or her, that I was looking for a way out. I figured it was something like that, but to hear Shelley tell it..." Tanner's eyes glittered with inner fury. "Tricia made Shelley believe that if I divorced her, then next I would look for a way to get rid of Shelley. Nice, huh?"

"Why would she believe that? She's your daughter."

"A daughter Tricia told her I never wanted. She even intimated there was another woman in my life. I think she even dropped your name once or twice." Tanner sighed. "The worst of it is that, after my accident, I didn't show either of them much attention. Shelley took that as a sign that her mother was right and Tricia made certain she believed it. I don't know why Tricia was so manic about that. Maybe she was afraid I would divorce her and that I would sue for custody." He drew a heavy breath. "I would have, too. But I wasn't looking for a divorce."

She felt his hands dig into her shoulders, and said gently, "Then Dr. Gaver was right. She was trying to be as miserable as possible, subconsciously setting up what she expected to happen."

Tanner nodded. "It's why she pulled all those stunts over being sick when she really wasn't." He walked with Maggie to the window, looking out at the lazy late afternoon. "Overhearing our conversation the other night was like a knife in her heart. She figured she'd leave before I tossed her out. I didn't love Tricia—by my own admission—and so I couldn't possibly love her." He winced. "I should have been more careful."

"We all should have," said Maggie.

"She's never taken her diabetes that seriously," Tanner went on. "I mean, she worries about it, thinks she's different, but she's never understood the consequences until now. She couldn't really conceive of going into a coma." He shuddered, and Maggie tightened her arms around him.

"Does she believe you love her now?"

"I think she's beginning to." Tanner heaved a sigh. "My God, how could she ever doubt me?"

Thinking back on her own fears and insecurities, Maggie murmured, "Oh, I don't know. Sometimes we just make mistakes."

Tanner brushed her hair back, thinking how much he loved her, how he couldn't go on without her. In his peripheral vision he saw his hand, wound in her hair. The ugly remnants of his operation were painfully visible, and he turned his hand over and said thoughtfully, "There's something I forgot to tell you."

"What?"

"Stay here."

In bewilderment Maggie watched him leave. What was he doing? Where was he going?

A few minutes later he returned, tossing a manuscript onto her desktop. "I finished the first third of it last night."

"Oh, Tanner." She read several pages in silence, amazed and thrilled by his tight dramatic style. Then she looked up, her love vivid in her eyes. "This is really good. You're going to finish it in your spare time?"

He nodded. "But I'll never be a surgeon again. That's over for me."

"Do you think I care? As long as you're happy, it doesn't matter to me what you do. Gerrard was the one who wanted you to be a doctor, not me."

He threw her a grin. "Maybe I can be a doctor and a writer."

She grinned back. "Maybe you can."

"Maggie." Tanner was suddenly very serious. "We've talked about marriage, but never about Shelley and marriage."

"Shh." Maggie pressed her fingers to his lips. "She'll live with us. There was never any question about that. As long as you accept another member of my family into the house, too."

Tanner's brows came together. "Con? I thought—"

"Not Con. This friend has orange hair and yellow eyes and walks on four legs."

"I'm dying to meet him," Tanner said dryly.

"His name's Alley Cat, for lack of anything more imaginative. He thinks I belong to him."

Tanner smiled, groaning a little as he pulled her closer to him, her warm scent enveloping him. "When you said another member of your family for a moment I thought that you might be pregnant."

Maggie's eyes danced. "Well, you never know," she said, then kissed him before he could waste the rest of the afternoon doing nothing better with his mouth than talking.

* * * * *

Silhouette Special Edition

COMING NEXT MONTH

#403 SANTIAGO HEAT—Linda Shaw
When Deidre Miles crash-landed in steamy Santiago, powerful Francis MacIntire saved her from the clutches of a treacherous military. But what could save her from Francis himself, his tumultuous life and flaming desire?

#404 SOMETIMES A MIRACLE—Jennifer West
Bodyguard Cassandra Burke wistfully dreamed of shining knights on white chargers. Cynical ex-rodeo star Alex Montana had long since turned in his steed. As they braved murder and mayhem together, just who would protect whom?

#405 CONQUER THE MEMORIES—Sandra Dewar
For social worker Carla Foster it was time to face the music. In an adoption dispute, Drake Lanning recognized her for the singer she used to be, and he vowed to learn why she hid her talent...and her heart.

#406 INTO THE SUNSET—Jessica Barkley
Lindsay Jordan wasn't just another city slicker playing cowgirl, no matter what ornery stable manager Nick Leighton said. And despite his sensual persuasion, she wasn't greenhorn enough to think of riding off into the sunset with him!

#407 LONELY AT THE TOP—Bevlyn Marshall
Corporate climber Keely LaRoux wasn't about to let maverick photographer Chuck Dickens impede her progress up the ladder. But traveling together on assignment, the unlikely pair found that business could fast become a dangerously addictive pleasure.

#408 A FAMILY OF TWO—Jude O'Neill
Hotshot producer Gable McCrea wanted newcomer Annabel Porter to direct his latest movie. But what inner demons prompted him to sabotage her work... and her growing love for him?

AVAILABLE THIS MONTH:

ATTRACTIVE, SPACE SAVING BOOK RACK

Display your most prized novels on this handsome and sturdy book rack. The hand-rubbed walnut finish will blend into your library decor with quiet elegance, providing a practical organizer for your favorite hard-or soft-covered books.

Only $9.95

Approximately 16" x 8" when assembled

Assembles in seconds!

To order, rush your name, address and zip code, along with a check or money order for $10.70* ($9.95 plus 75¢ postage and handling) payable to *Silhouette Books.*

Silhouette Books
Book Rack Offer
901 Fuhrmann Blvd.
P.O. Box 1396
Buffalo, NY 14269-1396

Offer not available in Canada.

BKR-2A

*New York and Iowa residents add appropriate sales tax.